SECRET AGENT "X"

THE MAN OF A THOUSAND FACES

Volume Three

Airship 27 Productions

SECRET AGENT X: VOLUME THREE

An Airship 27 Production
Edited by Ron Fortier
Designed by Rob Davis
Cover and interior illustrations ©2008 Rob Davis

ISBN: 978-1-969285-03-5

Second Edition

Produced in the United States of America

10 9 8 7 6 5 4 3 2 1

SECRET AGENT "X"
Volume Three
CONTENTS

Chapter One

"**S**o, Charley, when are you going to be making an honest woman out of that Ruth of yours?"

The question was a frequent one, asked at least once per dragging shift. Charley took his feet down from the table that filled the small coastal rescue station's combination kitchen and main entrance room, and sighed. Folding his paper and setting his coffee to the side, he rubbed his bloodshot eyes and put his elbows on the table.

"Jesus, Benny, when are you going to stop repeating that damn question? Is she slipping you a sawbuck for every time you ask me?"

Benny Thatcher smiled, comforted by the fact he had managed to get a rise out of his watch partner. They had been stuck together on the midnight shift here for four months now. Neither complained too much about the work, since there wasn't a lot of it to go around in these hard times. With the Depression on, and no end in sight, both were glad just not to be in the soup lines that were widely featured in the newsreels.

Unfortunately, their nightly duties put them in close proximity, and familiarity had bred Benny's slight case of contempt for Charley and his lifestyle. Benny was a devout Catholic, and disapproved of Charley's cursing and living in sin with his long-term fiancée, Ruth Badermann. Benny hoped his long-filed transfer would go through soon to another coastal watch station, one in a higher traffic area, with more action, and higher pay.

"Relax, Charley, I'm just passing the time. We've still got four hours until Manny and Joe show up for shift change. Did you ever work out that bug with the wireless radio?"

"Nope, we can still only receive, not transmit. I've put in a repair notice to Regional two weeks ago, but you know the Captain's a lush. He won't process any request unless it's wrapped around a bottle of hooch."

Benny grimaced and smirked at the same time, hiding his expression behind the mug of coffee as he brought it up to his lips. He admired Charley's ability to cut to the heart of an issue, but found his methods rough, and what was the word? Uncouth. Uncouth: there was a twelve-dollar word if he ever heard one.

"So, we're still stuck with just the hand-cranked phone, huh?"

"You got it, mac."

"Well, it's better than nothing."

"So you say."

Benny took the remark as an excuse to step outside into the cool night air. The kerosene lamp kept the small watch station warm and lit, but tended to make the place stuffy. Benny stared out at the sea, at least what he could see of it reflected by the watch station's lights. It was a moonless night out here on the Long Island sound, and the low sound of crashing waves pulled his gaze towards the sea as much as the gray smudge of breaking surf did.

Something caught his eye, silhouetted against the flashing light of the Block Island lighthouse, a few miles across the water. For the briefest of instances, a square shape flickered in the darkness, dimly backlit by the distant, rotating strobe. He squinted, trying to focus on the shape even as it appeared to sink below the waves.

Stepping back into the doorway of the watch station, he called to Charley, "Hey, Charley, hand me those binoculars up on the shelf, would you?"

"Why, whattaya see out there? There's no moon. Is the lighthouse on fire?"

"No, wiseacre, I thought I saw a square sail or something sinking between us and Block Island."

"Square? Did it have hard edges like a sail, Benny, or rounded edges like a-"

"The binos, Charley, quick. I can barely see it, and it's fading fast."

Charley handed Benny the optics with a grim reluctance. He wasn't in the mood to shove their rescue boat into the surf, especially at this time of night. Hopefully, it was nothing.

Benny kept looking out the door towards the water, reaching back for the offered binos.

"Holy smokes, Charley, I think it might be a-"

A drilling whine registered in Charley's head, like a mosquito had flown down his ear canal. The sound crescendoed violently, and the back of Benjamin J. Thatcher's chest exploded over Charley and the rest of the small room. A window on the far wall shattered at the same time, directly across from the doorway. Benny slumped against the door jam, sliding down it at a jagged and tortuous pace, and fell backwards into a pool of his own fluids.

Charley was rooted to the spot, shocked, the binocular case still held out at arm's length. Shredded bits of bone, blood, and other parts of Benny covered him. By the time the stricken man finally hit the floor, Charley was snapped out of his stupor by a thunderous report that came through the doorway three or four seconds after the initial event.

"…Subma…rine…Charley…," Thatcher's last words rasped out as his pupils dilated. The sound seemed to come from his gaping chest wound as much as it did his blood-filled mouth.

"Oh, sweet Jesus, Benny, what the hell-"

Benny's lips mouthed "submarine" one last time as he faded away. Charley dove for the floor, and began to slip and slog across the gore-soaked kitchen towards the wireless radio set in the next room. The station was built from brick and mortar to withstand pounding surf and driving winds that would come with seasonal Nor'easters. Those had been rifle shots. The lag between impact and the rifle's report meant the shooter was some distance away. Charley had been a veteran of the Great War. He knew he would be safe from long-range rifle shots if he kept low, behind cover.

The seemingly-strong walls now began to explode. Every terrifying concussion of brick and dust would be followed later by thunderous gunshots in rapid succession. They happened at such a rapid pace that they began overlapping each other in a frenzied drumbeat of fury and thunder. Charley screamed and covered his eyes and ears from the assault of stinging pieces of brick and splinters of wood from the kitchen table. After a tortured eternity of seconds, the fusillade stopped.

Charley crawled to the wireless set, his ears ringing. He never noticed the snaps and pops coming from the pool of kerosene spreading from the shattered lamp. He picked up the wireless radio's microphone, but remembered as he touched it that it was unable to transmit. He reached for the hand-crank telephone mounted on the wall nearby. A few fearful turns of the manually-powered phone produced a low growl, and a loud click as the party on the other end picked up.

"Long Island Office of Public Maritime Safety, Lieutenant Pudlowski speaking, how can I-"

"Pud! Pudlowski! It's Charley, Charley Morgan, out here at Green Hill Beach Station! Me and Benny need help! Benny's dead, but he said he saw a su-"

Half a dozen gunshots rang out again, but this time from within the station. Charley felt a slick stream of liquid heat pouring down the side of his face, and faintly heard Lt. Pudlowski's frantic "hello's" coming from the earpiece. The telephone dropped as his arm failed to respond to his mind's commands, useless from the new perforations in his shoulder, deltoid, tricep, and neck. The massive influx of pain forced him to turn around, to face this new attack, but his body fought him every excruciating degree of rotation. His eyes widened in shock at the fire slowly filling the kitchen. Looking through the blaze, the doorway was filled by a giant of a man, dressed from head to toe in black. Even his face was smeared black. Only a pair of piercing blue eyes, highlighted by the fire, gave any variation to his form.

Others dressed like him stood behind in the doorway, some facing into the room, others outward towards the building's surroundings. Some pointed their weapons at him, others watched their assigned sectors of overwatch. The large man raised his pistol, and surgically put a pair of rounds into Charley's face. The fire from the lamp became a roaring pyre as it found new fuel throughout the shattered kitchen. The hulking figure stooped to pick up his ejected shell casings.

Giving a signal with his hands, he and the small team pulled back, moving in a column up the dirt road that led from the coastal bluffs down to the remote rescue station.

Minutes passed. The small group of killers formed into an ambush pattern without a word as a rumbling canvas-backed truck came down the road. They disappeared among the low dunes and scrub pines that dotted the beach. The truck squealed to a stop on worn brakes and turned off its headlights. A rotund figure dismounted from the truck, comically clad in some semblance of a military uniform. He was nervous, looking around the beach and back towards the main road with great hesitation, bathed in the orange glow of the burning station. He put a small brass whistle to his lips, and blew softly.

The team's leader appeared from nowhere, startling the truck driver. The pudgy man attempted to draw himself up, and threw his right arm up in an outthrust salute. The giant team leader clapped his massive hand down upon the driver's forearm, issuing a terse foreign profanity. The team loaded into the back of the truck, their number increasing by one as a sleek, similarly-outfitted figure joined them. The newest member moved swiftly, but was visibly burdened by the long case held in one hand. The case was slid into the back of the truck, and the marauders rumbled away into the night, the rescue station falling in on itself in a sudden gush of sparks and flame as its roof collapsed.

Chapter Two

A mortician's duties are burdensome and dark, and are never made easier when the man he must bury is loved so dearly, and taken so unexpectedly. The family of the man lying before him, sealed in an economical pine box, had been devastated by the vicious loss that had been visited upon them. He had comforted the weeping widow, had tried to assure her with gentle words and scripture that her beloved husband was now in a better place. The man's sons were too young to understand that daddy was not coming home. The ceremony had been solemn, bleak, and they had fidgeted, giving curious looks to the grieving adults that surrounded them. The memorial service had drawn to a suffocating close, and soon the funeral procession to the hole dug in the graveyard outside would commence.

After performing his duties as undertaker and master of ceremonies here at Westbrook Memorial Home, he was finally alone with the corpse. He sighed, and reached into his coat pocket for a small prybar, no more than six inches long. Opening a nailed-shut casket containing the grisly remains of what once was a man is never a silent operation. The nails yielded with a low moan, slowly at first, then all at once in an outpouring of noise that he did his best to contain. He looked to the doorway, saw no one was coming, and went back to work. He reached into another jacket pocket for a special container. Good. It was still there. He had felt it move when the traumatized widow had been weeping into his chest.

He placed the lid of the pine box to the side, next to a beautiful display of flowers sent by the dead man's mother-in-law, and was confronted with the blackened sight of Ben Thatcher.

Murders happen every day in New York, Connecticut, and Rhode Island, just like the rest of New England, just like the rest of America. Gangsters machinegun each other down in restaurants. Pimps strangle unproductive members of their street harems. Mothers smother their babes in desperation or drunkenness. The mid-1930's dark economic situation had been hard on the entirety of the populace, and the result was often the shedding of innocent blood.

"The nails yielded with a low moan, slowly at first, then all at once in an outpouring of noise that he did his best to contain."

What didn't occur too often, however, was the unusual, the bloodthirsty, the brutally grotesque. Two coastal rescuemen found at their remote station on Long Island sound, mercilessly drilled with gunfire and left to burn, had somehow prodded even the jaded Gotham public into paying attention. Newspapers from Manhattan flooded the seaside towns along the quiet coastline with raucous reporters, each trying to scoop their competitors.

The fervor for the story had lasted more than the usual couple of days, when it was usually banished to the back pages by another atrocity. Something about the story, filtered through his ever-working subconscious mind, also refused to settle into the muddled background of normal, everyday life. That last rumination made him smirk despite his somber undertaker's disguise: "normal, everyday life." As if there was such a thing for him, the man known as Secret Agent "X".

This case resonated something in him, something that clawed and whispered in the back of his brain. Spree or thrill killers were often sloppy. They were usually deviant youth, seeking to offset their hollow, privileged upbringings by debasing themselves in the blood of others. This crime was unlike something along those lines.

The two men, Thatcher and Morgan, had both been killed by gunfire, but there were no casings found. Residents of a small hamlet of Charleston, some six miles away, reported being awakened by a cavalcade of shots, describing it, "as if an army of them crawling tractor-tanks had landed on Green Hill beach, by God," as one aging resident had told the papers. Assuming the killers had used conventional weapons, the Charlestonians shouldn't have heard a thing, considering the sizeable distances involved. Another piece of the puzzle that didn't fit.

Charles Morgan's corpse had yielded few clues from the examination Agent "X" performed this morning after a similar memorial service. The more-than-half dozen shots he took to the rear torso, punctuated by the twin wounds to the face, appeared to be pistol rounds. Pistol rounds definitely would not have been heard miles away. Something was wrong.

Opening the once-displaced container in his vest, Agent "X" took out a plug of special wax and placed it on the edge of Thatcher's now-open coffin. Lifting up one side of the body, Agent "X" evaluated the horrific exit wound. The man's right lung was completely gone, along with the surrounding ribs and musculature. Thatcher's body was spared from the punishing heat of the fire and trauma of the watch station's collapse, since he was killed in the doorway. The wound channel carved by the projectile was huge, far larger than any rifle strike Agent "X" had ever seen in his years of fighting crime. The only thing comparable was referenced from his years overseas, fighting the forces of Kaiser Bill. Because of its size, the exit wound was useless for the purposes of forensic detective work, short of the declaration that Thatcher had been hit with something on par with an elephant gun or a small cannon.

The entry wound on the front of his torso, however, was more promising, and not nearly as traumatic in scope or measure. Warming the special wax in his gloved hands, Agent "X" pressed the semi-solid solution against the wound. After a moment, the wax cooled and hardened, and he pulled the plug out gently. There, in his hand, was a positive impression of the cavity formed by whatever had snuffed out Benjamin Thatcher, created just after the projectile had hit him, but before it had yawed, tumbled, and turned his insides and rear torso to human hamburger.

He measured the smoothest, most cylindrical section of the plug with a tiny caliper, and came up with a measurement of just over 520 thousandths of an inch. Roughly thirteen millimeters: that had been a monstrous bullet. No wonder the exit wound had been so traumatic: in the world of man-portable weaponry, Thatcher had been hit with the equivalent of a freight train.

Agent "X" placed his forensic and precision items back into their varied hiding places on his person. Stripping off the gray mustache and wig he wore, he strode to the broom closet against a far wall in the small memorial hall. Inside, he retrieved a small briefcase and gently placed it on the lap of the seated, sleeping man who also occupied the closet. After another quick look to the door of the room, he opened the attaché, and placed the hair devices in their respective pouches. He donned a pair of thick, black-framed glasses containing clear lenses with no prescription. It was a simple, yet effective device that would enable him to slip out of the building unnoticed.

Taking a small capsule in hand, he crushed it while holding it under the nose of the unconscious man. It snapped with a small puff, and an acrid, piercing smell filled the closet. The real undertaker stirred to groggy consciousness. The powerful chemical stimulus caused his own, quite real, gray mustache to twitch.

"Mr. Westbrook, time to wake up, sir. I hate to leave you in such a quandary, but my presence is required elsewhere. I do hope you understand."

The mortician and funeral home director blinked and rubbed his eyes, not noticing the folded wad of hundred-dollar bills being pressed into his vest pocket. By the time he was able to focus his attentions and rise to his feet, the studious-looking man of average height and average build was gone from his funeral home, briefcase in hand. Westbrook emerged from the closet just as the widow Thatcher came back into the room, her eyes drawn immediately to the forced-open coffin. He slowly followed her gaze, and swore profanely as he lurched to grab for the coffin lid. A clamor arose as members of the bereaved family flowed back into the room, drawn by the crashing noise of Mrs. Thatcher fainting into a row of chairs as she fell to the floor.

Chapter Three

After an hour of nonchalant searching in an ever-widening pattern, Secret Agent "X" believed he had at last found the spot. The elevation, cover, and concealment were perfect. The only thing that puzzled him was the distance involved: over 1100 yards. Walking along the beach that stretched in front of the ruined rescue station, he had been stopped by a policeman who was assigned to the crime scene. His disguise was simple work clothes, a cosmetic dental bridge of stained teeth, and a workman's wool cap. The trappings were secondary, really, since he was hauling around a surveyor's tripod and sighting glass, or transit. His explanation that he was scouting a location for the new rescue station had easily passed muster with the beat cop, and his discreet search for the shooter's perch was now complete.

The location was in a thicket of low seaside grass, interspersed with patches of sand here and there. Like the rescue station, no empty cartridge casings were found. Thankfully, though, a weapon that was able to hit a man from over a half-mile away with enough force to turn him hollow was just as equally rough on the environment from which it was fired. Even days later, despite the constant wind coming in off the sound, Agent "X" could see the patterns of the weapon's muzzle blast in the driven sand and crushed vegetation. Small indentations a foot behind the blast patterns showed the gun had been mounted on a bipod. Each violent recoil forced those bipod feet to move incrementally, and come to a rest as the weapon had bucked and roared. Agent "X" counted ten distinct stops and starts in the miniature trenches. Ten shots from 1100 yards and change; no wonder the folks in Charleston had heard the cannon's discharges.

Where had the remaining shots gone, if it took only one to dispatch Thatcher? Morgan's wounds were inflicted from a pistol, and close. Yet another piece of the puzzle.

The energy required to send a projectile measuring more than a half-inch in diameter this kind of distance was monstrous. Elephant guns and the like were large, but usually suited to shots of 100 yards or closer. Besides, their projectiles were usually solid brass, and would have been easily recovered at the crime scene. Here, he stood eleven football fields away from where a man had been torn to pieces with a single hit. This was military-grade weaponry, probably some form of anti-tank rifle. He mentally ticked off the short list of countries that possessed such powerful man-portable cannons. The list was short, and grim.

To confirm his suspicions, he knelt to the ground, clipping a small tuft of grass. The blasted and pulverized vegetation was impregnated with the residue of the gunpowder that had launched the projectile. Agent "X" placed the grass in a small tube of special solution. He replaced the cork top of the glass vessel, and shook it vigorously for ten seconds. The liquid reacted to the powder residue on the blades of grass, and turned a virulent purple.

A smirk signaled his annoyance at having been proved right, once again, especially when he didn't want to be. A dark blue would have meant British cordite. Light blue that turned to red after prolonged shaking would have meant American propellant. The powder was German, based on the mixture of nitrates and trace elements that resulted in the noxious violet color. It fit, now. Thatcher had been killed from afar by a powerful rifle and an accurate shooter, while Morgan had been finished off up close. That is where the remainder of the heavy rifle shots had gone: the shooter had been trying to flush Morgan from inside the rescue station, or keep his head down long enough for the pistol shooter to finish him off. The building's collapse had hidden the remainder of the heavy impacts.

The tactics were standard doctrine from the Wehrmacht field manual: establish a volume of powerful suppressive fire from a distance, while another element moves in close and finishes off the target.

Since the location was so close to water, insertion of the German force must have been from some passing ship, or even a U-boat, if the operation was important enough. The hows and whys of the rescue station slaughter now fell into place. Thatcher and Morgan had seen a group of individuals come ashore that they shouldn't have, individuals who were German, armed, and ruthless. Now to find out why these Teutonic murderers were here, on American soil. He had a good idea where a group of German commandos could hide, and who would harbor them.

Agent "X" took down the tripod, and began the long walk back to the rescue station and the pair of cars parked there. The policeman folded up his paper and rolled down the window to his police car.

"Say, mac, how goes the surveyin'?"

Agent "X" pulled his mouth down at the corners, affecting the same peculiar Mainer's drawl he had used earlier with the lawman, "Aw, you know, officer, anothah fine day at the office. I'm just about to wrap it up."

"Another day at the office, that's good. Damn shame what happened to these boys out here, eh?"

"It's an ugly world, officer, full of bad people. Your department any closer to figurin' it out?"

The policeman blanched, giving him an embarrassed shirk and grin. "We're a tiny little seaside department. We're not used to seeing this kind of action. Stuff like this happens in the big city, what with all those closed factories and folks out of work."

"Well, officer, you know this stuff just happens, sometimes. I'll be going, now. You have a good day."

"Ain't that the truth. Say, mac, one last thing: ain't there usually some other guy with you when you go surveying, holding a pole and chain, or something?"

Agent "X" kept smiling at the officer, looking him in the eye as he casually placed the tripod and sight glass in the trunk of his black, non-descript car. A small, pistol-shaped tool was fastened to the inside of the trunk lid, out of sight. It quickly found its place in Agent "X"'s left hand, tucked in the small of his back.

"It's a new technique, officer. That sight glass lets me take my measurements without an assistant carrying a surveyor's pole, or a Gunter's chain, as it's called."

"Hmm. What will they come up with next? The times we live in, huh?"

"Indeed. Well, goodbye."

"So long."

Agent "X" relaxed. The policeman appeared to be a decent man, and it would have been disappointing to use the device he pulled out of the trunk. He put the car in reverse, and looked in his rear view mirror. A harsh tap on his car's window told him that things weren't going to work out as neatly as he hoped. Agent "X" found himself staring down the barrel of the policeman's service revolver.

The officer spoke calmly through the glass, "I called the chief while you were out there in the dunes, scoping out the place. The surveyors don't come until next Monday. Get out of the car."

"Very well, officer, you've got me. I'm a reporter for the Herald, just trying to get a scoop."

"I figured as much. I'm from up around Bangor. That fake accent of yours is horrible."

Agent "X" smiled. His drawling Mainer Yankee accent usually worked. He'd have to work on it in the future. He feigned tugging at the inside release of his car door, "Officer, the door handle of this car is broken. You're going to have to open it from the outside."

Shifting his revolver to one hand, the policeman reached for the car's exterior door latch. As he did so, Agent "X" jammed the electric stunner he held into the door. The current shot up the officer's arm, causing him to fire a round involuntarily into the air as his back arched and his neck muscles went taut. The man dropped backwards like a rock, his head thumping against the fender of his own police car.

Agent "X" swore quietly to himself, and got out of his own vehicle. He looked at the back of the patrolman's skull. It was going to rise up and be tender for a while, but it didn't look like a concussion, nor did it require stitches. Agent "X" propped the stunned policeman up against the side of his patrol vehicle, careful to bring the helpless man's legs out of the path of Agent "X"'s tires.

"Easy, there, officer, you took a nasty fall. I must admire your initiative and vigilance, but I'm afraid I don't have time to go back to the station with you. Do have a nice day, now, won't you?"

Agent "X" placed the policeman's revolver back in its holster, got back into his car, and looked around to see if there was anything else he should notice before another surprise reared its head. His eye was drawn to an article in the policeman's paper folded on the dash of the car, one titled "Famed Weapons Inventor To Re-Open Gov't Armory." He retrieved the paper from the car, and sped back up the access road to the main highway.

Chapter Four

A thunderous roar erupted after the singing of *Das Lied der Deutschen*, or, "The Song of the Germans," better known by it's opening lyric "Deutschland Über Alles." As the fat man on the podium wished them all goodnight, the evening meeting of the local German American Bund

Chapter drew to a close. His garish uniform and appearance were not quite military issue from any one nation in particular, but his personal swagger and barking tone gave anyone listening substantial reason to believe he was capable of martial force. Imprecise, ham-fisted force, borne more of thuggery and brawling than military discipline, but force nonetheless.

The meeting place was a large, well-worn tent, stained in spots, and frocked in red and black bunting on one side, red-white-and-blue bunting on the other. The crowd of men had listened to the meeting's proceedings while sitting on bales of hay arranged like church pews. Flags from various periods in Germany's history were arranged on a small wooden stage, flanking a simple podium. A draped American flag adorned the front of the speaker's pulpit. Bright bulbs run by a generator outside filled the tent with light, though these shut down with a long-winded whine as switches were loudly thrown somewhere behind the stage.

The thirsty membership, numbering a couple hundred men or so, retired in due haste to the plush beer garden set up for them next to the large meeting tent. German jokes and curses flew amidst the thick clouds of cigarette and pipe smoke. Only a smattering of English was heard, here and there, and only among the few second or third-generation immigrants.

Many of the men here were relatively new residents of this country. Most left Germany during the dark years of the Weimar Republic's collapse. Almost all were unemployed, or destitute, or an angry boss's whim away from those conditions. The ruinous times made their lives hard, but tonight the large steins of free-flowing beer helped ease their burdens.

The beer garden was a comfortable affair, complete with long pine benches and tables, a rough-hewn bar, and high stools. Tapped beer casks set up behind the meeting tent filled the steins of the men waiting in line. Young men in passing semblances of uniforms cheerfully filled the large mugs of the waiting meeting attendants. Once served, the Bund members sat at the benches and talked of their memories of, and hopes for, the old country.

The meeting's leader made a genial entrance to light applause and hoisted mugs. He moved with ease through the midst of the crowd, his sizeable bulk giving him little hindrance even amongst the close-packed tables. Here and there, he shook hands, clapped men on the back, and drank from his own large mug while engaging in lively conversation. The men regarded him with an eager respect, careful to laugh loudly at his jokes, and to nod when driblets of wisdom fell from his lips. His connection with the rising power back in their Fatherland made him an important man, one who must be followed. Whispers of some impending event made him an even more compelling figure. All present wanted to help further the cause of a stronger Germany, as well as helping their own situation in this new land.

Secret Agent "X" brought a large pewter stein to his lips, and pretended to wipe the foam from his mustache as he brought his hand up to his mouth. The beer was excellent, served at just the right temperature, but too heavy a drink would loosen the spirit gum holding the disguise together under his nose. Upon securing the bushy device, he resumed his conversation in fluent German with Horst, the affable man seated across from him. Horst was halfway through his third stein, and was feeling no pain.

"What…what did you say your name was, again, friend?"

"Willy. Willy Krupp, from Saxony, by way of Pennsylvania." Agent "X" had known a Wilhelm Krupp back in the Great War, a German officer advising the Ottoman Turks. The name was easy enough to remember: Agent "X" had been forced to kill him in a duel.

"Ah, Krupp, like the ironworks. Any relation?"

"We are distant cousins, but we're from a poor branch of the family. My pappa came over in the 1890s, and built railroads."

"Ah, railroads. I bet your pappa was a good man, working with his hands, yes? He would have approved of our cause here?"

Agent "X" played along, drawing what he could from the inebriated man without raising suspicion, "Pappa was many things, but no matter what, he would have fought and bled for a stronger Germany. He and I have that much in common."

Horst grinned, glad to have found a fellow traveler, "Ah, Willy, a strong Germany is coming soon. I have seen it with my own eyes. The Fatherland's economy is strong, the Jews, curse them, are put back in their place, and the Fuhrer now looks to wipe away the last twenty years, starting with that damnable treaty signed in that damnable railroad car.

"I was there, Willy. No, not at the car, but I was there in the trenches, in the last days of the war," he hissed. Horst thumped his chest as a bit of beer rebelled against him, and let out a burp. He leaned in closer to the man he believed to be the son of a German immigrant.

"...And let me tell you this, Willy: I was a corporal in the service of the Kaiser. The Ardennes. Verdun. The Argonne. I was there. I was Fifth Army. These Americans, they don't know how close they came to losing it all. Not to worry. Things will be different the next time around."

Agent "X" leaned in as well, winking as he feigned drunkenness. He slurred his words slightly, "So tell, me, Horst, what's going to be so different the next time around? What's going to keep the Americans and English from stopping the new Reich?"

Horst took a deep drink of beer, and brought his stein to the pine table with an abrupt thump, "The difference, Willy, is that the Fatherland's forces won't be stuck with the same old bolt-action rifle that I was forced to use twenty years ago. Something's coming, and it's going to put the German soldier in at the top of the food chain, where he belongs, mark my words. The damned doughboys will be stacked up like cordwood when the Fuhrer's new weapons are brought to bear!"

Horst's drunken speech turned into a bellow towards the end, drawing attention from those around him. Little did he know that Jacob Heinz, sitting behind him, had also been at the Argonne, though Heinz, like Agent "X" for a short time, had been there under the command of American General John Joseph 'Blackjack' Pershing.

Heinz had never been much for words. Instead, Agent "X" saw the man's knuckles whiten around his beer stein's handle. In an instant, Heinz stood and turned. Others reached for him, but before they could stop him, he smashed his heavy mug to pieces across the back of Horst's head.

Horst's lips were bloodied, since he had been drinking from his own stein when the blow landed. Spewing German curses through broken teeth, he launched himself at Heinz. The two of them grappled between the pine benches while others roared with laughter. No one noticed the mustachioed man who had been talking to Horst disappear.

Agent "X" broke away from the melee before Horst had even turned to face his angry attacker. Taking advantage of the chaos, he made his way back into the darkened main meeting tent. He took a small black cylinder from his jacket pocket, twisted one end of it, and placed it under the podium. He paused for a moment, studying the speaker's platform. On a whim, he ripped down the American flag from its place on the podium, bundling it quickly inside his coat. After the speech he sat through earlier, Old Glory did not belong in this canvas temple of idiocy and hatred. A number of identical devices were inserted into random hay bales throughout the hall. He then made his way out of the structure, under the cover of darkness, to his car in the dirt parking lot.

Looking vigilantly over the dashboard, Agent "X" brought up a pair of binoculars from a special case beside his seat. He hooked a small set of earphones into the side of the binoculars, enabling him to hear through the tiny, powerful directional microphone built into them. The advanced surveillance device let him follow the action from a safe distance, both from the members of the Bund, and the fire that was about to erupt in their meeting place.

The Bund leader had managed to make his way through the throng of laughing, shouting members surrounding the fight. Swinging a riding crop, he broke the two combatants apart. Two pairs of young men in uniform held the arms of each of the fighters.

"Damn it all, Horst, you're a mess. What was it this time? The Argonne again?"

Horst spurted and burbled through shattered teeth, "Werner, that sh... schweinhund there cracked my skull when I wasn't looking. I was just talking to my new friend, Willy, about the Fuhrer's new weapons-"

The Bund leader known as Werner turned to the bloodied man, and silenced his drunken rambling with a hard strike from his riding crop, "Shut your mouth, Horst! I knew you talked too much! I knew I shouldn't have told you a damn thing!" The blow drove Horst to his knees with a moan, and he was promptly kicked in the ribs by the fat man's black jackboots.

The leader nodded to the Bund members holding the two men. They shuttled them away, to the far side of the meeting tent, hidden from the view of the beer garden, but still in sight of Agent "X" in the parking lot. The celebration at the benches and beer barrels slowly resumed, with one man in pseudo-uniform leading the group in a drunken German folk song. The Bund leader, Werner, made an upwardly-rolling motion with his hand to the conductor of the folk song, a combination of "keep it going" and "sing louder." The man nodded at the signal, and urged the group to belt out another, louder, round of the bawdy, raucous song.

Upon another signal from Werner, Horst and Heinz were put on their knees with a pair of punches to the kidneys. From the shadows, a number of men emerged to surround the Bund thugs and their two problem members. No, not all men,

Agent "X" observed. One of them was a stunning blonde, her hair cropped short, her figure revealed, even enhanced, by the cut of her uniform.

The remaining members of the squad were tall and broad, purposed for battle, unlike the softer Bund civilians. Their uniforms weren't facsimiles or faux imitations. They wore the real item, Wehrmacht gray-green field utilities. They bore pistols, modified German Lugers with silencers attached to their barrels. They advanced menacingly towards Horst and Heinz.

Werner spoke tersely in German, "These two nearly gave everything away. Dispose of them."

The largest of the men spat back at him, "We were not dispatched here to be your death squad, Herr Mannheim. Our mission orders are clear, as is your supporting role. You deal with your own problems."

The woman spoke next, "Besides, how did these two know anything about why we are here? Have you been running your mouth about the American weapons designer, Mannheim? If you can't control your tongue, perhaps we should cut it out." She drew a blade from her belt, holding it in her left hand while the pistol in her right trained itself onto the Bund leader's forehead.

Agent "X" saw Werner Mannheim stiffen and turn white as the blonde toggled the safety on her pistol. Deciding he had seen enough, Agent "X" flipped the top off yet another small black cylinder. Though it looked the same as the devices he planted in the meeting hall, it was actually a remote radio detonator. With the push of a red button, the meeting tent exploded, the incendiary bomblets bathing everything within their blast radius with fuel and flame.

The mixture of Germans and Bund men on the far side of the tent scattered into the woods. Agent "X" was glad to see Heinz and Horst make it away safely. The Bund leader's bulk had taken the brunt of the fireball that had burst from the tent. Agent "X" was even happier to see that Mannheim was a bit singed, madly beating his backside to put out a small, intimately personal fire. The Wehrmacht men and woman made their way to a truck hidden in the once-shadowy treeline with lightning speed. They moved with a purpose, without fear, without hesitation. Agent "X" knew with a glance they were the killers at the coastal rescue station.

The rest of the men from the beer garden fled the scene, a crazed mob running from the horrific sight of their meeting hall engulfed in flame. The dirt parking lot was filled with dust as dozens of cars left deep skid marks in the dry earth, each spitting gravel and sod as they jockeyed to be the first down the dirt road to the remote spot in the woods.

Secret Agent "X", despite his reputation, was woefully ill-equipped to take on a squad of Wehrmacht special troops. Undoubtedly, he knew they had that monstrous rifle nearby. Countering firepower like that required special measures, using methods he did not have on hand. Besides, he now knew their target.

He turned the car's motor over, and sped quickly from the parking lot, joining the maddening throng tearing their way up the dirt road.

Chapter Five

Secret Agent "X" finished scanning over the last of the article on the front page of the newspaper, and looked again at the byline: 'Betty Dale'. He smiled, despite himself, at the thoughts that bubbled to the forefront. He had known Miss Dale since she was a young girl whose family he had helped in a moment of trouble. He had kept tabs on her over the years, making contact in various guises, though his various missions and crusades forced him to keep her at arm's length.

He had seen her bloom from awkward teenager to beautiful young woman, though it wasn't just her visage that kept her in his thoughts. She had become a stubborn and forthright reporter, fighting twice as hard as her male counterparts to get and keep the tough stories. He assisted her in her pursuit of truth, as best as he could, and she was one of the few voices in the news media that provided favorable coverage to the otherwise-dastardly public menace known as Secret Agent "X".

Now, as before, he was in disguise, not more than a dozen feet away from her. He had donned his familiar persona of being A.J. Martin, the Associated Press correspondent. Being Martin was easy, like putting on a comfortable pair of slippers, yet always slightly painful: as A.J., he was often near Betty Dale, but the closer he found himself, the more distant he felt. Donning the A.J. Martin mantle felt like a heavy burden to him at times. Someday, things would change, and the situation would be different between them. Today, though, was not fated to be that day.

Instead, today was a humid scorcher of a New York City Friday, with dark, scudding clouds overhead that allowed just enough of the sun's heat through to make the city an oven. Agent "X" felt sweat trickle down his ribs and back as he stood with the rest of the press corps, though he doubted the rest of the journalists were weighed down with the same implements he kept hidden away on his person. They were all awaiting a speech from the famous weapons designer, John Garand, the genius behind the U.S. Army's newest mechanical marvel, the M-1 self-loading rifle.

Betty Dale caught his eye as he folded the newspaper, winking as she pointed to the article he had been reading.

"Nice choice of reading material, there, A.J. What are you trying to do, pick up some pointers on real reporting?"

Agent "X" smiled, playfully returning her wink as he pretended to once again be someone he was not, "Not a bad score, kid, landing that Garand piece, but you need to work on that punctuation of yours. Who's editing your work these days, the Marx Brothers?"

Betty feigned hurt, playfully pouting, "Oh, A.J., you're just pulling my leg because I landed that feature, and you're stuck chasing your tail with that rescue station ugliness up the coast. Not to worry, dear, I'll crack that case next, once I'm done with mister rifle maker, here."

"Careful, there, Miss Dale, you wouldn't want to worry your pretty head about such things. You should stick to more important stuff at the gossip columnists' desk, like socialites and cheating politicians. Leave the real stories to me."

It was innocent banter, standard kidding amongst professionals. More than anything, it gave him a chance to interact with her, even if it was from behind the mask of A.J. Martin. To her, Martin was just a competitor in the news business. Secret Agent "X", though, was this mysterious shadowy figure that captured her thoughts. He knew from past conversations, from other press conferences or crime scenes where they had met, that Agent "X" was someone she held in more than just high esteem. Knowing she longed for him, when he had to be someone else, sometimes hurt all the more.

"Oh, quiet, you, the press conference is starting," Betty hushed him before he could say another word. She stuck out her tongue, causing him to laugh as he shook his head and turned his attention back to Garand.

John Garand may have been a genius, but his appearance lacked any ambitions of matching his grandiose reputation. He was a small, bookish man, Canadian in origin, with a dark shock of hair and circular wire-framed glasses. He had spent the better part of the last decade perfecting the M-1 rifle at the Army's behest, and the weapon was now making its way into full production for the armed forces.

Like many men of skill and talent, Garand also had his quirks. Agent "X"'s research had brought a smile to his face when he found out Garand often flooded his basement in the dead of winter, and would ice skate on the frozen water to collect his thoughts. Despite his eccentricities, the man was an asset to his country, and Agent "X" meant for him to stay in this country. Being kidnapped or killed by a team of Hun saboteurs was not going to happen to John Garand on Agent "X"'s watch.

The rifle maker emerged from an awaiting olive drab car, with a white star on the side, and proceeded towards a cluster of reporters and large crowd waiting for him. The press conference was being held on the steps leading to the Herald Building, one of the larger newspapers in the city. Betty Dale wrote for the Herald, and landed a feature story on Garand that ran in serial segments leading up to this news briefing. He was here to announce the re-dedication of a number of shuttered factories, both here in the city and upstate as well, that would produce copies of his new rifle. The scene was an ideal location to start watching over the man, since as a member of the press, he could shadow the government executive without raising suspicion, as long as he asked the occasional question or two.

Garand stepped up to the cluster of chromed microphones assembled to broadcast his announcement over the airwaves. A low squalor of feedback came from the pair of large speakers set up for the assembly, on the corners of the steps' top landing. The crowd murmured and twittered at the audio barrage, then settled down as the noise subsided. John Garand smiled, nodded to the gathered mass of citizens, cleared his throat, and pulled a small set of cards from his suit jacket's inside pocket.

He began to read in a dreadfully serious monotone, "My friends, my name is John Garand, and I have worked for this nation in the capacity of a humble ordnance engineer for more than two decades."

A smattering of polite applause followed the introduction. He nodded his thanks, and continued, "The rifle I have designed for the Army is not meant as a tool of empire. Rather, it is meant as a sword in the hands of the forces of liberty-"

A woman's piercing scream cut the little man's dry oration short. A policeman near Garand cried out in pain, holding his face as blood spurted past his fingers. Agent "X" grabbed for Betty, but a sudden swell from the crowd tore her from his hands. The policeman knocked Garand down as he fell, and the two of them rolled over the podium full of microphones in a cacophony of noise.

Pandemonium reigned as Agent "X" saw the source of the policeman's fatal wound. The Wehrmacht raiders must have read the newspapers as well, for here they were, in broad, scorching daylight, weapons at the ready. The largest of the Germans, with flashing blue eyes and short blond hair, pointed as he gave orders to his men. The pistol in his other hand was smoking, the noise of its discharge contained by the suppressor threaded to its barrel.

Agent "X" had not expected the killers to be so bold as to strike their target in public, especially during a press conference. His attack on their hiding place last night must have flushed them out, hastening their plans to abduct the weapons designer.

The large crowd of media and civilians continued to run about madly, screeching and screaming as a string of loud, unsuppressed gunshots erupted. One of the Germans was gunning down a pair of men emerging from Garand's car. They must have been his escorts from the Ordnance department, for Agent "X" saw their drawn revolvers just as they were torn to pieces. The hammering of the unmuffled submachinegun drove the crowd into a deeper frenzy. Agent "X" saw Betty make her way to the dazed John Garand, helping him up as she pulled the bloodied policeman off him.

Indecision and rage tore at him. Was he to engage the murderers in plain view of the press, or should he protect Betty and Garand from the onslaught of the Germans, all the while as his A.J. Martin personality? The decision was made for him when the Germans began to machinegun the crowd. A man caught between him and the Germans threw up his arms as his throat and lower jaw splattered over Agent "X", covering his face and chest with crimson. His disguise, including his false nose and cheek pieces, loosened as he wiped the blood from his eyes. No one noticed amidst the screaming pandemonium, so he peeled the mess away, and reached into his jacket.

With one hand, he placed a dark pair of sunglasses over his face. The other hand held three steel rings, their edges honed to a surgical sharpness. He threw the ring blades with great precision, severing the tendons in one German's forearm that had been gleefully shooting the panicked crowd. The man cried out as he dropped his weapon, drawing the attention of his teammates. The hulking team leader motioned to two others, one armed with a submachinegun, the other with a pair of knives. Agent "X" dove up the steps, bullets chasing his heels as he rapidly closed the distance with the knifeman. The gunner shifted his fire too late, and caught his companion in the leg just as Agent "X" reached him. "X" snapped the man's wrist with one deft move, twisting the knife from the now-useless hand holding it. He hammered the German with the pommel of the blade's handle, knocking him out. Agent "X" took the other knife, and threw it into the upper shoulder of the gun-wielding German.

While occupied with those two, the leader of the terror squad had picked up Garand and Miss Dale with a single beefy paw. Putting the pistol to Betty's head, he asked the weapons designer, "Herr Garand, the Fuhrer requests your presence and talents to be put to use in the service of the Reich. What shall I tell him in response to his kind invitation?"

Betty Dale spit on the giant man, telling him, "You monstrous swine! These people you killed today don't care about your petty Reich, or your petty, goose-stepping little Fuhrer!"

A backhand from the goliath knocked her into the arms of the small weapons designer. Agent "X", his fury uncontainable, yelled as he threw the second knife directly at the man's head. The Aryan brute, alerted by the sound, deflected the blade with his pistol. He continued and focused the gun's parry, and put four shots directly into Agent "X"'s chest. The quartet of hammer blows dropped his bloodied figure backwards, draped over an older woman gunned down by the Nazis during the previous butchery.

A black car roared up from the street to the base of the steps of the Herald Building. Police sirens wailed in the distance as the blond commando hustled Miss Dale and Mr. Garand down the steps. Everywhere, the screams of the wounded and frightened were heard. Most huddled in fear, or wailed over the bodies of their slain loved ones. Others were shot by the remaining Germans if they stood in the way, whether they were brave or shell-shocked.

The black car was driven by the fierce-eyed German woman. She nodded to the team leader, motioning the pair of frightened abductees to the back seat while she revved the engine. The big German entered the passenger side of the car, his pistol trained on Miss Dale. Once they were inside, she tore off down the crowded city street, fleeing pedestrians bouncing off the fenders and hood of her sedan.

The world congealed before Agent "X"'s stunned eyes. He was gasping for air, the wind driven out of him by the rapid succession of gunshots he had taken. He felt for his chest by instinct, his heart hammering in his ears as he struggled to breath. His fingers brushed over the four stubs jutting from his lightweight armor, their ferocious energy transferred into the special woven material instead of his person. He stumbled to his feet, just in time to see a second black sedan tear away from the carnal scene with the remainder of the German assault team. The people around him were too busy saving their own skins to notice his Lazarus impersonation. He staggered to the olive green government car. It was riddled with bullet holes, but its tires were intact, and the only fluids leaking under it belonged to its former occupants. He scooped up a fallen agent's revolver as he dove into the car, pushing the body aside roughly. Good, the keys were still in it. He started the

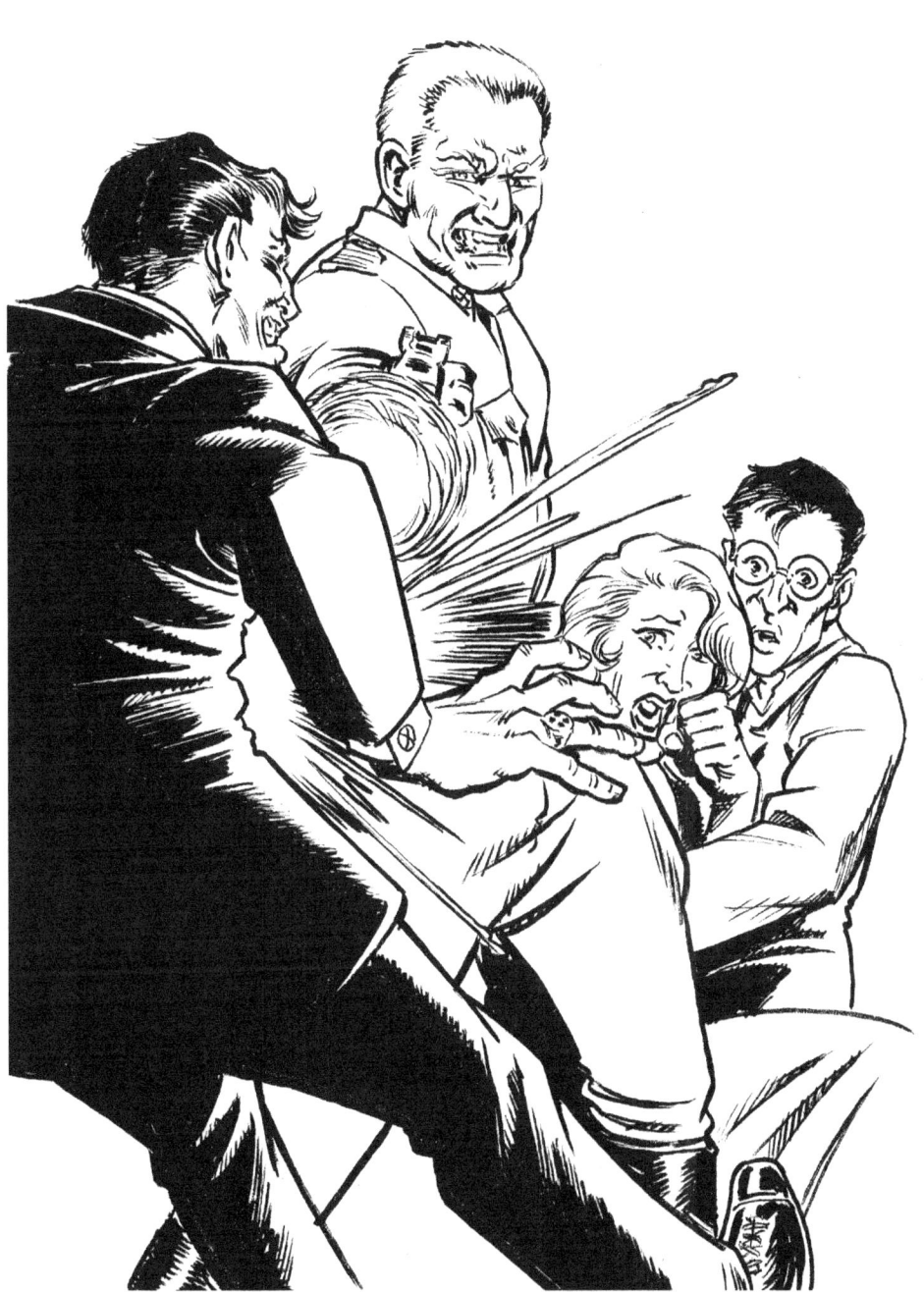

The Aryan brute put four shots directly into Agent "X"'s chest.

engine, slammed the car into gear, and took off in pursuit of the pair of sedans.

Chapter Six

The two large sedans had a good fifteen or twenty second lead on him. Barging through mid-afternoon traffic was never easy, but these murderers were making good time by rear-ending other cars into intersections, driving through flimsy newsstands, and barreling the wrong way down empty one-way streets.

Agent "X" was driving nearly as recklessly, grinding gears as he struggled to move his vehicle through the debris and carnage caused by the escaping Germans. The killers in the rear car, closest to him, had slowed down now, and Agent "X" could see one of the men in the back seat knock out the rear window with the butt of his submachinegun. Glass flew in a cascade of twinkling shards, and a brutish black muzzle emerged from the rear of the speeding car.

Flame and chattering thunder erupted, stitching the hood and windscreen of his car with bullets. Agent "X" slammed on the accelerator, ramming the back of the black car just as its driver had to step on the brakes to avoid a large truck. The collision of the two vehicles sent the German spilling out of the back of his own vehicle, onto the hood of Agent "X"'s car. The truck moved from the path of the two cars, and the black sedan tore away, leaving the Aryan killer stranded and weaponless.

Agent "X" kicked his bullet-riddled windscreen out, and reached for the dazed man on the car's hood. Pulling him towards him, he slammed the man's forehead into the car's body where it met the top of the windshield. The blow knocked the German out, and "X" followed through the assault by pulling the man into the green sedan with him. He folded into an unconscious heap in the passenger footwell.

Fishtailing quickly around the truck, Agent "X" caught sight of the two cars again, half a block ahead of him. They were headed for a small public market. Produce and people flew as the lead car barreled through the crowded square, bashing carts and bodies aside with sickening regularity.

Agent "X" followed his car through the melee of wounded market-goers and squashed groceries. There was no time to stop to help the injured, though he saw many who needed help. He gritted his teeth, and leaned harder on the gas pedal.

The Germans' cars were now exiting the market, and were headed for the docks down by the East River. Narrowly avoiding a bus, he managed to draw even with the rear car. The two of the three men in the vehicle brought pistols to bear on him. Their silenced Lugers spat projectiles into the side of his already-mauled government sedan, the impacts rattling the cab of the vehicle.

Agent "X" braved the hail of fire, keeping his car abreast of the Germans. Between shots, he saw ahead that the two-lane road they were on narrowed to one lane. The lead car had already shot through the narrows, barely missing another car. Agent

"X" pulled his steering wheel hard into the other car, causing the two vehicles' sheetmetal to scream. Sparks flew from the hubcaps as Agent "X"'s momentum carried the German car against the curb. The narrowed lane loomed closer as the two speeding juggernauts hurtled down the street, parts of running board and pieces of tire flying.

The German driver was unable to push back against Agent "X"'s lateral assault. His car jumped the tall curb, and "X" saw all three men throw up their hands as the black car hit a thick stone staircase leading up to an apartment building. Agent "X" looked back at the shattered wreck, confident that none of the men were going to walk away from the high-speed collision. The police would deal with them. He had Betty to save.

The remaining German car was more than a block ahead of him now. The giant Aryan trooper kept his pistol pointed at Betty's head, but his gaze never left Agent "X". Seeing half of his squad knocked out of commission caused his stern expression to twist and harden. He barked an order, and the shorthaired woman spun the steering wheel, causing the car to heel right and disappear from view.

As he pushed his embattled car harder, the folded-up German in the seat beside him began to stir. Agent "X" had saved the pistol from the press conference for shooting out tires. It now served handily as a club. The German let out a small squawk as he painfully exited consciousness, courtesy of the butt of the revolver's grip.

Agent "X" caught sight of the fleeing black car when he rounded the corner moments later. The two Germans had switched positions, the hulking male now driving. As the sedan continued to speed away, the woman emerged slowly from the passenger side window. Her sleek upper body seemed to slither from the escaping car's window, twisting to face backwards at him even as she hurtled down the road. Her serpentine motions were not just for display, however.

A long, black, cylindrical shape emerged from the window, impossibly large. The shape resembled a weapon, but it was almost an oversized caricature. A muzzle brake resembling a miniaturized artillery piece was soon pointed at him, and he saw one of the blue eyes of the German woman disappear behind a large sniper scope. She cocked the weapon, and smiled as she found a favorable sight picture.

The world closed to just the two of them, hunter and prey, both hurtling down a New York City street at breakneck speeds. The Aryan woman squeezed off the massive rifle's trigger just as her driver was forced to hit the brakes to avoid a collision, throwing off her aim. The detonation of the cartridge was deafening, despite the road noise and moderate distance of 75 yards or so. The shell flew high, but the boom and crack of the projectile deafened him.

She chambered the next round easily. Agent "X" saw the empty brass cartridge fly from the rifle's ejection port. The empty brass casing was the size of a small bottle. It fell by the wayside, bouncing noisily into the storm drain as he continued his mad pursuit down the crowded street.

He feared what would happen when her driver gave her an opportunity to make a more steady shot. He didn't have to wait long. The cannon thundered again, a blazing gash of flame burning from its muzzle. Agent "X"'s car shuddered like it had been hit with a boulder. The middle of the car's dashboard exploded, blowing out the radio and clipping the stem of the gear shifter. He stared numbly at the shifter knob he now held in his hand. As he brought it to his face for closer inspection, he noticed the flames and smoke emanating from the sides of the car's perforated engine compartment. She had split his engine block and crippled his car with a single shot.

Cursing, Agent "X" hit the brakes. He raged and hammered against the steering wheel, tormented by the last glimpse he caught of Betty Dale looking back at him, desperation in her beautiful eyes. The black car continued its rampage down the street, disappearing into the concrete and steel canyons of New York.

People on the street emerged from their hiding places, yelling at each other to compensate for the ringing in their ears. Men ran to the olive green car that was now engulfed in thick black smoke. Flames shot out of the engine compartment, and a pair of construction workers managed to brave the heat to open the driver's door. The smoke cleared momentarily, letting them survey the inside of the car before the fire forced them back. They saw only bullet holes, an empty pair of seats, and an open passenger side door.

Chapter Seven

It had not been easy, carrying the unconscious German commando through the back alleys of the packed Italian immigrant neighborhood. The commotion he left behind him distracted the people for blocks around, but he had to find a safe place to hole up soon. A blood-covered man with four gunshots in his suit jacket, carrying an unconscious German soldier, tended to stick out in people's minds.

He continued down the alley, half carrying, half dragging the wounded Wehrmacht commando. He came to the rotted back door of a repair garage. Hearing no noise, he peaked through a small hole in the door. Nothing. Good. It must be closed down, a victim of the times.

Propping the Nazi against the wall, Agent "X" kicked the door in. It yielded with a crack of sodden splinters, the lock and hasp tearing out of their aged sockets with a single blow. "X" dragged the slumping man inside, and evaluated his situation.

A chain hoist, usually meant for pulling engines out of cars, was attached to a steel beam that traversed the width of the garage. It would do for what he hand in mind. Agent "X" rolled his unconscious prisoner onto his belly. Removing the man's belt from his trousers, he pulled the man's arms back and folded them across the small of his back. Agent "X" fastened the belt tight around the man's forearms, so that his limbs were locked uncomfortably behind him. The brute began to stir.

Agent "X" then attached the J-hook from the hoist to the belt. Hauling on the hoist's second chain, the hook began to rise. The soldier was dragged slowly until he was sitting upright, his arms at a peculiar angle behind his back. The pain awoke him from his daze, but before he could regain his composure or let himself off the hook, Agent "X" had him suspended.

The man's arms threatened to dislocate from their sockets as he rose higher and higher. He bellowed in agony, dangling in midair. Agent "X" lowered the chain slightly, so that the majority of his weight was still carried by the torturous belt and hook, and just the tips of his boots scraped oil-stained concrete.

Speaking in German to the man, "X" said, "Your name. Your mission. Your rendezvous point. Give them to me, and the pain stops."

The man swore at him, casting aspersions about his ancestry. A "nein" through gritted teeth was the only non-profane response he gave.

Agent "X" ratcheted the chain back up, and the man howled. "X" left him there until one arm popped and hung at a sickening angle. The other shoulder socket nearly gave way as well, but the German was lowered until again only his toes touched the ground.

"Your name. Your mission. Your rendezvous point. I will not ask again."

Moaning, trying to aggravate the flaming pain in his shoulder as little as possible, the man gasped out, "My name…is Mickey…Mouse." The German then made a vulgar menu suggestion for Agent "X" of the scatological variety.

Agent "X" reached into one of his many pockets. Finding the right set of capsules, he snapped one loose from the others, and crushed it. Instead of emitting a puff of gas, a pale orange paste oozed into the palm of his gloved hand. He showed it to the German, "This is oleoresin capsicum. Very hot. Very painful, especially in this concentrated form. Let me know in a few minutes if you're willing to talk."

"X"smeared the searing concoction over the German's eyelids, working the concentrated chili residue into the tear ducts, corneas, and eyebrows with vigor. The man began to scream, an unholy sound that echoed through the garage. The jagged note doubled in volume as "X" began to lift the man higher in the air. Soon, rank, name, organization, and chain of command began spewing from the man's lips. He was a corporal in a special unit of advisors, helping General Franco's troops in the bloody Spanish Civil War. His name was Klaus, Klaus Mueller to be exact. They had been ordered, as Agent "X" had already deduced, to kidnap John Garand and bring him back to build a new rifle for the German Army.

Agent "X" brought him back down with the hoist, lowering him until he was sobbing on his knees. The fearful pain in his eyes was diminished by a cupful of water from a filthy garage sink. Agent "X" had the man hold still, and pushed his arm back into its socket with a deft movement. The throbbing pain in his shoulder suddenly stopped, like a switch had been flipped. Agent "X" held the hoist's chain plainly in view, the threat to use it more than implied, and began to ask questions.

"Tell me, Klaus, who is the woman with that rifle? What is her name?"

"I only know her last name is Gerheim. She was attached to our unit after we received orders from Berlin to go on this mission. I know she is an amazing shot, far better than any sniper or Olympian I have ever seen before. They call her the Valkyrie."

"The Valkyrie? Like Brunnhilda?"

The soldier grimaced through the pain radiating from his eyes, "One of the stupid U-boat crewmen asked her that, and she broke his jaw in three places."

"And the rifle?"

"I have never seen anything like it. It must be experimental. You should have seen what it did to the first man we dispatched at a small boathouse when we came ashore."

"I did. Nasty piece of equipment, there."

The man sniffled, snot pouring from his nose and hot tears still streaming from his eyes. The oleoresin capsicum was non-lethal, for the most part, but packed a terrible wallop, especially when it made contact with the eyes or nasal passages. Agent "X" walked over to the sink again, and filled another cup with water.

As he poured the water over the German's head, flushing the compound away, he soothed, "There, there, Klaus, not to worry. This burning compound is rather unpleasant, yes?"

"Yes. I have never felt this much pain before, in all my years of service and training."

"Yes, well, Klaus, what you experienced there was just the beginning of what I can do to you if you don't answer my next question. I am not a sadistic man, but as we both know, I have ways of finding out what I want."

Klaus stiffened, listened very carefully to the question, and gave a very detailed response to the man who had filled his life with pain for the last hour. Agent "X" popped another capsule under Klaus' nose, one that knocked him out instantly.

"X"stripped the man of his uniform, gun belt, and other accessories. Taking a small, palm-sized camera from his vest, Agent "X" took profile shots from every angle of the man's face. He dragged him out into the alley, and left him, his arms still bound behind his back. Klaus would be found soon enough, but Secret Agent "X" would not be there when the police or another agency scooped him up. Agent "X" had an appointment with the Valkyrie.

Chapter Eight

Surprisingly, the vast majority of the information Klaus Mueller provided was true. The uniform Klaus had provided happened to be a bit small, though, and required a small amount of altering for his larger frame and accompanying gear. Though needle and thread had helped with the uniform, the Wehrmacht-issue hobnail boots the man wore were not as forgiving, though Agent "X" had tried repeatedly to muscle his feet into them. A similar pair was substituted from his supply reserves. They weren't identical, but they were good enough to satisfy a passing glance. "X" hoped it was enough.

Like Mueller's boots, Agent "X" found his rushed plan to rescue Betty Dale and

John Garand a bit hard to squeeze into as well. He pushed his doubts aside, and sifted through the large amount of information with which Klaus had deluged him. The concentrated pepper extract exerted quite a formidable influence upon the young man. Agent "X" used the stuff previously only as a distraction device. He would have to remember its use as an induced duress when extracting information in the future.

He had found the abandoned factory easy enough. What had delayed him was developing the photos he had taken of Mueller, and fabricating a disguise based on them. Even more time was spent waiting for night to fall, giving him cover to ascend to his perch here on the roof, high above the factory floor. It turned out to be one of the facilities Garand was slated to re-open on the lonely New Jersey waterfront to produce his rifles. Whether this was intentional irony on the Nazis' part, he did not know.

Night had now fallen, and gray clouds hid the thin sliver of rising moon. He peered through a missing skylight, careful not to put his weight on any of the rusted patches that dotted the corrugated roof. A boot sticking through the factory's ceiling, whether it looked like Wehrmacht issue or not, would draw gunfire.

The Nazis had taken refuge at the remote industrial site but they did not look interested in staying for long. They were packing their supplies, arranging their saboteur materials in long rows that were illuminated by worklights on stands. Agent "X" saw a multitude of explosives in various shapes and sizes, cases of ammunition, and other military supplies. The sheer amount of material was too great to have been simply rowed ashore from a submarine. A great deal of preparation had gone into this misadventure. He took a small bit of grim satisfaction knowing that he had disrupted it. Now to finish it.

The unit's commander, the large Aryan he now knew as Captain Donner, continued his attempts to raise their U-boat on a bulky short-wave radio transmitter. The Valkyrie lounged about, smoking a cigarette while lying across a small stack of duffel bags. A large case nearby undoubtedly contained that cannon of hers. Betty Dale and Mr. Garand were held a short distance away, in what used to be a floor supervisor's office. They sat on the floor, gagged, blindfolded, and bound back to back.

Seeing Betty like this made Agent "X"'s blood boil with barely-contained rage. He focused his anger, channeled it, steeling himself for this final reckoning with the Wehrmacht commandos. It took considerable effort, and he was unsure if his control was just a self-imposed illusion. Regardless, it would have to do.

Klaus said their numbers were few, and again he was right. They were even fewer now that there were only four of them left, from the original team of ten. The other two troopers busied themselves, one tearing down briefing displays and boards with newspaper clippings and intelligence photographs on them. The other moved around nervously, peering through windows that looked out to the waterfront. Occasionally he would walk away from the windows, and move wooden boxes next to the other long arrangement of explosives. Between boxes, he invariably returned to the window, his hands straying to the submachinegun slung across his back.

The radio stations across the nation had blazed with breaking news announcements since the shootout erupted on the steps of the Herald building. Dozens were dead or injured. Foreign soldiers had been found along the course of a maddened car chase like breadcrumbs strewn along a path.

J. Edgar Hoover's G-men had swooped down on the captured Germans, and had gone so far as to physically pull them out of New York police department squad cars and holding cells to place them in federal custody. They, like he, had a job to do, and even though they had arrived to the party late, they still played their part. He knew many F.B.I. agents personally, through his many aliases and contacts, and found them to be good men. The high-profile nature of their organization made them effective as a national agency, but unwieldy when dealing with specialized situations such as this. Unrestrained and unencumbered, Agent "X" was able to move through the underworld like a ghost, in places they could not follow.

Being a ghost was lonely, though, and his unorthodox tactics often put him at odds with public opinion, even if he served the same common good. It was a hard road, one he knew was best walked in solitude.

Thoughts of being alone also brought back thoughts of the lovely Miss Dale, wondering if there was ever going to be a day when things would be different, and he wouldn't have to hide from her in plain sight anymore. He shook his head, and focused on what he had to do.

Agent "X" slowly backed away from his high vantage point. He slid softly to the steel access ladder he had come up. He padded softly down to the bottom rung of the ladder, moving from shadow to shadow as he began his final approach. His concentration and night-vision was spoiled as headlights suddenly flashed across him. The sight of Betty had distracted him, and a diesel-powered vehicle's rumble had gone unheard until it was close to the facility.

The headlights of the truck did not dwell on him, though, and he moved to the edge of the building to see the same large truck from the Bund meeting backing up to the factory's loading dock. As "X" watched, young men jumped down from the back of the truck and quickly began loading the supplies. The portly Bund leader, Werner Mannheim, wriggled down from the driver's seat and greeted the large Wehrmacht leader with a crisp Nazi salute. The giant man returned the salute, though with less pomp and circumstance. Agent "X" could not hear their conversation, but they walked around the material and towards the Valkyrie. The large commando waved one hand broadly and slowly, indicating that it all must go. Mannheim must have said something less than agreeable to the request, because the Valkyrie leapt up and slapped him while pulling her pistol.

The Bund members froze, their work of loading the truck nowhere near complete. The two other Wehrmacht troopers brought their weapons to the ready, and motioned the lot of them up against the wall.

The Valkyrie pushed her pistol against the now-blubbering Mannheim's temple. She led him over to his men, and stepped away.

The crying man managed a loud, "But Captain, I swear I did not fail you!"

The Captain barked an order, and the eight men were machinegunned down before the fat Bund leader could elaborate. Their bodies fell in an awkward heap, and a survivor who tried to drag himself clear from the pile was dispatched with a single shot from the Valkyrie's suppressed pistol. The large officer ordered the two troopers to burn the bodies in a smelting pit on the far side of the factory, and they grimly set themselves to the task.

Agent "X" decided it was time to make his move. Placing his arm into the sling he wore around his neck, he limped into sight of Captain Donner and the Valkyrie. They instantly turned their weapons on him, but relaxed when they saw he wore the bruised and battered face of their own Corporal Klaus Mueller. The facial disguise had taken hours to prepare, but the investment in time and effort paid off when they instantly lowered their weapons.

"Klaus, you bastard, how did you manage to escape?" was the large Captain's stunned question. The incredulous grin on his face showed that Agent "X"'s ruse was working, at least for now.

Agent "X" feigned injury as he drew a ragged breath. He limped over to a stack of boxes, and sat down with a great deal of implied misery. He gritted his teeth, and ground out the pain-laced words, much like Klaus had done in the garage.

"It was not easy, sir," he motioned to the artificial bruises and cuts on his face, "the other men in my vehicle were not as lucky as I was. They were pinned in the car. That madman chasing us left us for dead, and I managed to pull myself from the car before the Amerikanner police arrived. I hid in an abandoned garage until night fell."

He gestured with his free hand at the sling, "I think my arm is broken, as well. It was difficult to steal a car and drive here, but I did."

The Valkyrie spoke, eyeing him coldly. She must have seen his/Mueller's pain as weakness, or never had a high opinion of Klaus to begin with.

"He chased us as well, but I stopped him. I put a round into his car, and it caught fire. Those idiotic briefings about the supposed American vigilante proved true after all."

She shifted her gaze, "Your uniform is a mess, Mueller. Where is your belt?"

Agent "X" shrugged his acted response of indifference, and gave a low moan as he shifted his weight. "I don't know, Madame Valkyrie. It must have come off when I pulled myself out of the car wreck."

The Captain came close, and laid a beefy paw on his shoulder. "Never mind that. It's good to see you again, Mueller. Help Dieter and Paulsen with the bodies of those morons we shot. We'll talk later on the U-boat."

"Jawohl, Captain. Right away."

As he turned, he caught the slightest glimpse of the Captain and Valkyrie exchanging an icy look. The hairs on the back of his neck stood up. Did they know? Continuing the pained routine, he shuffled off slowly, joining the returning pair of troopers as they loaded up another set of bodies. They were glad to see him, but he begged off their questions by telling him that he was hurting too much to talk, and that they should just complete the task at hand.

Troopers Dieter and Paulsen made quick work of the pile of carnage, taking the victims to the back of the factory, one by one. Agent "X" dragged one of the smaller young men by the collar, following the other two Nazis. It was slow going as he tried to keep his arm in the sling, tugging at the dead weight. He recognized the youth as one of the beer servers from the Bund meeting. Eventually, he and the corpse arrived at the back of the factory.

He set the young man in a newly-formed pile of dead traitors. He groaned, and sat down at a desk in what was once a machine shop. The other two men piled body after body back in a giant smelting crucible. The huge vessel was reminiscent of a cup, though a thousand times larger. It had once held tons of molten steel. Now it was to be pressed into service as a crematorium for the bungling Bund Judases.

Their task nearly complete, the two Nazis struggled to put the last body, the late Herr Mannheim, into the pit on top of his men. Two gas cans were poured over the bodies, and lit with a tossed match. The two men stood over the funeral pyre, smoking and making small talk while they watched the bodies burn, casting occasional looks over at him at the desk as they spoke in low voices. Satisfied that the fire could be left to burn untended, they made their way back to the assembly area. Agent "X" stood up, limping to join them on the walk back.

He slowly pulled a large pair of abandoned slip-joint pliers off their dusty rack on the wall, freeing his arm from the sling as he did so. The pliers were formidable, meant for gripping various sizes of large pipe, and would serve well for what he had in mind. He let the first man pass him, and swung the heavy metal pliers for all he was worth into the back of the second man's knee. The blow crippled Paulsen, sending him to the ground with a shout. Dieter turned in confusion, but Agent "X" had popped the pliers open to the widest they would go, and viciously grabbed the man's elbow. The powerful tool's jaws crushed the complex joint with a wet, slow popping sound. As the man's eyes widened in pain, Agent "X" pulled him hard into his fallen compatriot. The two soldiers butted heads violently, knocking each other out. Agent "X" relieved them of their weapons, stripping them apart expertly and tossing the separate parts into the darkness.

Agent "X" made his way back to the loading dock area on the other side of the facility, slowly settling back into the pained limp he had shown before. He slipped his arm back into the sling, careful not to disturb the other things concealed within it. The German Captain was back on the radio set, deeply involved in his work. The Valkyrie was nowhere to be seen. Agent "X" shambled past a stack of rusted barrels that took him near the floor supervisor's office. He peered through smudged windows at the captives held within. Both were awake, though it was pointless for them to struggle. The ropes holding them were strong, with thick knots binding them. The rage in him bubbled up again as Betty tried desperately to shake her blindfold off, though the effort only whipped the back of poor Mr. Garand's head with her hair.

Agent "X" looked through the far windows of the office, and saw that the Captain was no longer at his radio. Looking up in the reflection of the window closest to him, he saw the muzzle of the Valkyrie's cannon, and her distant, distorted image. She was up high on a gantry, above and to his left.

He pulled himself down just as she fired the massive rifle. The round cracked by the back of his neck, creasing the top of his right shoulder as he dove for the floor. The windows of the office exploded, showering the bewildered captives with tiny pieces of glass.

As she reloaded, Agent "X" made his way to the stacks of barrels, trying to get out of sight of the lady sniper. The Captain was waiting for him as he rounded the corner of the office. He pulled his arm from the sling, and braced himself for combat.

"How did you know, Donner? Was it the belt, or the boots? It was the damn boots, wasn't it?"

"Nein. Klaus was a whiner. Burning bodies was beneath him. You agreed far too easily."

Agent "X" smiled and lunged, knocking the pistol from the giant man's hand. The move left him exposed, and the Captain's heavy fist crashed into "X"'s face. Stunned by the ringing blow, Agent "X" found himself being crushed in a bear hug by the big man. As his last bit of breath hissed out of him, he pulled back, and head-butted the goliath.

Blood shot from the man's broken nose. The pain caused his grip to loosen, and Agent "X" slipped loose from the constriction hold. "X" felt the cheek-piece of the Klaus Mueller mask peel back, hanging by a thin section of rubber. He instinctively reached for it, but then realized it was no time for keeping up appearances. The Nazi snorted crimson, and charged him.

A pair of solid punches to the man's midsection yielded nothing but hollow thumps. The German was a powerful specimen, a fact he demonstrated with a solid right hook that sent Agent "X" reeling into the tall stack of barrels. The pile came down with a large clatter, separating the men for a moment. A noxious fluid poured from the rusted containers, some sort of petroleum product that burned the eyes and nose. Gallons of the stuff formed a small lake as it glugged and flowed from the tumbled containers. Taking a pause from the brawl, Agent "X" reached into the sling that once held his arm, and pulled items from small pockets sewn into the cloth.

The Valkyrie had reloaded another shell in her rifle's chamber, and scanned for the intruder among the clutter of fallen barrels and spreading pool of chemicals. The Mueller imposter was impressive, undoubtedly the same mystery man she had nearly dispatched earlier. She tracked a gray-green blur of a Wehrmacht uniform, and swung to follow it. A sudden puff of smoke blocked her scope's vision, but she instinctively hammered a round into the center of the cloud, hoping to hit the man. Another smoke cluster popped up nearby, and she again reloaded and fired her huge weapon in one smooth movement. She saw the man flash by her magnified sight picture, and fired again, but missed. The relatively close distances here in the factory were not conducive to her riflescope's powerful magnification, and shots that were easily taken at hundreds of yards went by too quickly at a distance of less than two hundred feet.

She grinned ferociously as the Captain found the false Klaus amidst the swirling

Agent "X" found himself being crushed in a bear hug by the big man.

cloud. Her smile faded as the smaller man punched the large officer in the throat with frightful speed. He was quick, she must admit, but Captain Donner had brute strength and years of special training. The Nazi lifted the smaller man up over his head, driving him with a splash into the now-slick factory floor. A pair of punishing elbow strikes followed the maneuver, but the mysterious man remained in the fight. A swift kick from the downed imposter sent the Captain staggering backwards in the smoke, his cheekbone shattered. She watched in disbelief as the man pulled a knife, seemingly from nowhere, and leapt into the fog after the Wehrmacht commando.

For an instant, nothing but smoke filled her vision. A pair of footsteps splashed in the spreading puddle. Then, a cry of pain, then nothing again. She braced herself, her finger taking up the slack in the trigger, and probed the artificial mist for the man.

She heard more splashing footsteps. Then, a faint silhouette with its arm in a sling lurched from the swirling chaos, and she fired without hesitation or evaluation. The anti-tank rifle bucked and roared, and the round streaked unerringly to its target.

Too late, she saw her Captain drop to his knees, a knife sticking out of his left shoulder, his wounded arm hastily shoved into the sling once worn by the ersatz Mueller. The Valkyrie shrieked in anger as her team leader flopped over, his sternum neatly punched through by the half-inch bullet. As the sight of her leader held her gaze, she heard the noise of a small metallic clatter. Looking through the grate of the catwalk, she saw the mystery man now beneath her position. He was holding a length of steel cable attached to a small grappling hook. The hook ran through the grating by her. With a mighty tug, the rusted bolts holding her catwalk to the factory's wall groaned and shrieked as they gave way, sending her plummeting to the floor fifteen feet below in a pile of twisted steel.

Screaming and baring her teeth, her usual cool beauty turned to fury as she pulled herself up from the tangle of scrap metal. She yanked her pistol from its holster, and swung the weapon up, firing it reflexively as it rose up its arc. The man deftly moved aside, rotating into a kick that sent her against another stack of barrels.

Her burst of pistol rounds caused sparks to fly as they hit the concrete floor. Vapors from the eye-stinging chemicals lit, and the pair of them watched a ghostly ring of blue fire expand away from her errant rounds. The flames reached one barrel that still stood on its base. The flames swept up to the barrel, and it promptly exploded in a geyser of thick black smoke that launched the barrel to the factory's high ceiling.

The Valkyrie leveled the pistol at him again, and pulled the trigger just as he flung a razor ring at her. The hammer of the pistol fell on an empty chamber, but the circular blade bit severely into her hand, causing her to drop the pistol with a curse. Agent "X" advanced at her, a second razor ring about to be thrown, when another barrel exploded. It, too, launched like a rocket, landing on the thin roof of the floor supervisor's office.

Spitting blood from his mouth, his eyes stinging from the leaking chemicals,

Agent "X" turned in horror as the ring of fire expanded to other barrels. The paint and rust on their surfaces began to blister. A few wooden boxes that had not been loaded on to the truck were burning as well. Boxes that contained more than just reeking solvents or abandoned turpentine. Oh my God. Betty and Garand.

Agent "X" kept his hands in loose half-fists, and quickly evaluated the Valkyrie. She was hurt, but her combat posture told him that she was trained in more than just expert marksmanship. There was no time for brawling. He had to move back to the hostages. Snarling, he broke contact with her, and bolted for the office.

He jumped through the shattered window, and quickly cut Garand loose just as another barrel detonated. It was followed in quick succession by another, and another. Agent "X" pushed the little man out the office door, carrying the still-tied Betty over his bruised and bloodied shoulder. The lip of the loading dock was so far away, and the flames dancing on the explosive-loaded boxes were so close. Blasts detonated back in the area where "X" had knocked the Valkyrie into the barrels. With luck, she was caught in those flames, but Agent "X" knew better.

"X" roughly lowered Betty over his shoulder ahead of him. Her blindfold had worked its way loose while he had struggled to carry her. He saw her eyes widen as she disappeared from sight. Agent "X" looked back as he scrambled down over the loading dock to follow her. Garand had fallen, just out of arms reach. Agent "X" glanced at the explosives, lunged for Garand, and caught the back of his collar. Pulling with all his wounded might, Agent "X" hauled the weapons designer over the edge of the loading dock just as the pile of wooden crates touched off.

The concussive wave blew the contents of the Bund men's truck over the apron of the loading dock, and peeled the cab loose from the frame like a giant child snapping a toy. The items in the truck's bed flew for yards, but the shockwave passed over the three figures huddled under the lip of the dock. Wave after wave of explosions went off on the factory floor, causing the foundations of the building to buck and heave. Finally, the man-made storm subsided.

Agent "X" grunted as he cut the last of Betty Dale's rope bonds. His bloodshot eyes, reddened by the former contents of the barrels, regarded her kindly. A wry grin crossed his partially disguised, explosion-scorched face.

"Miss Dale, may I suggest in the future, you choose your feature articles with a bit more care."

Her confusion from the earlier abduction and slaughter on the Herald's steps deepened. Here she was, staring at a Wehrmacht trooper who had just saved her from a detonating factory. She took in his weary frame, his peeling face, and suddenly, her confusion melted away in a moment of clarity.

"It's you, again, isn't it? I knew it was you in that car, and now here you are. Oh, Secret Agent "X"...I don't know what to-"

"Say nothing, especially if it's 'thank you'. It's just what I'm called to do, Miss Dale."

Garand piped up, "Well, Secret Agent "X", please permit me to express my gratitude, if you will not allow it from the lovely lady. You saved me from a fate that is too cruel to ponder."

"Besides," he added, a mischievous look overtaking his normal bookish expression, "I can't stand German food."

Agent "X" allowed a small chuckle as he stood up, then grimaced in pain as he gripped his bullet-creased shoulder. He looked at the blast-devastated factory, and saw no sign of the German woman with the short blonde hair and the flashing eyes. A length of twisted pipe near the lip of the dock drew his eye, and he reached for it. Pulling it from the wreckage surrounding it, he examined its ruined length for a brief moment, then passed it to John Garand.

The ordnance man hefted the weight of the smoldering portable cannon. He looked it over, taking in every detail, every curve, every line. His lips began to move as he made quiet calculations and observations. Agent "X" smiled as the weapons designer turned to look at him through cracked glasses, giddy as a schoolboy.

"It's a recoil-operated action, with delayed blowback. Look here, see how this cam rotates the bolt, and opens the chamber? And here, the rotating bolt face looks like it's based on the Mauser action. It extracts and ejects automatically, but a new round must be chambered by hand! It's-"

"It's something you need to reverse engineer, my dear Mister Garand, for the coming storm," Agent "X" interjected. Sirens began to wail some distance away. Whether they were fire or police, he could not stay to find out.

"The coming storm, yes, quite. There's not a lot here to work with, but I've already got a few ideas. Let see here…what happens when I push this button," a piece of the ruined weapon unlatched, accompanied by a giggle from the weaponsmith.

Betty stood, a wistful look in her eyes. She looked at the pulverized factory, and the shattered truck, and then to him. She brushed back a hanging bit of the Klaus Mueller mask with her hand, exposing the all-too-real bruises underneath the disguise. Her soft palm stayed on the side of his brutalized jawline.

"Agent "X", there's so much I want to tell you…and yet I don't know where to start…"

He found his own hands approaching her waist. He halted them, then gently took her hand from his cheek. He held it with his two hands, and slowly let it slide from between them as he backed away.

"Good-bye, Betty. I shall be seeing you from time to time, though I doubt you will recognize me. Do take care of Mr. Garand, here, and see to it the proper authorities are notified that the Valkyrie is still on the loose. In the meantime, I'll continue the chas-"

One last barrel cooked off within the depths of the shattered factory. The explosion caused Garand and Betty Dale to reflexively pull back behind the concrete loading dock's protection. The blast caught them unprepared. Blinking and coughing away the last of the foul black smoke, they stood and looked around in vain: the battered man in the Wehrmacht uniform was gone.

The End

Don't Worry, I'll Get To It:
Of Anti-Tank Rifles and Looming Deadlines

What can I say, I'm a procrastinator. More on that in a minute, but first I wish to thank Mr. Ron Fortier for the chance to write for him. I landed on Ron's radar because of Chad Hardin, a damn good friend whom I've been bouncing ideas off since we first met in high school, more than 16 years ago as of this writing. Chad introduced me to Ron, and I introduced Ron to some of the short stories I've self-published. He asked me if I would be interested in doing a Secret Agent "X" story for an upcoming anthology. I usually deal with science fiction and superhero adventures, but I welcomed the chance to stretch my horizons with pulp heroics, and took the job.

Back to the procrastination bit. Ron gave me this assignment in the spring of 2008. I researched, and read similar tales to make sure I wasn't retreading someone else's story, and researched some more. A month or so of grappling with the pulp concept later, and I didn't even have an outline. The deeper I delved into pulp writing, the more doubts I had. How was I going to put words in characters' mouths without them sounding like bad gangster caricatures from old Bugs Bunny cartoons? Ron's deadline of Labor Day loomed large, but by mid-June something finally emerged, a vision of a stunning blond Nazi sniper with our hero in her crosshairs.

Well, this being the pulps, no ordinary rifle would do. I'm a firearms enthusiast, like my father and grandfather before me, so the natural choice for a larger-than-life portable weapon from the 1930's was, of course, an anti-tank rifle. The story's rifle is an imaginary experimental hodgepodge of a few real weapons from that time period, though most weren't equipped with scopes like the one in the story. Most A-T rifles were brutal, sewer-pipe affairs, none nearly as elegant as the imaginary long-distance killing machine that the Valkyrie wielded. Their latter-day descendents, .50 caliber rifles, are still with us, but tanks designers have long stopped worrying about simple ballistic rounds fired from man-portable cannons.

I focused on what such a round was capable of doing to a man, and how using an anti-vehicle weapon tends to demand respect when it's used for sabotage and crime. The story grew from there.

June again. I knocked out a quick outline, roughed out a few characters and high points I wanted to hit, and the idea sat, percolating in the back of my mind. I swore to myself I would hammer out the story before the San Diego Comic-Con, at the end of July, and all would be right with the world.

Well, needless to say, July came and went. Before long, August was staring me in the face. I buckled down, upped my caffeine intake, and knocked out the full text of the story over the span of a couple weeks.

It was an enlightening experience, writing for the pulps. I was intimidated by the character of Secret Agent "X", mainly because he seemed so unstoppable, and had such a wide variety of tools, secret contacts, and other fantastic means and methods at his fingertips. I decided to strip much of that away, and wrote an action story that not only allowed our hero to stop Nazi saboteurs, but also showed Agent "X"'s subtle longing for his long-time unrequited lady love, Miss Betty Dale. By endangering Betty, I hoped to unhinge the normally cucumber-cool Agent "X", forcing him to take shortcuts and risks he normally would forego.

Is my story a full deconstruction of a revered character from days of yore? I hope not. Instead, I just wanted to give a small peek behind his normal façade, to show that even though he wears many faces, he's a human being capable of self-doubt, fear, and minor mistakes, just like you and me.

Well, thanks for putting up with my screed. Please let Ron know if you enjoyed it, via his Airship 27 website, and maybe I'll get the chance to tell you another two-fisted tale here in the pulps.

I'd also like to take this last moment to dedicate this story to my wife, Rachel. Like Agent "X" and his Miss Dale, thoughts of Rachel tend to unhinge me as well. Thanks for your support through the years, gorgeous.

I'm **JOHN BEAR ROSS**, and I write and work in Southern Nevada.

I've worked a variety of jobs, from delivering newspapers as a kid to carrying an M240G in the Marine Corps Reserve. I now work for the Department of Energy as a maintenance contractor, and write when I have ingested sufficient amounts of caffeine.

I'm married to my wife, Beautiful Rachel, and we have two kids together. My work is dedicated to them. My main website is www.johnbearross.com I'm also on Facebook.com/johnbearross and @johnbearross on Twitter.

Thanks for your time.

Chapter One

William Haines was a lucky man and he knew it. Born to a moderately well-off family, his parents' connections assured him a spot in Princeton and a 3rd Vice Presidency at the Murdstone Bank. His mousy wife Agnes was well-bred and completely focused on her various charities and social clubs, allowing William a chance to indulge in less respectable pleasures.

Take tonight for example; five minutes into hitting "Fingers" Creel's night club and he literally ran into Helen…or was it Ellen? Haines didn't know or really care. She was astonishingly shapely with golden blonde hair and catlike green eyes. The accidental meeting proved quite lucky, because a few moments later they were leaving the night club and heading for her nearby apartment.

"You live alone?" William asked, not really interested in Helen/Ellen's living situation.

"Yes, all by myself honey. It's so lonely." She said, her voice a whispery coo.

"Maybe I'll come visit you once in a while. I wouldn't want you to be lonely, my dear." William said. This woman was exactly what he needed as a respite from his dull wife and job.

"Oooh, I'd like that, sweetie!" Helen/Ellen said, snuggling closer to William.

Her musky perfume filled the air and caused William to feel light-headed. The street lights were dim and the area seemed deserted of all life. He was about to ask how far her apartment was from the club, not liking the current neighborhood. But a man stepped out of the alley, blocking their path. He was dressed in dark, rough looking clothes and possessed a hook-like nose and large powerful hands.

"Excuse me." William said, attempting to step around the man. But the woman on his arm held him tight, not letting him move.

"This is the one?" the man asked, his accent not American, but not unpleasant to the ears.

"Excuse me?" William asked, not understanding this at all.

"He's the one you paid for." The woman said her voice no longer musical. She sounded bored and a little annoyed. "Where's my money?"

"You get it from the boss." The man said and turned his attention to William. "You will come with me."

"I will not!" William said, pulling free of the woman. This was all a ruse to kidnap him. Well, William Haines knew the kidnappers hadn't taken into account who they were kidnapping! He was still in the same shape he'd been in when he'd won the middleweight boxing title in Princeton.

Putting up his hands and taking a boxing stance, William said, "Back off or I will make you wish you'd never been born!"

The hooknose man shook his head and stepped a little closer. William fired a quick jab feint at the man's nose and a right hook guaranteed to shatter his jaw. The man never put up his hands but merely moved a few inches to the right and watched as the fist missed him by mere inches.

William didn't lose his balance but shuffled a little closer and threw a jab, right cross and uppercut combo, the same combination that flattened Archie Whitcomb in the third round of the quarterfinals.

But the man wasn't there! Instead he took a slight step to the left and jumped over William. William was a tall man, a little over six feet, but this hooknose man had vaulted him as if he was fire hydrant!

William spun, swinging his arm wildly, but the hooknose man merely ducked and stepped in close. He jammed a wet handkerchief against William's face. The cloth smelled terrible and a second later the world began to spin, going black before he could attempt to get free.

✪✪✪

William woke a short time later, his head spinning and his stomach queasy. The world seemed to be vibrating, a low rumble from all directions. He opened his eyes slowly, feeling dizzy as he tried to sit upright.

"Don't bother." A voice said from above him. William turned his head that way and saw the woman. She was sitting a short distance away on a car seat, legs crossed and a cigarette in her mouth.

"What?" William managed to say, his voice sounding shaky even to his ears. He realized he was lying on the floor in the back of an automobile.

"He drugged you and we're heading to see the boss." The woman said, blowing a long stream of smoke out of her mouth.

"You! You set me up to be kidnapped!" William said and tried to lurch to his feet and throttle the treacherous woman. He stumbled forward, falling back to the floor of the car. His hands and feet were bound tight with thick, strong rope. William tried to struggle but realized the act was a futile waste of time.

"I was about to tell you that he tied up your hands and feet, so don't bother to struggle. And yes, I set you up. The money was very good." The woman said as the car came to a halt.

William lay still for a moment and watched as the door was pulled open and the hooknose man appeared with a younger, darker man at his side. The younger man waved the woman to exit and the two men pulled William to his feet. Moving close to him, the younger man pulled a long, silver-colored knife from his belt and turned it slowly before William's eyes. Any protest was caught in William's throat as he stared at the knife and cold, dead eyes of the man holding the blade.

"I am freeing your legs. If you attempt to run, Asterion here will hurt you very badly. Do you understand?" The older man asked. William nodded and felt his legs freed a moment later.

The room they were in was dark and smelled strongly of fish. Unable to speak, William found himself propelled down a long series of stone steps, finally stopping before a huge, rusted metal door. The older man knocked once and a small slit opened in the center, with one dark eye viewing them carefully for several seconds.

The door opened with a creak and William was pushed roughly inside a long, empty stone chamber lit by a pair of huge braziers. The fires in the braziers cast shadows throughout the room, causing William to shiver with greater fear than ever. There were slits along the floor for some reason and this mystery didn't help his nerves!

The young man pulled William to his knees, the huge knife still in hand, hovering near William's side. "Do not move." The young man said, his accent like that of his hooknose companion.

"We bring to you the one you asked for, Lord Minos." The hooknose man said, "The banker and the one who betrayed him for money."

"Money I want now! You men are bugsy!" The woman barked, standing and stepping forward.

William chanced a look and realized the room was not as empty as he thought. A lone figure sat on a chair set on an elevated platform at the far end of the room. William couldn't make out the figure, seeing only heavy robes covering the person from head to toe.

"Give her to the Minotaur. She is not worthy." The figure on the far end of the room said. "Leave the banker to me."

"Hail Minos!" Both men said and grabbed the protesting woman, dragging her out of the room. The door slammed behind them, leaving William alone in the room with the robed person.

🕈🕈🕈

"Let go of me!" Helen Thomas said, struggling against the two odd men to no avail. She'd tried vamping these two and was surprised by their total lack of interest. That just never happened to her, men always fell at her feet to give her what she wanted, all it took was a little smile and some clever talk.

Helen Thomas knew she was beautiful and had used that beauty since she was younger to get whatever she wanted in life. Need some money for rent? All it took was a smile and a few whispers. A new car, a mink stole. All she needed to do was ask the right way. But not today for some reason.

"Where are you taking me?" She asked, trying another tack.

"To the Minotaur. You are his now." The older man said, stopping before another metal door. A large key hung on a hook by the door and he took it and opened the door. Helen was roughly pushed inside, the door slamming shut behind her and the lock snapping shut a second later.

Helen was surprised to find herself in a well lit corridor with a sandy floor, many passages twisting off in different directions. She knew these men were odd, but this was unusual even in her experience.

"Hello?" she said as she walked forward. There was something very wrong here. Fear crept along her spine.

❊❊❊

William Haines was completely confused. The figure in the robes asked him a series of questions about the Murdstone Bank's employees and colleagues with which he socialized regularly. The questions didn't make any real sense, who cared about the dead heir of Murdstone's and William's busy social life? William gained back some of his courage during the questioning at least, sensing he wasn't being sought for ransom at least.

"Are we finished here? I have been very patient and answered all of your questions!" William Haines said, his bluster back in place. "I wish to return home!"

"I have one more use for you, William Haines." The robed figure said, rising and approaching in a silent glide.

"As a messenger." The figure said, stopping several feet away. "Are you prepared?"

"Yes, of course I am! What do you want me to tell and to whom?" William asked.

"Tell? No, you mistake my meaning, William Haines. The message you give will not use words." The robed figure said and pulled back its hood. "Gaze upon the Mask of Medusa, William Haines! Gaze on the face of death!"

William Haines screamed, loud and terrified, a sound that was cut off as soon as it started….

❊❊❊

"Help! Help me!" Helen Thomas screamed as she ran with all the speed she could muster. Kicking aside her expensive shoes, she ran for her life, trying to get away from that…that thing!

Turning a corner, she found herself in a dead end once again. She turned to retrace her steps when a huge shadow covered her face.

"NOOOOOOOO!!!!!!!!!" Helen screamed as huge hands descended toward her throat…

Chapter Two

❚❚Nobody allowed inside, Miss. Sorry, rules is rules." The patrolman said, looking down at Betty Dale with an apologetic smile. He liked the pretty, golden haired reporter, but he liked his job even more.

"Now Johnson, you know I'll get inside there sooner or later. Better to let me know what the big secret is now and save us both some time." Betty Dale said, flashing the patrolman a wide smile.

The county coroner's office was an unusual place for anyone to try and get into, the presence of dead bodies often made people nervous. But Betty had a hint something unusual was happening, beginning with Inspector John Burks

she screamed as huge hands descended toward her throat...

being summonsed from his fishing vacation. Burks, the well-known expert on the legendary Secret Agent "X", was often called in when an unusual crime appeared. He was often wrong in his belief that "X" was behind the crimes he investigated, but John Burks was an ace detective.

"Inspector Burks said…" Johnson began, but cut off abruptly, looking over Betty's shoulder.

Betty turned and spotted a tall, familiar figure, Police Commissioner Charlie Foster, the politically appointed leader of the police and considered by many to be one of the most important men in the state.

"I think we can allow Miss Dale entry into the chamber, patrolman. The story within will break in the papers and radio soon enough." Foster said and added, "But I'll remember your zeal at your duty."

"Yes, sir, Commissioner!" and Johnson stepped aside, allowing Foster and Betty to pass.

The antiseptic smell of rubbing alcohol and other chemicals struck Betty's nose, caused her to shake her head as she entered the examination area. An unpleasant location, but she'd been here in the past and knew it was a necessary evil in her job as a top newspaper reporter. Betty followed Foster to the far end of the room, spotting Burks and the Chief Coroner, Dr. Farmer leaning over a table. Farmer was an obese, balding man with an abrupt style of speech that made him a figure of respect among the police.

A large figure lay under a clean white sheet, its shape oddly unidentifiable even up close. Betty frowned but realized the reason for the secrecy was soon to become apparent.

"The white marks on the arm are chalk and volcanic ash according to the lab." Dr. Farmer said to Burkes, pointing to something on the table before returning the sheet, hiding it from view.

"What do we have here, Doctor?" Foster asked, his voice hushed.

"Good morning, Commissioner." Dr. Farmer said and glanced at the trailing Betty, "Are you sure you wish to discuss this in front of a reporter?"

"Yes." Foster said, his voice flat but allowing for no further discussion.

"Fine, fine." Dr. Farmer said and pulled back the sheet. Laying on the table was a man, his arms frozen in front of him as if to ward off something terrible. The man's face was frozen in a silent scream, his eyes wide with terror. The man was dead, seemingly from fright!

Betty was horrified by the look of fear on the dead man's face, but her instincts as a reporter prevented her from feeling anything more than the briefest revulsion. She examined the man's face and said after a moment, "That's Billy Haines, isn't it?"

Dr. Farmer looked at her for a moment, impressed by Betty's cool resolve. He nodded and said, "Yes, tentative identification is that this is William Haines, an officer in the Murdstone Bank."

"How do you know the victim, Miss Dale?" Burks asked, his eyes moving from the corpse to her and back.

"I went to school with his younger sister." Betty said, "He seemed more interested in booze than banks. Last time I saw him, he was bragging about befriending that monster, "Fingers" Creel. His crowd likes hanging with roughnecks."

"Terrible, quite terrible, but not very unusual, doctor. Why the veil of secrecy?" Foster inquired, stepping forward and examining the body again.

"Allow me to demonstrate." Dr. Farmer said, pulling a retractor from his pocket. He tapped the instrument against his hand several times, a soft slapping sound filling their ears. The doctor looked at the Police Commissioner and Betty for a few seconds and then moving closer to the body of William Haines raised the retractor and tapped the frozen hand closest to their eyes.

Instead of a soft slapping sound, Foster and Betty heard a loud clicking noise, like the sound of two solid objects striking each other. He tapped again and Betty suddenly realized the point the medical examiner was attempting to make.

"He's frozen solid as a rock!" Betty said, her hand covering her mouth as she fought back revulsion.

"Not frozen, that would imply cold. But yes, this poor man is encased in stone." Dr. Farmer said, nodding. "It's quite impossible, but true."

"Impossible?" Foster asked, sounding outraged, "Throwing victims into cement is a popular means underworld assassination, Doctor!"

"True, Commissioner. But the late Mr. Haines isn't covered in a cement jacket." Dr. Farmer said, "This man's skin has somehow been transformed into stone. It's a scientific impossibility!"

"Secret Agent "X" uses bizarre scientific devices. William Haines must have gotten in the way of one of his diabolical plans." Burks said. "If we discover the means he used to commit this murder, he'll be easy enough to catch!"

"Good man, Burks!" Foster said and looked to Betty, "I trust you'll be discreet, Miss Dale? Good, good! I'll escort you to your car!"

"Thank you," Betty said and allowed Foster to lead her past Officer Johnson and out the door a moment later.

"You're welcome." Foster said, glancing around and added in a different voice, "Burks is on the wrong trail."

Betty blinked with surprise immediately recognizing the voice of Secret Agent "X", "I knew he's wrong that you were behind the attack."

Who was Secret Agent "X"? Few in this world knew and they would never tell that tale. He was the Man of a Thousand Faces, an expert fighter and warrior against the hordes of evil forces in the world. Legends of his skills and powers were whispered in frightened tones by underworld figures, all of whom trembled at the very mention of his name!

"He's also wasting his time attempting to discover the means. The path to the murderer lies through the victim. We need to discover why William Haines was targeted and then the method will reveal itself!" Secret Agent "X" said.

"Where do we start?" Betty asked. The man beneath the disguise was the love of her life, but he would never acknowledge such emotions. "X" was committed only to his never ending struggle against the evils of crime and its many followers!

"You investigate the life of our victim, William Haines. I'm heading to a less savory location, the Murdstone Bank and then the bar owned by 'Fingers' Creel!" said Agent "X."

⊘⊘⊘

Why was "X" investigating this strange crime? Besides its strangeness, he'd been contacted by his mysterious Washington supervisor, the unknown man only known as K-9. They'd spoken only one hour earlier over a telephone line that was hidden from the phone companies and only known to a few select people.

"Agent "X", a strange situation has occurred. A banker named Haines was murdered in your area." The rough voiced K-9 said over the line. "He was employed by Murdstone Bank as vice-president."

"I can look into the death. Why does this concern you?" asked "X".

"The Murdstone Bank is a powerful bank that has strong ties to foreign powers. We suspect they're too close to countries which we believe may work against American interests." K-9 said to the top agent.

"Understood." Said "X" and disconnected. Reaching for the regular telephone, he dialed Betty's number and began assembling his latest disguise. Little did he realize how odd this crime would prove to be, a foul murder by a means unknown to science.

Chapter Three

❚❚Thank you for agreeing to meet me at such short notice, Mr. Murdstone," said "X" in his disguise as Dr. Elisha Pond, wealthy philanthropist. It hadn't been difficult to arrange a meeting with the chairman of the Murdstone Bank, just a simple request. The chance of receiving an investment from the legendary millionaire caused Jessup Murdstone to clear his calendar immediately!

"Yes, the timing was rather inconvenient. However with the death of that idiot Haines, I was able to reschedule several appointments," Jessup Murdstone explained. He was a short, round man with the broad flat face of a bulldog and the growling voice of the same breed of animal. Murdstone was universally reviled for his foul temper and brusque manner as he was revered for his financial acumen.

"I'll try not to waste too much of your time," said "X", "I was considering expanding my investments and your name was presented as one of the best able to assist me in this area."

"One of? No doubt some of my competitors denigrated my name as a means of attracting your business. Well sir, my advice to you is to invest in Murdstone Bank. Our investors currently receive 4% returns as of this morning." Murdstone boasted, thumping his desk for emphasis.

"Four and a quarter percent, Mr. Murdstone," said the man standing to the right of Murdstone's desk. He was a reed thin man with hunched shoulders, large round glasses and the quavery voice of a whipped dog. Introduced as Uriah Heath, third vice-president and personal assistant to the Chairman, Heath gave "X" a limp handshake before returning to staring at the floor.

"Four and a quarter, very good, Heath," Murdstone snapped, shooting his assistant an angry look. "Heath is our oldest employee. An excellent assistant, if useless in every other area."

"I see," the Agent said, disliking this man's bullying style. "May I ask the prime source of your investment direction?"

"Foreign investments, Pond, foreign investments! Place your money with the correct government and the returns far exceed that of this country's resources!" Murdstone said, thumping the desk again.

"Any countries in particular?" asked "X", knowing it was a clumsy question. This was an intentional ploy, a demonstration of weakness that would show more of Murdstone's true character.

"Why would you wish to worry about such information, Pond? My investments are legal and provide an excellent return on the dollar. If you provide us with capital, we would, of course, go over your investments in detail. But such boring details are best left in our hands." Murdstone lowered his voice attempting to sound soothing.

"X" didn't react, but internally he was grateful K-9 placed this assignment before him today. It was apparent that Jessup Murdstone was investing in governments that probably were contrary to American interests. He hid his barely legal activities under the guise of loud blustering and false promises, but in truth "X" judged this man little better than the gangsters he'd fought every day.

"Too true, too true." said "X", pretending to agree with Murdstone's statements. "One of your top men passed away recently. Will this affect future investments?"

Jessup Murdstone shook his head quickly, a look of disgust crossing his face, "Haines had no part of the bank's investments on behalf of our clients. His job was...what was his job again, Heath?"

"Property, sir. Mr. Haines was the third vice-president of the property division, Mr. Murdstone." Heath spoke with his eyes still on the floor.

"There you see it! Haines was little more than a functionary in truth, almost as useless as Heath here. Seemed to believe investing in warehouses in this city was a good direction for the bank." Murdstone said, "Rest assured we would place our best men in charge of your portfolio, Pond."

"That's encouraging." said "X", deciding to probe a little further. Occasionally by asking a very impertinent question, you discovered more about a person's character. "Still, I am concerned at two recent mysterious deaths in your bank, Mr. Murdstone. First your son, my condolences on your loss, and now Haines."

Jessup Murdstone's lips tightened and he said, "Thank you, Pond. But my son's passing was an accident while on vacation with his university friends. And you will probably learn through other sources that he was removed from his position prior to his accident. My son had radical notions regarding foreign investments."

"And Haines?" the Agent asked, nodding with sympathy. It was interesting that Murdstone's son died just after he disagreed with his father over bank policies.

"He was effective enough at his position, but as easily replaced as Heath here. Now if there's nothing else, Pond, I have to attend a board meeting shortly."

Murdstone face could barely hide his open contempt for Dr. Elisha Pond.

"X" stood and did not extend his hand in thanks. "I will discuss your proposals with my advisors. Good afternoon, Mr. Murdstone."

"Afternoon, Pond," Jessup Murdstone said, turning his back. "Heath will show you out."

"X" followed Heath out, pausing outside the closed office door. The smaller man seemed even more shrunken outside the chairman's office, his eyes barely rising up to the Agent's face.

"If I can be of any assistance to you, Dr. Pond, please contact me at your convenience."

"Thank you, Mr. Heath" replied "X". "What country was it that Mr. Murdstone and his son fought over, if I may ask?"

"Several. I believe the ones in question were Germany and Italy."

"Interesting. Thank you, Mr. Heath." "X" nodded politely and walked away. It seemed K-9 had reason to be concerned about this bank after all!

Chapter Four

It wasn't hard to find "Fingers" Creel, he was almost always in the same place every evening: Club Ritz. Club Ritz was a low-end dive that seemed to exist because it provided upper-class men and women the chance to rub shoulders with gangsters pretending to be classy. Originally a speakeasy owned by Joey "Big Ears" Collins, Club Ritz was filled with society types gambling shoulder to shoulder with men who would gladly rob the rings off their fingers. The only reason this never happened was because Creel didn't allow any violence in his club unless specifically ordered by him.

An example of that violence appeared just as "X" arrived. A pair of enormous men dressed in poorly fitting tuxedos burst out of the club's front doors, a struggling figure held in their huge fists. It was a man no older than twenty, his expensive suit torn, his face a bloody mask of bruises. He had straight blonde hair and thin, barely visible pencil mustache that was darkened with blood.

"You were told to stay out, swell. Now we got to break your jaw," the larger of the two thugs said, sounding almost apologetic.

"I told you, I'll pay what I owed! Please, don't do this!" The young man's voice was slurred with obvious pain.

"Too late, kid," responded the second thug, his gravely voice sounding amused. He giggled for a few seconds and added, "I'm glad you were too stupid to listen! Hold him still, Bobby."

"Alright, Jimmy. Make it quick," the thug named Bobby held the struggling man tighter. He glanced at his partner, a look of open disgust on his face.

"X", an expert at criminal behavior, knew instantly what he was witnessing. The thug named Jimmy was the worst type of criminal, one who enjoyed causing pain in others. Even among criminals, a cowardly and suspicious lot, a man who enjoyed hurting others was viewed with loathing and fear.

Jimmy raised a huge fist up and giggled again, "This is going to hurt you a lot more than it hurts me, kid! But do me one favor, scream loud for Jimmy….I like it!"

Just as Jimmy stepped forward to deliver his first hammer-like blow, "X" jumped into action! Grabbing the thug's enormous arm, the Agent slammed his hip hard into Jimmy's back, pulling the criminal off-balance and sending him flying to the pavement!

"What the…hey!" Bobby yelled, dropping his helpless victim and reaching a hand into his jacket.

"X" shuffled a few inches forward and threw a hard cross punch to Bobby's arm, an old boxer's trick that numbed the thug's arm. A pistol clattered to the ground as the Agent stepped a leg behind the thug's leg and sent him crashing to the ground!

"I don't know who you are, Mister, but you're going to hurt bad now!" Bobby snarled, climbing to his feet and pulling out a blackjack. Slapping it in his hand once, the huge thug grinned and stepped forward and swung the weapon in a fast arc at the Agent's head!

But "X" was more than ready, ducking the swing and driving a hard fist into Bobby's stomach. The thug gasped in pain, but the Agent wasn't finished yet. Grabbing Bobby's collar, "X" flipped the criminal through the air and caused him to land with a loud bang on his criminal compatriot's prone body!

Seeing both thugs were stunned, "X" helped their young victim to his feet, "Get out of here now and don't come back," he advised, his voice a harsh rasp.

"Um…okay…thanks, Mister…I think…" the young man stammered as he touched his bruised face. He backed away, seemingly as frightened of "X" as he was of the two thugs that almost beat him mercilessly.

The Agent nodded and waited until the young man was out-of-sight before heading into Club Ritz. The club was oval shaped and filled with more glitz and showy decor than most European palaces. The crowd was filled with tuxedoed men and women in expensive evening dresses, but the division went far deeper. Fully half of the crowd were part of the "too young, too rich", each seeking a cheap thrill by rubbing shoulders with the other group populating Club Ritz: Criminals. Hard-eyed men and flint-hearted women who pretended to befriend the young socialites while secretly plotting the fastest and best means to milk their victims of every dollar they possessed. Originally "X" planned to arrive disguised as a young socialite himself, an easy mark for one of the many thugs and hustlers that lurked on the edges of Club Ritz. But that might waste time, force him to swim through a sea of con-artists and gangsters in the hopes of discovering a link to "Fingers" Creel. Instead he came dressed as an infamous and somewhat legendary crime figure that "X" believed was currently hiding in Europe, Jack Diamond. Diamond would receive proper respect from a low-end boss like Creel, enabling "X" to close his operations right after he discovered who was behind the unusual killings of bankers.

Moving to the bar, "X" knew it wouldn't be long before he was propelled into the inner sanctum of "Fingers" Creel. Ordering a whiskey he had no intentions of drinking, the Agent smiled as he heard the heavy footfall of several approaching thugs. Reaching for his drink, he waited until a heavy hand landed on his shoulder.

Smiling to himself. "X" threw the whiskey over his shoulder and into the face of the man behind him. Spinning on his heels, the Agent swept the legs out from under this unknown thug, continuing to smile as Bobby and Jimmy began to advance.

"Hold it! Not inside the club." said a voice from behind two bruisers. A weasel-faced man in an ill-fitting suit pushed forward and stared up at "X", his eyes widening when he realized who he was staring at now. This was Creel's second in command, George "Razor" Davis, a cold-blooded professional killer who always carried several of his namesake weapons at all times.

"'Razor' Davis," the Agent said, his voice now the harsher tones of Jack Diamond. "You look nervous pal, cat got your tongue?"

"Jack Diamond? You cement heads started brawling with Jack Diamond?" "Razor" exclaimed, his voice a strangled rasp as he looked at Bobby, Jimmy and the unnamed third thug who was slowly climbing to his feet.

"He started it..." Bobby started to say, but was silenced by an elbow in his side from Jimmy.

"Your boys was about to beat down a swell in front of the club. You looking to get raided or something, "Razor"?" The Agent snarled.

"I'll deal with them, Mr. Diamond. If you'll have a drink, on the house, I'll let the boss know you're here." "Razor" Davis managed to say while shooting the large thugs furious looks.

"I'll come with you and surprise him." said "X" with a nasty grin.

Davis looked unhappy at the thought of surprising Creel with anything, the boss had a lethal temper and didn't hesitate to use it. But this was Jack Diamond, the man who took out the whole Gibson Mob single-handedly! You didn't make a man like that mad unless you wanted to wear a cement overcoat. "Follow me, Mr. Diamond," he said, pushing through the crowd around the bar.

Waving the bartender away, Davis knocked on a door in the floor and opened it up, revealing a set of metal stairs. "X" smiled to himself, realizing that Creel, like many gangsters, was terrified of his fellow man. Creel hid in a basement office and plotted to rob innocents, but he did so while hiding in the dark. The Agent followed Davis down a filthy dark hallway and waited as he knocked and entered the office.

"Boss, someone here to see you...it's Jack Diamond," "Razor" Davis said, trying not to sound so impressed.

"Fingers" Creel was a huge man, several inches taller and wider than "X", with enormous slab-like muscles and some of the biggest hands in the city. He had a bullet shaped bald head and a permanent sneer across his battered face. His deep-set black eyes never seemed to stop moving, always searching for a possible threat. Seated at his feet were a pair of black bull mastiffs almost as large as their master, Creel's only constant companions.

"Jack Diamond, eh?" Creel said, pulling out a cigar that looked like a matchstick in his beefy hand, "Okay, "Razor", you're forgiven for not warning me in advance. Get moving."

"Razor" Davis backed out the room, grateful he had escaped his boss's terrible temper. The metal door closed with loud slam and "Fingers" Creel waved "X" towards the room's only other chair.

"Grab a seat Diamond. But no fast moves. Dempsy and Tunney here will rip you apart, they don't like people," Creel said, grinning.

"Good protection. I heard you was smart." said "X", locking eyes with the dogs. Asserting his will, the Agent watched as both animals slumped slightly, control of their minds now in his hands.

"That I am, Diamond. That I am. Now, what do you want with me?" Creel asked.

"X" didn't bother to answer, he just reached under his jacket and pulled out his gas gun. He fired a burst full into Creel's face, just as the giant gangster yelled, "Dempsy, Tunney, KILL!"

The bull mastiffs didn't move, merely sitting in place like a pair of stone temple lions. Creel looked stunned for a moment then shook his head, the gas having a slow affect on his system. Seeing his dogs weren't coming to his aid, the giant gangster roared like a bull and charged "X", his huge hands reaching for the Agent's throat!

"X", not wanting to get caught in Creel's crushing grip, grabbed the crook's hands and pushed himself backwards in the chair. Using the momentum of Creel's charge, the Agent fell backwards fast while his legs kicked out against his enemy's rock hard stomach. This combination sent "Fingers" Creel sailing head first across the room, crashing into the heavy, metal office door. The impact, as well as the gas from the Agent's gun, caused the criminal boss to slip into unconsciousness. Knowing neither state would last long, "X" pulled out a pair of steel handcuffs he concealed in his jacket and cuffed Creel's hands behind his back. Flipping the giant onto his back, "X" knelt over the criminal and watched as the light of reason slowly appeared in Creel's eyes.

"You….you ain't Diamond!" Creel said, struggling against the cuffs to no avail.

"What was your first clue?" asked "X" in Diamond's harsh voice. "Here's how it works, Creel. I'm going to ask you a few questions and you'll answer them. If you don't, then I'll let Tunney and Dempsey here become…unpleasant."

"How'd you turn my dogs against me?" Creel asked and recoiled as both animals began to softly growl as "X" raised a hand. "Okay, okay, what do you want to know?"

"William Haines. What did you do to him?" The Agent asked, not really suspecting this thug, but knowing this line of questioning was the best tactic.

"Billy? Nothing! Why would I mess with a golden goose like that one? He makes me more green than almost anyone" Creel said, looking confused.

"He's dead and this is his last known location," said "X", using a lie to pressure the criminal. "You'll get the chair for this one…if you live through today, 'Fingers'."

Creel's face looked angry, as if he was going to spit out a curse and willingly accept his possible fate. That changed after "X" raised his hands, causing both dogs to step close, teeth bared as they growled. The sight was terrifying, even for their former master.

"Okay, okay! Call them off! Look all I know about Billy Haines is some foreign crumb who wanted to know the best way to get close to Billy Haines and Richie

Winthrop. Haines was easy, I pointed the crumb at that gold-digger, Helen Thomas. Richie was easier, just had my guys rough him up a little outside a little while ago and make him easy for a grab."

"This Winthrop? He's a fat man, balding and about 40?" asked "X", a sinking feeling in the pit of his stomach.

"Nah, he's a thin blonde kid, in his twenties. A real moron at the tables, doubles down when he should walk away." Creel said, shaking his bullet shaped head.

"X" wasn't listening to the gangster any more. Tossing the chair aside, he threw the door open and ran down the hallway towards the exit. Richie Winthrop was obviously the young man he rescued earlier and now his life was in danger!

Chapter Five

"**M**ore tea, Miss Dale?" Agnes Haines asked, gesturing with a pale, limp hand towards an intricate silver tea service on a nearby table. She was a tiny woman with light blonde hair and colorless skin that appeared even more pallid under her black mourning dress. An older maid hovered a short distance away, attempting to remain invisible but watching her mistress with open distress.

"No, thank you," Betty answered, not wishing to strain the woman any further. William Haines's widow appeared drained of all life, with every gesture an expression of her total exhaustion.

"I suppose you wish to know more about dear William," Agnes continued, closing her eyes and sighing with some effort.

"I'm sorry to distress you, but did Billy…I mean William, have any enemies?" Betty asked.

"As I informed the police, none. William was a friendly man, quite open with strangers. I suppose it was one of those mad creatures the newspapers place upon the front page," Agnes suggested, picking up her tea cup, but not raising it to her lips.

"That's possible," Betty agreed. "Who were his closest friends?"

"The Musketeers of course."

"Is that an organization of some type, Mrs. Haines?"

"No, no, nothing so…formal. Merely a group of friends from school that remained close through college and employment. William, my late brother, Jessie, and young Richard Winthrop. They became close in preparatory school and began calling themselves the Three Musketeers in the tradition of the French novel." Agnes leaned back in her chair. It seemed the flow of words exhausted her of most of her remaining vigor.

"Your late brother?" Betty asked, wondering if he too was a victim of the bizarre murderer.

"Yes," Agnes replied. "He was lost at sea several years ago, a storm off the coast of Greece. We searched and searched, but to no avail. William was prostrate with grief as was Richard. They were present when my poor brother fell overboard, a

Musketeers work holiday they called it."

"They worked together?" Betty blurted, trying to hide her excitement. The mention of Greece caused her to remember why the killing of Billy Haines appeared so familiar. Greece was the site of many legendary myths of heroes and monsters, but the most unforgettable was the story of terrible fiend named Medusa. Betty couldn't remember the full tale, but she did recall the most exciting detail; to look into the face of Medusa would cause a person to turn into stone!

"Yes. My father thought William and Richard to be wastrels and fools, but Jessie prevailed upon him to employ them all at his bank. The Musketeers remained together, even while employed."

"Thank you, Mrs. Haines. I'm sorry for your loss," Betty finished, getting to her feet. She now knew she had discovered the clues "X" was seeking by sending her to speak to Agnes Haines. The full picture was still unclear, but the strange murder of William Haines was now a little less mysterious. But more was needed. Details regarding the legendary monster Medusa could be found quite easily at the City's library!

"Yes, yes," Agnes Haines raised her hand in a feeble parting gesture. With a slight nod, a maid appeared to escort the blonde reporter to the front door.

Hailing a cab, Betty was off a moment later, unaware of the elderly roadster following a short distance behind. The driver remained within sight of the taxi, seemingly just another driver on the busy city roads.

A short time later, Betty arrived at the City Library, glad to see the lights still on within. Though it was past working hours, she knew the head of the special collections, Mr. Ernest Poole, was often remained pouring over his own research late into the evening. Poole was unknowingly an information source for "X", happy to help anyone interested in obscure facts. Moving quickly to the back door, Betty Dale knocked loud and smiled when she heard approaching footsteps. Luck was on her side tonight!

❉❉❉

The driver of the older car, parked a short distance from the library and quickly found a telephone booth. Dialing a number from memory, the other line was picked up without a word.

"Hail Minos. This is Daedalus. The woman left the Haines house and went immediately to the City Library."

"You have done well, Daedalus. This woman will soon meet the Minotaur and her inquisitive nature will be her death!" Minos' voice was filled with laughter.

"I can bring her to the Minotaur tonight, Mighty Minos," Daedalus suggested, smiling at the thought of this nosy reporter meeting the Minotaur.

"No!" Minos said. "Two more must fall to the Mask of Medusa, then this phase of our plan is complete. If this woman vanishes, it may cause suspicion and questions from her employers. For now she is shielded by her employment as a reporter. But soon, she will meet the Minotaur!"

Daedalus smiled, Minos was always a step ahead of everyone. "It will be my pleasure, Minos!"

Chapter Six

"X" ran out of "Fingers" Creel's underground, knocking aside several patrons as he took the fastest route to the exit. The life of the young man he had rescued earlier was in great danger from the same killers that had murdered William "Billy" Haines. Ignoring the yells of protest, the Agent headed through the doors and into the dark night, his quarry nowhere in sight!

Glancing around the sidewalk, "X" spotted the drying blood that fell from Richie Winthrop's face earlier and breathed a sigh of relief. The blood droplets lead into the distance, granting the Agent a clear and easy trail to follow. His tracking skills were expert, learned from tribesmen in North Africa who helped him recover from a bullet caused by a German agent. The tribesmen were able to follow any animal with only a few tiny signs of their passage, a skill he mastered thanks to the patient teachings of a witch doctor that claimed to be over 100 years old.

Slowing to a trot, "X" followed the trail down the street, heading towards a deserted street which many patrons used to hide their cars. The Agent hoped that Richie Winthrop was long gone, at home being treated by some underpaid servant. But he heard a sound in the distance that made him suspect this was a vain hope. A keening sound, like that of an animal in distress was approaching his direction, causing "X" to increase his pace. He might still have time to rescue the latest victim!

Richard Albert George Winthrop Jr., Richie to his friends, was not having a good day. First he was forced to listen to a long lecture about responsibility from that blowhard, Jessup Murdstone, then Club Ritz's gangsters had rejected his request for an extended line of credit! That would have been terribly embarrassing, but then that fool "Razor" Davis ordered him beaten and tossed out of the low-class dive!

But those were all minor inconveniences compared to the last few minutes. Richie, after being rescued by the well-dressed stranger, had fled into the night, only to stop at the sight of two swarthy looking men blocking his path. They were speaking in an oddly accented form of Greek, a language he'd learned after many trips on the family yacht to the Mediterranean. Richie wasn't the smartest graduate from Princeton, but his gift for absorbing foreign languages had enabled him to earn high marks in classes on that subject. Even Old Man Murdstone kept him close during negotiations with foreign investors, preventing the bank from missing any secrets.

"Is that the one?" The younger of the two said, looking at Richie as he came to a halt.

"Yes," said the other, unaware their intended victim could interpret their words. "Even with the blood hiding his face, I recognize that is the one sought by Minos. Smile as he approaches and I will apply the drug. Try to look friendly."

Richie was shocked to learn these men were going to try and kidnap him?

Why would they do that? For money? His father was a notorious skin-flint who would sooner let them keep him hostage forever rather than part with any money! And anyone who knew Jessup Murdstone would know he'd blame Richie for the problems and would fire him rather than pay any ransom. It didn't make any sense!

And that name they had mentioned, Minos. Richie vaguely remembered the name from the tour guide in Crete. Minos was a king of some kind who was famous years ago. In truth the guide's stories weren't important back then, the Musketeers had been too busy trying to see which of them could drink the most of the local rot-gut drink without becoming ill. Jessie won that contest.

But those thoughts were lost as the two men approached Richie, false smiles across their faces. Not willing to become a hostage, he turned on his heel and ran for his life! The two men, seeing their quarry fleeing, dropped their phony demeanors and pulled out the rope and drugged cloth used for kidnapping their victims. Their exchanged looks made it clear they blamed each other for revealing their intentions to the prey and that a reckoning over this mistake would come later. For now they had to capture this fool and satisfy Minos's commands!

"Help! Help! Someone help me!" Richie screamed, glancing over his shoulder. Both men were running now, their athletic strides causing them to quickly close the gap between them and Richie.

"Catch him, fool! Before his screams alert the police!" Damianos snarled at Asterion. The hooknosed older man never liked his young partner. Asterion liked using his knives far too much. Killing wasn't something to be enjoyed, just an act that needed to be performed as needed!

"This was your stupid plan! You are the one Minos will blame if he gets away!" Asterion snapped back. But secretly he was happy, seeing a way to eliminate his rival. Minos only required one strong arm, not an old man who complained constantly when work was to be done!

"He won't get away if you stop chattering and paid attention!" Damianos retorted. The young banker was running back and forth, screaming for his life and so far eluding their grasp.

With a wordless snarl, Asterion pulled out his knife and raised it above his head. Damianos's eyes widened, they'd specifically been ordered to bring the Winthrop idiot in alive!

But Asterion was a step ahead of Damianos. Throwing the knife at Winthrop, the handle struck the young banker behind his leg. Screaming, Richie was thrown off balance and crashed to the pavement, stunned. Asterion gave Damianos a triumphant look and placed a knee against the young banker's spine, pinning him down.

"Helphelphelphelphelphelphelphelp!" Richie screamed struggling and trying to free himself.

Damianos clapped the drugged cloth over Richie's mouth, cutting off his screams immediately. The young banker struggled for a few seconds and then went limp. Asterion reached for Richie's arms, knowing the drug would wear off in a short time. But he paused, hearing footsteps approaching quickly from the distance.

"Someone is coming!" Asterion warned, scooping up his knife.

"I have ears! Ready yourself! I will tie this one up!" Damianos ordered, taking the rope and encircling Richie's wrists.

Asterion stood up, smiling at the thought of some American idiot interfering with his work. Americans, even the professional criminals who relied on strength to get what they wanted, were poor fighters at best. Damianos and Asterion were skilled in unique forms of fighting that confused everyone they dealt with in this country. Yes, that huge gangster named Creel would be a challenge, but he was no more than a bull and they had defeated larger ones in the past.

"X" spotted the two men hovering over the body of a man dressed in a tuxedo. The older one was tying the fallen man with heavy rope that looked like it belonged on a ship rather than used for a kidnapping. The younger one was holding a long wicked looking knife and assumed a thrower's stance. "X" knew most people who attempted to throw knives were incapable of hitting any target, but this man's assurance made it clear he was well trained in the art.

Asterion drew his hand back and flung the knife at the man running at him at a surprising speed. But fast or not, a knife through the heart would end this meddler's life!

"X" didn't break stride, catching the knife with his right hand and tossing it aside. It was tempting to use such weapons for many, but not Agent "X". Weapons like knives and guns were only good for killing, a solution that usually caused as many problems as it solved. He had learned that all too well in the Great War and learned far greater skills since that time.

Asterion was shocked the stranger caught his knife, but was ready to defeat this man without weapons. Stepping forward, he leapt over "X" and kicked backwards, sending the Agent sprawling forward!

"X" was amazed by the man's leaping ability, which surprised him as an opening attack. Rolling to his feet, "X" was swept off his feet by Asterion, who pulled a second knife from his belt. Grinning, Asterion moved in to end this, happy to see that Americans were so easy to defeat.

But "X" was more than ready now, moving to his side and faking a kick towards Asterion's hand. Asterion slashed out, exactly what "X" wanted him to do and leaving him open. Pushing off the pavement with his hands, "X" rose to his knees and fired a hard uppercut to his enemy's stomach.

Asterion exhaled loudly, all of his air rushing out of his mouth in a rush. He gasped in pain and slashed out towards "X" with the knife he was barely able to keep in his hand. The Agent was forced to step back, but immediately stepped forward and fired a hard cross-punch to the side of his enemy's jaw.

Asterion was thrown sideways, sprawling onto his side, shaken by the power of the Agent's punch. His jaw felt like it had been struck by a bar of iron and might have even been broken from one punch! But he wouldn't give his enemy the satisfaction of knowing the blow actually hurt. Instead Asterion faked a slash and leapt over "X", landing on his feet and raising his knife to stab the American interloper in the back!

"X" was more than ready, no longer surprised by the amazing leaping skill of his opponent. Without turning, he shot a back kick into Asterion's shoulder, causing the knife to fly out of his now nerveless fingers. Turning towards Asterion, "X" used his momentum and fired a hard hook punch to his enemy's ribs.

Seeing his enemy was all but finished, "X" grabbed Asterion's arm and shoulder and flipped the man over his hip. The Agent's enemy sailed through the air and landed on his back, groaning softly in pain.

"Hey Mister, look over here." Damianos had not left Richie Winthrop's side. The hook-nosed man was impressed by this newcomer's fighting skills, he'd beaten Asterion with ease and seemed ready to advance and do the same a second time.

Damianos knew he was an excellent fighter, rougher than Asterion but not as flashy. Also Damianos knew he was far smarter, and there was no need to attack this excellent fighter. Instead a bit of brains usually worked far better.

Damianos placed his rarely used knife at Richie's throat and gave "X" a mirthless smile. "You're very good," he said in heavily accented English. "Now take three steps backwards and don't get clever."

"X" raised his hands, hoping to relax the man as he stepped back a short distance. The man's accent was a version of Cretan based Greek, not common in the United States. "I won't let you hurt him. I advise you drop the knife and back away now."

Damianos laughted. "I have the blade. That means I am in charge here. Unless you wish to see me cut his neck here and now."

"X" immediately knew this was a hollow threat, these men had gone to great lengths to kidnap Winthrop. Why, would they kill him now? No, they needed the young banker alive and the Agent was determined to prevent that from occurring!

"Minos…" Asterion gasped as he slowly came to consciousness.

"Fool," Damianos whispered, hearing Asterion's words. Fortunately Americans knew nothing of the Greatest King of all time, so the secret would remain safe. Turning his attention back to "X", he said, "My assistant is waking. He and I will leave or you will see this man's blood spill across the ground."

"I don't want that," said "X", dropping his hands to his side in feigned defeat. But he had a hand on his gas gun and in a moment, would capture both kidnappers.

"Good!" Damianos smiled while waving the dazed Asterion to his side. "Move fool! We must take this one away!"

Asterion shot enraged looks at "X" wishing for his knives but Minos's wishes always came first. Still, he memorized the American's face, determined to make him pay in the future!

"X" was about to raise his gas gun and fire at both kidnappers, when the screech of car's tires caught all of their attention. A large roadster stopped several feet away, the headlights illuminating them all in the darkness.

Out of the car hopped Jimmy, Bobby and "Razor" Davis, each carrying a Thompson Machine Gun. They aimed their weapons at "X", but didn't pull the trigger. A few seconds later, the back seat of the car opened and "Fingers" Creel stepped out, looking even larger in the shadowy darkness.

"You ain't Jack Diamond." Creel said, his voice tight with rage. "You played us

"X"Didn't break stride catching the knife...

all for a chump, now we're going to make you pay."

"We will leave you to your pleasure, Mr. Creel." Damianos said, smiling and pulling Richie to his feet. He and Asterion marched the young banker to a parked sedan and were gone a moment later.

"You got any last words before me and the boys ventilate you?" Creel asked, raising a pair of huge pistols and aiming at "X".

"X" knew he only had seconds to think fast.

Chapter Seven

"**T**hank you for agreeing to help me, Mr. Poole." Betty said, following the elderly scholar through the barely lit library. Poole moved at a slow, arthritic pace, unwilling or unable to rush into action in any way.

"No trouble, no trouble at all, Miss…um…Miss…" Poole mumbled, forgetting Betty's name again. He was a brilliant scholar, but prone to ignoring the rest of the world outside of his books.

"Dale," Betty supplied again, smiling. Many became frustrated with Poole's mannerisms, forgetting that the man was a renowned expert on ancient languages, consulted by museums and private collectors for his translations.

"Yes, yes, Miss Dale." Poole stopped before a desk which was piled high with papers and open books. Sitting down with a sigh, he said, "I was just translating a recently discovered copy of Ovid, if that's of interest to you."

"Possibly later," Betty replied politely. "Right now I just need some information on a character from Greek Myths. What can you tell me about Medusa?"

"Medusa?" Poole looked surprised. "What an odd question…but ours is not the reason why. Medusa you say?"

Betty nodded, "Yes, it may be connected to a recent murder."

"How…interesting." Poole was clearly perplexed by the notion. He shook his head and said, "What do you know of Medusa, Miss…um…that way I will not be covering ground you have already walked, so to speak."

"Well," Betty said, "I know she was a monster in ancient Greece. To look in her face would turn you to stone."

Poole nodded, "Correct, if limited. Anything further?"

Betty shook her head. "That's all I remember from school. I preferred the stories of Heracles."

Poole chuckled and shook his head. "Young people do appear to find the empty-headed muscleman to be a fascinating subject. But Medusa, a far more interesting subject, is often ignored."

Betty merely smiled and waited, knowing Poole was not to be rushed. Many lost patience with the elderly scholar, who would arrive at the subject at hand eventually. To attempt to hurry Poole was a fast way to lose an excellent source of scholarly information.

"Classically, Medusa was reputedly a beautiful priestess of Athene, the chaste goddess of wisdom. By committing an indiscretion, a subject I would not mention to a lady, with Poseidon, the sea god, she offended Athene. As a punishment, the goddess transformed Medusa and her two sisters into gorgons." Poole turned slowly in his chair and pulled out a large book for a nearby case.

"I never knew there were three." Betty confessed, writing this information down in her notepad.

"The other two are only ever mentioned in passing. Gorgons are women with lovely faces with hair made up of live snakes. To look upon their faces caused one to turn to stone. A popular subject of ancient artists, Da Vinci reputedly painted Medusa, but some doubt the veracity of that painting. Here! This is a photograph of Caravaggio's work, Medusa." Poole pointed to a picture of a woman with snakes for hair, caught in mid-scream.

Betty shuddered at the terrible image. "Terrifying! I can see why she's considered so frightening."

"Hmm, possibly so. Allow me to complete the classic myth. The son of the god Zeus, Perseus, was charged by King Polydectus with slaying Medusa. Using magic items of the Greek Gods, he snuck up close to the sleeping Medusa and, with the help of a polished shield, beheaded the gorgon. Perseus utilized the properties of the head to slay a monster and rescue a beautiful princess as well as destroy King Polydectus and his entire court." Poole finished closing the book. "That is the classic view of the tale. Heroic and filled with the elements of fantasy."

"There's another story about Medusa?"

Poole nodded and gave Betty a brief, knowing smile. "Several modern researchers such as Harrison believe that Medusa was a priestess of an ancient cult and that her horrific visage was in fact a mask utilized to ward off evil. The power of such ancient religious organizations lies in the maintaining of their mysteries. By slaying the leader of this secret priesthood, Perseus was in fact destroying their mystery, their power over the people."

"That doesn't explain how they were able to turn people into stone."

"That piece of the puzzle that is Medusa, remains part of her mysteries. If there were such a religious order, then it is critical to remember that their power lay in secrecy." Poole was already beginning to drift away from the conversation. His eyes sought out the pages on his desk and began to scan the written lines.

"One final question, what ever happened to Medusa's head or mask?" Betty asked.

"Hmm? Oh yes…classical works state Perseus gave the head to Athene, who placed it in her shield, the Aegis, to be used as a powerful weapon against her enemies. Some modern scholars propose that the item in question became the property of the kings of Crete, who utilized it to subjugate the Athenians several generations prior to the Trojan War." Poole lifted a page and a fountain pen and beginning to scribble a note. His dissertation was at an end.

"Thank you, Mr. Poole. I'll see myself out," Betty said, hoping this information would be of use to "X" in the current case.

"Hmm? Oh yes, of course. Good afternoon Miss…" Poole said, his voice trailing off. He was already lost in his latest translation as Betty headed for the door.

Chapter Eight

"X" sneered at "Fingers" Creel, knowing the giant's weakness and planning on using it against the criminal. Creel's reputation as an unbeatable and clever killer was renown in the underworld, a source of fear to his underlings and rivals. Many of Creel's competitors discovered that the giant seemed to feel no pain and would ignore major wounds, if only he could get his hands upon his enemies.

Using that knowledge, "X" just said one word, "Coward." His voice was almost a whisper.

"What? What did you call me?" Creel asked, his bullet head flushing bright red with rage. The deep-set black eyes narrowed, becoming tiny obsidian chips that glared at "X" with the fury of a rampaging bull.

"I called you a coward, Creel. A low, yellow, gutless, coward." "X" spat out the words with as much contempt as he could muster in each syllable. "You're supposed to be the toughest guy in the city with your fists, but you've gone soft since becoming boss. I beat you down easy and now you're too afraid to take a second chance."

"I'm gonna kill you for that, whoever you are!" Creel threatened, lowering his pistols and tossing them in the back of his car. "Keep your guns ready boys. If he tries anything clever, gun him down. Otherwise, leave him to me!"

"Okay, boss," "Razor" Davis said and smiled, "Leave a little for me to slice up nice and pretty."

"And me!" Jimmy chimed in and giggled. "You're gonna bleed bad, Mister Fake Jack Diamond!"

"Let me just take my jacket off," the Agent said as he pulled his tuxedo jacket off his shoulders. Holding the jacket in one hand, "X" tossed it in the air while drawing his gas gun with the other. All eyes were on the jacket for a split second, giving the Agent a clear quick shot at all the assembled killers.

"Get him! Get him!" "Fingers" Creel managed to cough as he reached for his pistols. "Razor" Davis fell to the ground senseless from the gas, while Jimmy and Bobby covered their mouths and tried to raise their machine guns.

"X", knowing an accidental discharge could kill him as easily as an aimed shot, dove to the ground and rolled forward. Several bullets whizzed over his head, bare inches from striking him! Then he rose up in one motion, grabbed Jimmy's gun by the barrel and shoved it back hard into the gangster's gut. He fell backwards with a gasp of pain and "X" leapt forward and sent Bobby reeling with a knife hand strike to the neck.

And just like that, the fight was over. This time, "Fingers" Creel had caught a full dose of the gas and was laying unconscious, half of his body in the car, the other half sprawled in the street. "X" was grateful to the Texas born gunslinger he had long ago met in the Afghan plains. The man, an expert with a pistol, had taught him the jacket diversion trick in case to be employed when facing overwhelming odds. It seemed the gunslinger's instincts were totally correct!

"X" picked up his jacket and pulled out a thin metal tube, extending it several feet. Pressing a button located at the tube's side, a crackle of static suddenly filled the air. This seemingly innocent tube was in fact one of the most advanced radios ever invented! An expert on electronic components, "X" discovered a method to miniaturize radio parts enabling a person to carry a device that weighed a few mere ounces! Though this device could have made the Agent a wealthy man, he refused to release the technology to anyone for fear it would fall into the wrong hands. Instead "X" reserved it for his fight against the evils of mankind!

"This is Police Commissioner Charlie Foster." Said "X" into the radio after dialing into the police band. "I've just been told by someone that "Fingers" Creel and his gang are causing a ruckus three blocks east of Club Ritz. You might want to send a patrol car to investigate. Also seen leaving the area at a high rate of speed was a car in which a young man has been kidnapped."

"I'm in the area, Commissioner." Inspector John Burks familiar voice sounded over the receiver. "I suspect Creel and his gang are having a falling out with their leader, the man known as Secret Agent "X"!"

"Good work, Inspector," the Agent said and after providing a description of the kidnapper's car, shut down his radio. Running over to where the sedan the two kidnappers drove had been parked, "X" shook his head in disgust. There were no tire tracks or clues as to where they were headed with Richie Winthrop. It seemed for now, the kidnappers had gotten clean away!

But "X" was closer to the secret behind this mystery than the enemy realized! The volcanic ash mixed with chalk, the Cretan accented English and name Minos meant that an ancient evil was rearing its head in the modern world!

"I need to test that chalk further and find out what Betty has learned!" thought "X" as he quickly left the scene and headed off to his base.

۞۞۞

Damianos and Asterion each told their version of the kidnapping to Minos and Daedalus. Daedalus, as always, hovered near Minos's chair and only spoke when Minos asked a question directly.

"Asterion over-estimated his skill and risked the life of our prisoner." Damianos spoke in Cretan accented Greek, shooting the younger man a murderous look.

"Damianos's plan was foolish and the greater risk. We nearly failed because of the interference of this outsider," Asterion replied, his accent smoother than Damianos's.

"Silence!" Minos thundered. "Daedalus, what is your opinion of all this?"

"Mighty One, they both failed your will. Asterion did overestimate his fighting skill against this stranger and Damianos's plan was quite poor." Daedalus bowed to the robed figure at the far end of the room.

"I agree," Minos nodded. "Daedalus, you will discover the identity of this mysterious stranger."

"I already know, Mighty Minos. Before we enacted your wise plan, I studied possible organizations or men who might attempt to interfere with your will. Asterion's description of this warrior leads me to believe we face none other than the criminal mastermind known as Secret Agent "X"!"

"The presence of the one known as "X" does not disturb me. If he attempts to find us, we will give him to the Minotaur!" Minos enjoyed seeing both Asterion and Damianos shudder at his words. "And if either of you fail me again, then it is the two of you who will meet the Minotaur!"

"We hear and obey, Mighty Minos," Damianos said and they both bowed.

"Good!" Minos turned to Daedalus. "Capture the third one as well as the reporter, Betty Dale in the morning. Damianos, Asterion, leave now and return when I summons you."

"We hear and obey, Mighty Minos," Damianos repeated and they exited the room quickly.

Richie Winthrop knelt on the stone floor, shaking with fear. The robed figure the two men hailed as Minos hadn't spoken to him or even acknowledged his presence. Richie could sense he was being watched by a pair of malevolent eyes under the heavy hood. After the two men and the robed one called Daedalus departed, Minos began to address him.

"Richard Winthrop, heir to the Winthrop fortune, banker, Princeton graduate and upstanding member of society."

"That's me, yes. Please, you can have anything you want, just don't hurt me!" Richie pleaded, beginning to weep.

"Richard Winthrop, drunkard, womanizer and…murderer!" Minos continued, his voice becoming crueler with each indictment.

"What…murder? No…I never…" Richie moaned, unable to look at the robed figure before him.

"Confess, Richard Winthrop! Confess and Minos will be merciful!" Minos offered as he rose from the throne and approached in a silent glide.

"I never…I swear…" Richie denied the charges, his body quaking with terror. How did this person know?! Only two other people knew the truth and one was now dead!

"Look at me, Richard Winthrop. Look up to me and confess."

Richie looked up and fell backwards, "You! How? Why?"

"Confess Richie." Minos cajoled, not moving any closer. "Confess."

"Okay! But please don't hurt me! We did it, Billy Haines and me…we killed Jessie Murdstone in the Med! We pushed him overboard after drugging him! We didn't have a choice! Believe me, we had to do it!" Richie continued weeping as he fell backwards. "I'm sorry, I'm so sorry."

"I cannot forgive you, Richard Winthrop. But I can grant you a merciful end." Minos said, putting on the Mask of Medusa and stepping closer to the fallen banker. "Look upon the Mask of Medusa, Richard Winthrop, look upon your final fate!"

A few seconds later Richard Winthrop screamed, which was cut off abruptly.

He was later found on the front steps of his family's Park Ave. mansion, his body a stone corpse!

Chapter Nine

"X" hit a button built on the side of his private telephone, connecting the machine to two large speakers. This enabled the Agent to continue working without being forced to stop and lift the receiver.

"Yes?" asked "X" as he waited for the alcohol burner to heat up the chemical solution in the test tube he had placed above the flame moments earlier. By discovering the type of chalk, Secret Agent "X" knew he was closer to discovering the location of this Minos character and his crazed helpers.

"Betty here. I have some information you may wish to hear." She began relating what she learned from Agnes Haines and Mr. Poole.

"That confirms what I learned earlier. This is not merely an attack on bankers, but the first step in a larger plan!" "X" was beginning to put the pieces together thanks to Betty's information. There were still a few unanswered questions, like the location of the criminal's hideout!

"How does that follow? I'm sorry, but this all appears to be a confusing mess to me." Betty said. How one, possibly two, bankers had been murdered by mysterious and terrifying means connected to an ancient monster and cult made no sense to her at all.

"It all begins with the death of Jessup Murdstone Jr., better known as Jessie, as well as the bank's policies on foreign investments," the Agent explained. "From there, everything else is connected."

"X" was writing down his findings as he spoke. The chalk was used in agricultural products, shipped to farmers to lower the acidity in soil. The volcanic ash and fit similar samples discovered in caves off the coast of Greece. But it was demonstrating several properties he hadn't seen before despite his expertise in toxicology.

"If you say so," Betty replied, clearly not following his reasoning. "What do we do next? I'm surprised you're not tearing apart the city for Richie Winthrop."

"I contacted Burks and he has the police searching everywhere at this point. If the auto is on the streets, he'll find it." What he didn't tell the tenacious blonde was that he also decided to contact Harvey Bates. Bates was the head of a network of operatives the Agent used in his crusade against evil doers. The network was very secretive, with operatives forced to learn new passwords regularly to identify themselves to each other. This was just one more tool Secret Agent "X"'s sophisticated, crime-fighting arsenal.

"There's nothing else you can do?" Betty asked, trusting "X" completely but feeling defeated by this terrible foe.

"Until someone discovers the location of the car the kidnapper used or Minos and his gang make their next move, no. But there are steps I can take to prevent more deaths! I'll contact you at the paper tomorrow with another assignment."

After a brief word of farewell, Betty disconnected and "X" dialed up another number he knew by heart, Harvey Bates! Hearing the line picked up with no greeting, "X" said, "The Congress shall have the power to lay and collect taxes on incomes, from whatever source derived."

The quote was his latest password, the first part of the Sixteenth Amendment of the United States Constitution. It was as unlikely a statement to be made over a telephone line as any and therefore the perfect password! Bates recognized the code and knew it was his mysterious chief.

"Send your best operatives out to the homes of Jessup Murdstone, Agnes Haines and Uriah Heath," directed "X". He gave Bates the home addresses he had for each individual. "Be on the lookout for two individuals, possibly Cretan Greeks, who wish to kidnap these people. They do not appear armed with guns, but are expert knife throwers and bull leapers."

Bates didn't answer as he copied down the description of the men "X" fought earlier. "Bull leapers?' he finally queried. "What the hell is that?"

"An ancient Cretan sport, also known as bull dancing that still exists on a few small islands. A man is placed in the ring with a bull and jumps over the beast acrobatically. A bull leaper makes a dangerous opponent. I met one during the Great War, he helped us fight the Turks." As he talked, Secret Agent "X" was mentally recalling the most famous legend of ancient Crete, that of the Minotaur!

The Minotaur was a creature that was half-man, half-bull and resided in a maze connected to King Minos's palace. Every seven years King Minos demanded seven girls and seven boys from the Greek city state of Athens, feeding them to the terrible monster in its maze. If the leader of this terrible criminal conspiracy was known as Minos, "X" knew it was safe to believe the Minotaur would play some part of their plans!

"Sounds bugsy." Bates said, obviously unimpressed by the information regarding bull-leapers.

"Contact me by radio if anything unusual occurs." "X" disconnected. The data he was recording from his tests on the volcanic ash was proving more useful than he imagined and might present the final piece of the deadly puzzle!

"Filters," the Agent said aloud, reading the data a second time. "Filters!"

Chapter Ten

B etty Dale enjoyed the walk from her family's brownstone to the newspaper where she was employed. Except in snowy weather, it was a pleasant walk through familiar neighborhoods and she knew several short cuts that got her into her office in less time than the bus or subway.

One of her best short cuts was to walk down the steps of a nearby subway station and bypassing the subway entrance and heading down the station's hallway to a distant exit. This way she avoided two very busy avenues and a social club frequented by less savory types. This rarely used subway exit faced a small cobblestone street and was rarely used by anyone other than the residents of a series of moldering apartment buildings.

Exiting the subway station, Betty stepped around a tramp sleeping near the stairs and headed up the street. Stepping around the sleeping tramp, she ignored the screech of tires from the street and continued on towards her office. After all, this was a Manhattan street and sounds like that were as commonplace as the yells of anger from the many taxi drivers.

A movement from the street caught the corner of Betty's eye, causing her to spin that direction with her hands up. Her movement was fast enough for her to catch sight of two men running her direction, their hands extended and reaching for her! Betty stepped back, raising her hands defensively, but the taller of the two men, a younger man with no expression on his face, grabbed both of her arms. His grip was powerful and painful, holding Betty in a viselike grasp that caused her to gasp in pain.

"Hold still and you will not be hurt. Scream and we will cause you much pain, Miss Dale." The second man, a hook nosed individual who appeared older, said in a soft voice.

"Help!" Betty yelled, kicking the man behind her as hard as she could muster. She struggled to no avail as the hooknosed man pulled out a damp cloth and extended it towards her face. Knowing this man was probably intending to drug her. Betty continued to ignore his advice and struggled to escape. But it was all in vain, the man holding her was far too strong!

Just as the cloth was about to press against her face, a filthy hand grabbed the hooknosed man's hand and pulled it back fast! The tramp, who moments before was sleeping on the bench, kicked the hooknosed man in the chest and send him flying backwards. The second man released Betty, causing her to stumble and fall to the ground. He stepped back and pulled out a long knife and took a vicious swing at the tramp's neck!

The tramp ducked beneath the blade and grabbed the attacker's wrist, slamming it down against his knee. The knife flew from the man's hand and the filthy derelict fired a powerful punch to his opponent's ribs, causing the man to gasp in pain. The tramp then grabbed his enemy's collar and with a spin of his hips, flung him across the pavement sending him head first into the side of the parked car at the curb. The attacker crumpled to the sidewalk unconscious!

The hooknosed man was also moving, having produced his own knife and circling carefully around the battling bum. The tramp stepped between Betty and stood still, his hands extended in a classic fighting pose.

Damianos didn't like this situation, not at all! Asterion defeated with no effort by this beggar, who was now protecting the woman Minos had ordered them to kidnap. If Damianos returned without Betty Dale, he would either meet his end at the hands of the Minotaur or the Mask of Medusa! Dying by either means was a terrible thought and he knew he had to kill this stranger fast! Damianos was an experienced knife fighter, learning his skills on the docks of Greece and Crete. It should be an easy victory.

Circling and making quick feinting gestures, Damianos tried to keep his enemy's attention on the knife. Meanwhile his free hand reached into his back pocket, retrieving a packet of chalk he had collected at Minos's hideout. Damianos palmed the packet and continued to make little quick mocking swings of his knife, not committing to any attack yet. But now he was ready! Feinting towards the stranger's chest with his knife, Damianos flung the packet of chalk in the stranger's eyes and smiled in triumph as he heard the yell of surprise! His enemy was blind and now would die!

The tramp stood still, yelling and rubbing his eyes, seemingly unaware of his impending doom. Chalk covered the man's filthy face and clothes, making him look older and cleaner to Damianos's amused eyes.

"Time to die, American fool!" Damianos snarled and stepped forward. He swung his knife up, intending to stab his opponent in the heart thereby killing him instantly!

The tramp didn't move out of the way, but stopped yelling as the knife approached on its lethal course. Suddenly he leapt backwards, causing Damianos to stumble forward off balance when his attack missed. The wily bum raised a hand and with a loud exhale of breath, swung the knife edge of his hand down onto Damianos's wrist. The wrist shattered with a loud SNAP!

"AAAHHHHH!" Damianos shrieked as the knife clattered to the ground. He grabbed his hand and doubled over with agony!

"Are you okay, Betty?" asked the tramp in the voice of Secret Agent "X". He kicked the knife out of the way.

"You were here all along!" Betty exclaimed, amazed as always by his skill at disguises.

"This seemed the best location to ambush you. I was ready in case they made an attempt. The other sites are being watched by my agents. "X" pulled out a pair of handcuffs from his filthy, battered clothing.

"You are quite clever," said a voice from behind them, emerging from the front seat of the car. "Sadly for you, not clever enough. Agent "X", I presume? You may turn slowly, but if your hands or feet move, I will shoot you both."

"X" and Betty slowly turned to see a hooded figure leaning out of the passenger side of a black sedan. A pair of small gloved hands held a sawed-off shotgun, both barrels aimed at the Agent and Betty. The face was hidden in the dark folds of the robe's hood and the person made no attempt to move into the light.

"He broke my arm!" Damianos howled, still clutching his wrist in pain.

"You were foolish enough to attempt your fighting tricks on the infamous Agent "X", Damianos. You get what you deserve. Take some smelling salts from the first aid kit in the back and wake Asterion. Then tie up Agent "X" and Miss Dale, hand and feet. Minos wishes to see them immediately!" The hooded figure sounded both amused and annoyed at the same time.

"And you are?" asked "X".

"You may call me Daedalus, advisor to Minos. Now please stop attempting to distract me, sir. We can talk once you're in our custody."

The shotgun did not waver as Damianos revived Asterion and they quickly tied up "X" and Betty. The gas gun and several lock picks "X" kept secreted in his clothes were taken after a quick search and both were shoved to the floor of the automobile at Damianos's feet. He continued to clutch his broken wrist, staring at "X" with angry, murderous eyes.

"You're American." Betty guessed, trying to crane her neck up to catch a glimpse of Daedalus's face. "How did you become a part of an ancient Greek conspiracy?"

Daedalus didn't turn, but replied, "Perhaps Minos will inform you about such information. It is not my place to say. Now, remain silent or I will have you gagged."

In the mean time, "X" was slowly working on escaping from his ropes. Trained in the art of escape by several professional magicians and a retired criminal, he carefully worked on loosing the bonds around his hands. It would take several minutes to loosen them enough for a quick escape, though "X" knew he would still need to wait for the right moment. Too soon and Daedalus would simply shoot them dead!

The car rumbled through what sounded like several major avenues and districts, before slowly pulling into a building near a body of water. Given that Manhattan was an island, this provided few clues for "X" or Betty. The building they had entered smelled strongly of fish and, to the Agent's sensitive and well trained nose, of fertilizer.

"Damianos and Asterion will carry you into the presence of Minos. I do not trust either of you free, hand or foot." Daedalus said and they heard him leave the car, his footsteps trailing away.

The back door to the automobile opened up and Asterion appeared, grabbing "X" and throwing him over his shoulder as if he was carrying a sack of potatoes. He paused to lend a hand to the injured Damianos, who carried Betty in the same fashion. Damianos tensed several times in pain as he carried Betty down a long series of stone steps and through a rusted metal door. The captives were unceremoniously deposited on the stone floor, several odd slits on the floor near where they lay.

"Bring the other." Daedalus said. Asterion and Damianos appeared a moment later, carrying a large burlap sack with someone inside. The person in the sack struggled and faint cries of fear and rage emerged, the words muffled and lost. Damianos and Asterion ripped opened the top of the bag and dumped this third prison onto the ground.

"What is this? Why are you doing this to me? This is an outrage! The Governor shall hear of your actions if I'm not released! Kidnapped from my very home…" Jessup Murdstone cried, sounding outraged as he tried to rise to his feet.

"Silence!" Minos said from across the room. "We are not here to listen to you bluster, Jessup Murdstone!"

"Are you in charge here? You'll be hearing from my lawyer as well as the Commissioner of Police and the Governor! You made a mistake, thinking you can hold me! I'm Jessup Murdstone, Chairman of Murdstone Bank and friend of the President of the United States!" Murdstone spat back as he was pushed back to the ground by Asterion.

"And a murderer," Minos accused, voice barely above a whisper.

Murdstone seemed taken aback by this statement and stared at Minos for a moment, "I don't know what you're talking about…whoever you are."

"I am called Minos." The cloaked figure stood and approached them. He stopped next to Daedalus where they all lay on the hard stone floor. "But I believe the time for honesty is at hand. Jessup Murdstone, learn the truth of the identity of Mighty Minos, ruler of the Cult of Medusa!"

Minos reached up and pulled back the heavy hood. Betty stared open-mouthed at the head and face that emerged, shocked into silence. Jessup Murdstone fell backwards, his face turning pale in shock and fear.

"You! How could it be you?" Murdstone gasped, looking sick and terrified.

Chapter Eleven

"It was easy, Father," Agnes Haines said, her face twisted with disgust. "You always believed I was a weak, frightened little mouse, neither strong nor smart enough to do anything. But you never realized that was an act, a ploy that fooled everyone! First I married Billy Haines, an idiot but one I could manipulate easily. He would have been your perfect replacement! But that all changed when you forced my stupid husband and Richie Winthrop to murder my brother! Your own son!"

"I didn't…" Murdstone argued, his voice weak.

"Yes you did! They both confessed to their crimes! You ordered them to murder Jessie because you disagreed with which country he wanted to invest the bank's money with! Your own flesh and blodd!" Agnes shouted, spittle flying from her mouth.

"I didn't have a choice!" Murdstone moaned, "He was going to destroy all the family built…"

"By opposing your investments in Germany? A country filled with madmen intent on ruling the world!" Agnes' voice was filled with venom.

"Opposing?" Murdstone repeated, looking confused. He then began to laugh weakly. "Oh, you poor deluded fool. Jessie didn't oppose investing in Germany and Italy He was the one that believed Germany's new ideas were correct! Your brother wished to help the Germans take over the world!"

"Lies!" Agnes hissed, "Lies!"

"Why don't you tell her whether it's true or not, Daedalus. Or should I call you Uriah Heath!" "X" pointed to the other robed figured.

Daedalus/Heath threw back his robe and gave "X" a small tight smile. "Very clever Agent "X". How did you know my identity?"

"A famous detective once taught me to discover who benefits from a series of crimes. You, as one of the most senior bank officers, would be the clear replacement should something happen to Murdstone."

"Correct," Agnes acknowledged. "Uriah will take over the bank, after a suitable period of mourning of course. Later we will be married." She turned to her father again. "You drove us together, Father. Sending Uriah with me to search for poor Jessie. We learned we had much in common, including our hatred of you. Then when we discovered the truth of your destruction of my brother…"

"Destruction?" Betty cut in. "That's an odd way of saying he was killed by Billy Haines and Richie Winthrop."

"Not if you knew the whole truth, Miss Dale. My brother was pushed into the sea, but they didn't realize he wasn't fully unconscious. He was barely able to keep afloat, until he washed ashore in a cave on a small island. There the gases of the cave destroyed him…twisted him…my brother died in that cave…" Agnes's voice trailed off, her eyes looking into nowhere.

"And what emerged was a creature of legend…the Minotaur!" Heath finished loudly, his voice triumphant.

Agnes came over and took Uriah's hand in hers as she picked up the story. "The islanders shut him away in a labyrinth, built by the original Daedalus. There we found him and I was able to calm him, keep him under control. The cultists knew only Minos could control the Minotaur. Jessie still somehow recognized me and listened so the cultists taught me their secrets. They gave to me the Mask of Medusa!"

"Take the woman to the Minotaur," Heath ordered Asterion and Damianos, "These other two will die by the Mask of Medusa!"

Asterion picked up the struggling Betty and with Damianos behind him, departed, followed by Heath, who slammed the door behind him. Soon the last of their opposition would be destroyed and anyone that opposed their will would follow!

Chapter Twelve

Alone with the mad woman, Secret Agent "X" knew their survival depended on turning the tables on the murderous lovers.

"Heath never denied what your Father stated. That it was your brother Jessie who wanted to give money to Germany."

"He didn't have to, Uriah would never lie to me!" Agnes began reaching into her robe.

"Heath isn't smart enough to lie!" Murdstone boomed. "With him in charge, the bank will fail in less than a year!"

"I am through listening to your lies, Father! It is time for you to gaze on the Mask of Medusa! Time for you to pay for all your sins!" Agnes declared as she placed a tarnished gold mask on her face. The mask was that of a woman with snakes instead of hair and jewels for eyes.

"X', his hands free for a while now, exploded into action! Swinging an arm, he caught Agnes behind her knees and swept her to the stone floor. She screamed incoherently as a small box fell from her hand, skittering across the floor. The Agent yanked the rope off his feet and reached into his coat, ripping open the lining. Pulling out a cloth mask, he covered his face with even the eyeholes blocked by large pieces of special hardened glass. A second mask was on the other side of the coat and he pulled it out, tossing it to Jessup Murdstone.

"Put that on!" said "X". "She's trying to release volcanic gases that will turn you to stone!"

It was the toxicology work he had done the night before that revealed the final piece of this puzzle. The volcanic ashes contained an odd series of elements which, upon entering a person's body, would destroy skin cell tissue at a rapid rate! Jessie Murdstone had apparently only received a lesser dose, which twisted him into some kind of horrible monster according to Agnes and Heath.

Oddly enough, Murdstone didn't pick up the mask. He let it fall to the ground as Agnes picked up the box and pushed the button!

"Now you die, Father!" Agnes decreed as gases began to emerge from the slits cut from the stone floor.

"Yes I do." Jessup Murdstone said and walked over to his daughter.

"No Murdstone, don't!" The Agent yelled, picking up the fallen mask and running to the banker.

"Go!" Murdstone said and lay down on the ground, his breath now coming in gasps. "This was all my fault. I belong dead!"

"As do you, Agent "X"!" Agnes screamed from beneath the Mask of Medusa. She pulled out a knife, similar to the one carried by Asterion and ran at "X". He knew immediately she was trying to cut open his gas mask and kill him by turning him to stone!

⓵⓵⓵

Betty struggled in vain against Asterion, but the man's hold on her was far too tight. They stopped before another metal door and Damianos took a large key off a nearby hook. Unlocking the door, Heath quickly opened the door as Damianos sliced the ropes holding her prisoner. With a quick, practiced flick of his shoulders, Asterion deposited Betty on the sandy floor near the door. The heavy metal door slammed shut with a loud BOOM and Betty could hear the lock snapping back in place.

The corridor was well lit and she could see it twisting off in many different directions. Betty knew this was the maze of the Minotaur and Minos meant her to be the creature's prey! Throwing off her shoes, Betty began to walk forward, having learned from "X" that panicking would only lessen her chances of survival!

Outside the door, Heath stepped back and said, "Check the lock and hinges. We cannot risk the Minotaur getting loose!"

Damianos and Asterion shot him a surly look, but turned back to examine the door. They didn't like Minos's advisor, but she was the ordained leader of the cult and this Uriah Heath was her second in command. As Master of the Minotaur,

Minos had that right, but they didn't have to like this nasty little man!

Reaching under his robes, Uriah Heath pulled out his sawed-off shotgun. These two men were becoming a problem, their unimaginative actions had brought them all to the attention of Secret Agent "X"! Once Asterion and Damianos were dead, he would have Agnes send for two others from the island, more compliant servants this time.

The click of Heath's gun cocking caused both men to spin around, pulling out their long knives. Heath fired both barrels just as Damianos and Asterion threw their knives! The bullets struck both men in the head and chest, hurling them back against the labyrinth's door where they slowly sunk to the ground dying! But before entering that black void of no return, their eyes did register a final, welcomed sight; their knives striking Uriah Heath, aka Daedalus, in each of his eyes!

۞۞۞

Betty, remembering some of the stories of the maze of the Minotaur, tore a strip of cloth from her blouse and placed it on the ground behind her. If she marked her trail, she might be able to prevent herself from getting lost. Of course that did mean the Minotaur might be able to find her faster. But she had no other choice. Getting free of the maze had to remain her number one priority.

From somewhere within the maze, Betty could hear a deep, inhuman roar. The Minotaur was roused and hunting his prey!

۞۞۞

"X" backed away from Agnes' wild swings with her knife. She wasn't skilled like her henchman, Asterion, but her insane rage made her attacks harder to counter. Still, "X" was an expert when it came to fighting people with knives, sane or not. Stepping in and blocking her swing, with his lead hand, "X" struck Agnes in the face with a palm-heel strike. The lower and harder part of his hand hit the Mask of Medusa, causing the ancient, brittle porcelain to shatter! The Mask fell from her face, exposing Agnes Murdstone Haines to the horrific volcanic gases she'd used to murder people!

"NOOOOO!!!!!!" Agnes screamed, reaching for her shattered mask. She held the pieces in her hands, her moans of terror cutting off a few second later!

"Killed by her own weapon," thought "X" as he headed for the door Heath and his men had taken Betty through. Next stop, the Minotaur!

۞۞۞

Despite her pieces of cloth, Betty was growing more lost by the minute. The maze seemed to have no end. Three times she found herself stopped by a blank wall! The inhuman howls from behind her appeared to be growing closer by the second, but Betty did her best to remain calm.

She was trying to cut open his gas mask and turn him to stone!

Then it appeared at the far end of the corridor. The Minotaur was over eight feet tall with powerful oversized muscles and a huge bull-shaped head! The creature was covered in filth and it was breathing heavily as it slowly moved towards her.

Betty Dale screamed with terror and backed away fast! This creature was monstrous, a terrible being that didn't belong on Earth! She continued to back away, but found herself trapped in another dead end as the Minotaur slowly approached, reaching out for her!

Just as the Minotaur's enormous hand reached for her neck, the creature reared up and roared! As the howling creature turned away from her, Betty caught a glimpse of "X" standing behind the monster in a classic fighting pose!

The Minotaur roared with rage and swung an enormous arm at the Agent, its speed surprising even "X" who was sent reeling across the corridor! The Minotaur grunted and lumbered after "X", who rolled out of the way and back onto his feet. This monster was more powerful than nearly any opponent he had ever faced!

The Minotaur turned towards "X" and lowered its enormous head. A second later it was charging, moving a lightning speed! The Agent was barely able to dive out its way, crashing into a wall as the terrible man-thing turned again for another attack! If this charge was successful, "X" would be crushed to death!

Feigning injury, "X" remained in place as the Minotaur charged again. At the last minute he dropped to the ground and rolled forward, out of the way and into safety! But the momentum of the Minotaur's charge sent it crashing head first into the wall and it fell to the ground, momentarily stunned!

"Its head, it fell off!" Betty called out, amazed to see the bull-shaped head crack and fall to the side. All she and "X" could see was the back of a misshapen skull, large patches of white bone visible!

"That's a helmet!" said "X" as he took Betty's hand and lead her through the maze. He had studied all the details available on the original maze after learning someone was calling themselves Minos was involved in the case. Fortunately for Betty, Agnes Haines and Uriah Heath had constructed a maze that was an exact duplicate of the original built by the King Minos thousands of years ago.

"I can hear him coming!" Betty whispered, but wasn't surprised that "X" seemed already aware of this knowledge.

The Minotaur appeared from the maze, only a short distance behind them. The bull-shaped helmet appeared bent out-of-shape, but it continued to pursue them at a ground eating clip!

"X" pushed Betty to the side and ran towards the Minotaur, matching its charge. The inhuman creature bellowed and increased its speed, determined the destroy its foe!

"X" was ready again! At the last second, he dropped to his hands and knees, cutting the legs out from underneath the Minotaur! It flew several feet through the air before crashing to the sandy ground! But to the surprise of "X" and Betty, it quickly leapt to its feet and snarled.

This time the Minotaur did not charge, having learned from its past mistakes. Instead it turned and reached for Betty, intent on destroying her first! But "X" wasn't about to let the monster get her! He ran forward and kicked the Minotaur in its rock-hard ribs!

The Minotaur roared, but didn't appear injured by the attack. Reaching behind it, the creature grabbed the Agent's leg and swung him through the air! "X" slammed into the wall, feeling several ribs break with the impact!

The Minotaur howled with delight and swung "X" again, but this time he was ready! Using the momentum of the Minotaur, "X" kicked off the creature and broke its hold, rolling away and slowly getting back to his feet. The Minotaur snarled with anger and moved towards the Agent, slowly this time.

"X" knew the Minotaur was far too strong, the volcanic gases had twisted Jessie Murdstone into a nearly unstoppable force! But these gases also limited Murdstone's intelligence, which was any man's best weapon. Now the poor soul was clearly more savage animal than man. The Agent would use that fact against it!

"Come on! Come on and catch me!" teased "X", grabbing some sand and throwing it at the Minotaur as a taunt. The Minotaur howled again, but still maintained its quick, controlled pace.

"X" emerged out of the maze a few seconds later, leading the Minotaur past the dead bodies of Asterion, Damianos and Heath and up the hallway. Stopping halfway down the hall, he assumed another fighting pose and when the creature got close, kicked it hard in the stomach. The blow hit its intended target and "X" felt as if he was striking a brick wall! The Minotaur swung an arm out in response, but "X" ducked back and avoided the blow.

"Don't follow me!" yelled "X" to Betty as he opened the door. Pushing back, he quickly pulled on his makeshift mask and filter and rolled into the gas room. Ashes filled the air and the frustrated Minotaur followed, snarling and reaching again for "X".

"X" rolled past the Minotaur and slammed the door shut. This would protect Betty in case her reporter's instincts got the better of her and she tried to enter.

Unfortunately this gave the Minotaur a chance to reach out and grab "X" again. The Minotaur swung "X" through the air, sending him crashing to the stone floor. The Minotaur roared happily and swung "X" again, slamming him hard into the ground.

The creature was about to swing him a third time, when it suddenly faltered. Its movements became sluggish and it moaned with fear and pain. A few second later the moan was cut off and the Minotaur fell to the ground, frozen in stone!

"X" searched for several minutes, the broken ribs causing his movement to be sluggish and painful. He eventually discovered the box Agnes used to activate the volcanic ash. A second button was visible on the top and he hit it, hearing fans activate immediately.

The ashes and gases were sucked down the slits in the floor, their suction great enough to stagger the Agent. Soon the room was clear and he opened the door, seeing Betty waiting, wide-eyed and hand to her mouth.

"Is it...dead?"

"Yes, but Jessie Murdstone really died falling overboard in the Mediterranean

Sea. This twisted abomination was just his remaining anger and betrayed feelings."

"X" looked down at the frozen body of the Minotaur, sympathy etching his features.

Betty sighed with relief, seeing Agnes was also a stone corpse as well. It was all so sad and pointless in the end. "It's over then."

"Over? No, Betty not quite. The Cult of Medusa still exists out there, somewhere. Their evil must not be allowed to continue! One day I'll find their island and their twisted ways will not be allowed to destroy others!"

"X" took the blonde reporter's arm and together they exited the still room. This Chapter of the Agent's fight against evil was done, but the war continued!

THE END

Frank -
How I Got Here

Every time I read a story about how a writer took the first step towards producing pulp stories, I'm amazed at the depth of details. From discovering treasured collections of rare issues in family attics to rare discoveries in used book stores... the stories seem to take on an almost Norman Rockwell style. I wish I could match these tales with one of mine, but honestly my tale comes down to one person... Phillip Jose Farmer.

Let me set the scene for you...typical New Jersey kid Frank Schildiner, one of those teens who always got the "does not live up to his potential" reports, more interested in girls, Raymond Chandler and Donald Westlake novels, and Bruce Lee movies than homework. Pulp was a vague concept, the word cropped up without a lot of meaning to this kid, mentioned while reading old detective novels or Robert E. Howard, but not something said teen pursued. The Shadow was a cool old radio character who appeared in DC comics, Doc Savage was an odd colored guy who once appeared in a Spider-Man comic...get the picture?

Then enter said teen's friend, who handed him a book that would change everything. This book was "Doc Savage: His Apocalyptic Life" by Phillip Jose Farmer and everything changed in this teen's world. Suddenly young Frank Schildiner was transported to an art-deco world of the 1930's and 40's, where heroes fought for good against terrible men and women, intent of ruling or destroying the world. Pulp now meant more than just paper, it was a form of literature that became a life focus...

And that's the tale in basic, from Doc Savage I began to search for others, the Shadow, the Spider, the Avenger, G-8, Secret Agent "X"...the list goes on. To this day I'm still digging out long forgotten characters and feeling the same delight I experienced after reading Farmer's biography of Doc.

Secretly I wished I could have been one of those amazing creators, earning immortality reserved for greats like Lester Dent, Maxwell Grant, Hugh Cave...so when the offer to write a Secret Agent "X" tale by Ron Fortier, the Dean of Modern Pulp in my opinion, I was walking on air to say the least. It's a rarity to see someone fulfill a lifelong goal, but that's what happening since the day a former friend handed me Phillip Jose Farmer's tribute to a pulp giant.

FRANK SCHILDINER -has a BA in Criminal Justice and a Master's in Public Administration from Seton Hall University. He is a 15+ year veteran Probation Officer in the New Jersey Criminal Courts, a mixed martial arts instructor at Amorosi's Mixed Martial Arts and a writer. He was first published in *Tales of the Shadowmen 5* and has also written non-fiction articles on Hellboy and the Universal Frankenstein series. A long-time pulp fan, he resides in New Jersey.

CHAPTER ONE

Wilfred O'Malley went about his usual rounds in the museum. He was a new hire and took his job very seriously for a couple of reasons. The first reason being that he needed the money. Bad. Life had thrown him a curve and the Great Depression took everything he had. He never really recovered from it and took to living on the streets recently. Pure luck had thrown him this job and he planned on keeping it. He needed to get back on his feet.

The second reason he took this job seriously was all the rumors about shady dealings that went down in this place. When he first got the job, he asked what happened to the last guy. He was told succinctly to mind his own business. The people he knew on the streets heard everything from robbery to betrayal to black magic. He didn't know what to believe, but he wasn't going to let anything, supernatural or not, get in the way of guarding these treasures.

Wilfred O'Malley was ready for anything. Which is why he was so surprised when he caught a whiff of jasmine. It wasn't threatening. It was quite pleasant. Peaceful. Relaxing. He saw just the faint outline of a shadowy figure before his eyes rolled to the back of his head and blackness overcame him.

"What's happening here, Officer?"

Officer Frank Wyatt turned at the familiar sound of the suave voice. Standing behind him was AP reporter A.J. Martin. Frank smiled and rolled his eyes at the tall man.

"Trouble, now that you're here," Frank replied.

"Oh, come now, Frank," said Martin, "what could I possibly do that hasn't already been done here tonight?"

"Burks is here," was all Frank needed to say. Detective John Burks had a single, overriding mission in his life as a dedicated member of the police force. That mission was to bring to justice the mysterious Sedret Agent "X". The very man who was at this moment masquerading under his nose as A.J. Martin. Burks didn't care for Martin either, but considered him more of a nuisance than a threat.

"Can you give me the skinny before he sees me?" "X", as Martin, asked.

"Sure," said Frank. "New night watchman says some boogeyman waylaid him and stole a funky object. Never saw the guy. Keeps goin' on about some sweet smelling perfume or something."

"Tell you what," said "X", "the guy's a friend of mine. Think you can get me to him unseen?"

Frank looked a little worried at that.

"You lookin' to get me fired, Martin?"

"Easy Frank," assured "X", "just point me in the right direction."

Frank gave him a nod toward the back of the building. "X" saluted him and skirted the edges of the investigation, trying to stay in the shadows until he found O'Malley. Out of the corner of his eye he noticed that Betty Dale had arrived with her usual perfect timing. Her reporter's instincts were sometimes better than his. All eyes were drawn to her natural beauty and perfect figure, making it simple to get access to the watchman.

O'Malley was a sorry sight. Head hung in his hands, he was the poignant picture of failure. "X" had met him before while in the guises of a street tough. "X" was on assignment to uncover a plot by German infiltrators to capture homeless vagrants and experiment on their bodies with vile mutagenic solutions. "X" saved O'Malley from certain, agonizing death and appreciated the bravery O'Malley displayed when the going got rough. He didn't know that it was "X", as Elisha Pond, who set him up with the night watchman job in the first place. "X" planned to keep it that way. A man has his pride after all.

"Chin up pal," "X" said to the forlorn guard.

O'Malley looked up and just shook his head sadly. "Who are you?" he said. "Another copper looking to kick a dog when he's down?"

"Nothing of the sort friend. Name's Martin. A. J. Martin. I was just hoping to ask you a couple of questions. That's all." "X" put out his hand to shake.

"You one of them reporter types? I don't need my shame on the front pages, Mister." O'Malley turned away.

"No, you don't understand, Will," "X" used his familiar name. That gave him the reaction he wanted. Interest. "I want to put a good spin on how tough your job here is. But for that, I need to hear from you how things went down."

"Fine," O'Malley said. "If you can keep me this job with your fancy words, I guess I can lay it out for you. Though, I don't know what you'll get out of it more than them coppers did."

O'Malley gave his account. "I was doing my normal rounds and then, blam!, right on the back of my neck. I blacked out. There's nothing more to it. When I woke up, I called the coppers right away."

"Was there anything missing from the museum?" "X" asked.

"Oh, yeah," remembered O'Malley. "They took that old Buddha looking guy. The head of a statue. Ancient Indian or something."

"That could be important, old friend," "X" said. "Were there any other details that you can remember before the attack?"

"Do I know you from somewhere?" O'Malley asked.

"X" looked around discreetly and whispered to the watchman. "You used to know me as Ruggles, from the streets." A look of quizzical wonder came over O'Malley's face. "Yes, my friend. This is my real life. A.P. Reporter A.J. Martin."

"Holy cow," O'Malley breathed. "And I never even guessed."

"Quickly man. Details." "X" knew he didn't have too much longer.

"You know, there was something just before the attack. I caught a whiff of some kind of perfume or something."

"What did it smell like?" "X" asked.

"Jasmine."

"Hey!" the familiar deep voice of Detective Burks roared out. "Martin! Who the hell let him in here!" Burks was storming over to where "X" and O'Malley were sitting.

"X"stood up casually. "Nobody, Detective. You know I usually just let myself in when the people's right to know is at stake."

Burks grabbed him by the collar and shook him like a rabid dog shakes a live rat. "I should run you in for interference, Martin!"

"You know it wouldn't stick, Detective," "X" tried to keep his composure. The straight-laced Detective must be really strung out to loose his temper like this. "X" didn't want to start trouble when he seemed to have another case on his hands that needed dealing with. "But don't worry. I'll play nice and leave."

"You'd better," the Detective released him quickly, coming to his senses. He turned around and bellowed. "Wyatt! Finish up with the statements and let's get back to the station."

"X"made his way out to his sleek, black sedan. Pulling out of the parking lot, he sped down the empty roads while tuning in his radio receiver. The crackle of reception resounded throughout the vehicle until he got a clear signal to the headquarters of Harvey Bates at the Colonial Research Foundation. This bogus cover, set up by "X" through his financial resources as Elisha Pond, allowed Bates to hire people as permanent operatives under the guise of doing 'research' for the foundation when they were actually getting the information "X" needed to complete his various missions.

"What's the scoop?" Harvey asked.

"Get me any information you can on Southeast Asian artifacts that were stored at the International Antiquities Museum," "X" ordered. "Specifically, the heads of statues."

"Sure thing," said Harvey. "Anything else."

"Yes. Find out who's in charge tonight down at the docks. I may be going in that direction later."

"X"went to his personal lab to do some research on his own. He was an expert in toxicology and thought there was something familiar to O'Malley's claim that he scented jasmine before the attack. Sifting through notes that went all the way back to his days as a young man traveling throughout Asia, he finally found an obscure reference to emotion altering compounds. The compound consisted of crush Kapok seeds boiled down to a powdery essence mixed with a secret ingredient that supposedly came from a rare flower shaped like a crane. This created a colorless gas that was then scented with jasmine to make it detectable to the user. This gas affected the pleasure centers of the brain, making the imbiber instantly relaxed and off-guard. Entering into a fighting situation after getting a whiff of this stuff would be virtually impossible.

The origins of the flower were not Indian, as the uninformed O'Malley had blurted out earlier, but Southeast Asian, as "X" suspected. More specifically, the flower grew in the Mekong River delta region where it was jealously hidden from the eyes of the west by the local inhabitants. "X" had only seen it once in his travels, and that was only because he took the time to learn the Khmer language and customs while there.

While musing over such past experiences, the radio let out a trickle of static before Harvey's voice sounded out.

"I've got something boss," Harvey said.

"Go ahead," replied "X". "I'm listening."

"Bentley's on duty tonight at the docks."

"Good. That should make things easier. Anything else?"

"Yeah, apparently, one of those artifacts was from some ancient kingdom called Angkor."

"I figured as much," "X" said. "I'll be in touch."

Before leaving, "X" made extensive use of his supplies to disguise himself as Beady McNulty, a persona he has made use of in the past to get jobs on sea going vessels as a deck hand. Beady was an Irishman with a shock of red hair, tattooed forearms, a pock-marked face, and a thick accent. He parked his black sedan a few miles away in a safe spot and walked to the docks with that distinct swagger only sailors acquire after months at sea. As he neared the harbor master's office, he stopped short. There was Betty Dale making her own way to the office, probably following her own leads. This wouldn't be the first time Betty figured something out before he did. She was probably the best beat reporter in the city. She was definitely the best looking.

"X"hurriedly approached her. "Hey, doll," he said in the thick Irish accent. "Looking for a good time?"

"Excuse me!" Betty said, backing off.

"X"looked around quickly, making sure nobody was within hearing distance.

"Betty," he whispered. "It's me."

"Oh," Betty dropped her guard. She instantly recognized "X"'s normal voice. It's the one voice she was always listening for. "Are you here about the theft?"

"Yes," he said. "But there's something else going on as well. The manner of the theft doesn't fit."

"That's what I thought also," Betty replied.

"Good work," "X" continued. "But let me go in first. I know this guy. He'll talk to me."

She agreed, but added, "When you get back, I've something to show you."

Sedret Agent "X" smiled. She really was good at what she did. He nodded his ascent and left.

Ronald Bentley was an old scrapper who made his way up the ranks of the shipping magnates the old fashioned way. He fought tooth and nail for it. He worked a hard twelve hours a day and made damn sure everything was in order when his shift was over. He left nothing dangling that would worry him off-duty. He like to play hard as well, and that meant no loose strings to keep his mind on something other than hard drinking, fast women, and playing his horn like a madman at the local watering hole.

He was all business on duty, and that meant all cautious as well. When he heard a sudden knock on the door, it raised his hackles. There were no ships unloaded at this time of night, and no shift changes either. A knock meant something unexpected, and something unexpected usually meant trouble.

He grabbed his machete and went to open the door.

Standing there was a mug he hadn't thought to see again.

"Beady!" he yelled in surprise. "What in all the hells on Earth are you doing here, boy?"

"Ah, ha, ha!" "X" yelled back, pouring it on thick. "Bentley old man! You'd a think I'd be risen from the dead by your reaction. Let me in you old dog!"

"X"walked in the door and embraced the old man in a bear hug. Bentley threw the machete down and returned the embrace, patting him on the back. About a decade ago, "X" was on a mission on a freighter to the South China Sea. His boatswain was Bentley. They hit it off well after some initial friction. When "X", as Beady McNulty, came aboard, Bentley immediately took a disliking to him based on his 'heritage'. He gave him the most menial jobs and threatened to have him keelhauled when he didn't finish fast enough, even though "X" worked faster than any other man on the boat. All that changed when their boat was attacked by Japanese privateers looking for loot for their imperialistic nation. Bentley had been knocked over board during the fighting. "X" jumped in after him and pulled him out of the depths of the ocean. He managed to find a stray lifeboat and paddle them away from the melee unseen as the freighter went down in flames. They spent two months on a deserted island while "X" nursed Bentley back to health. Finally, a lone fisherman found them and brought them back to civilization. Bentley was forever grateful to Beady McNulty.

"So what can I do you for?" asked Bentley.

"I be looking to return to Singapore and was hoping you could of helped me out," "X" said.

"Boyo," replied Bentley. "You just missed the boat. Had one sail out of the harbor not an hour gone."

"X"slapped his forehead in mock frustration, not actually surprised by this revelation. "Figures. When does the next leave out?"

"Not for another month yet. It's a long journey and not a popular destination these days," Bentley said. "If you need help getting by until then, you know I can get you work."

"Tis not the work I need friend, but the journey," "X" held a mock sadness in his voice, working up the story.

"Why would you return to such a place?" Bentley asked.

"I be living there," "X" said. "All proper like. I got me a porcelain doll of a lass whom I aim to marry. I only be back here to tie up me loose ends."

"God in Heaven!" exclaimed Bentley. "I never thought to see the day when Beady McNulty settles down! This calls for something special!" Bentley reached under his desk and retrieved an exotic looking bottle with a bead covered sheath. He wiped off two dirty shot glasses and poured out of the bottle an amber liquid.

"My best Cognac," Bentley smiled. "Here's to Beady McNulty! The best sailor on the seven seas!"

"Here, here!" "X" agreed. There were many nights spent in Singapore just like this after their rescue off the island. "X" couldn't refuse the hospitality now.

"By the by," "X" inquired. "What be the name of that boat which left dock?"

"The Sacred Heron, my boy. The Sacred Heron."

CHAPTER TWO

"X" met up with Betty outside the docks.

"So," Betty started. "Is A.J. Martin going to get the scoop on me with this one?"

"Would I do that to you?" "X" asked.

"If it suited the mission," she added. "You would."

"Well," "X" continued. "Not this time. He's all yours as soon as we're done. Now show me what you have."

Betty drew some photographs out of a large envelope. "These are pictures I was able to dig up on the piece of the statue that was stolen. I did some research on it. It is a bust of Jayavarman VII, a Khmer emperor who ruled around the late 12th century. He also built a lot of the temples that are now sacred ruins in Cambodia."

"X"studied the photographs while Betty relayed the information, which he had already known about, but was too respectful of her work to interrupt. While he studied them, his eyes kept locking on one photograph in particular. It was a picture of the bottom of the head where the neck would have snapped off from the rest of the statue.

"Betty," he said. "Look at that. There are two holes leading up through the middle of the bust, as if it had a trachea and an esophagus. Then look really close at the nostrils and you can see two holes there as well."

"What would be the reason behind those?" she asked.

"I'm not sure, but it's very unique. To figure out anything else, I'd need to see the rest of the statue," "X" surmised.

"And that's just not possible," Betty said. "Is it?"

"Oh, it is. Bentley just informed me that the Sacred Heron has to go through the Panama Canal before moving on to Singapore. I've got to intercept that boat there." "X" slapped his fist into his hand to emphasize his determination.

"But why?" Betty asked. She didn't want "X" gone for so long. It was bad enough that they couldn't acknowledge their love for each other, but to have him out of the country again for so long a time was unthinkable to her.

"Betty," "X" explained. "You must understand. Everything is connected. There are forces building all over the world that mean evil things to others, and those forces are going to affect even us, here in the United States. This simple theft may seem insignificant now, but I have this sinking feeling in my gut that there is more

The Sacred Heron, my boy. The Sacred Heron.

to it. I plan to find out at any rate."

Betty nodded, understanding, but still not happy about it.

"I'll need you to cover for A.J. Martin while I'm gone," "X" said. In the past, Betty had ghost written articles for him when his duties as Sedret Agent "X" took him elsewhere. It was yet another measure of her effectiveness.

She nodded ascent.

"Good," he said. "Now I need to visit the First National Bank."

Bank manager Eddie Frieze looked like a slimy toad. He was short, squat, had greasy hair and a wide smile that gave expectations of a darting tongue. Despite his looks, the man had a heart of gold and was the soul of discretion. He welcomed Elisha Pond with enthusiasm and a hearty handshake. Knowing the millionaire didn't like to waste time, he led him immediately to a private vault where Elisha often liked to make transactions without witnesses. Considering the amount of business Elisha did here, Eddie felt he practically owned the bank anyway.

Sedret Agent "X", as Elisha, thanked the man and sealed the vault door behind him. Once secure, "X" went about opening the various boxes that would grant him access to enough hard cash to make a trip around the world, including international currency. He often wondered what his benefactors thought about his liberal usage of these funds, whether their replenishment was grudging or completely trusting and altruistic. It didn't really matter to "X" though, as long as it got the job done.

When he finished with the cash funds, he used a special key to open the message box. This was how his benefactors communicated with him. Inside was a letter. He opened it.

The news was shocking.

The letter read:

"Agent "X",

Terrible news. One of our own has been murdered. His body was found washed up on the distant shores of Siam. Whoever did this was looking for money. A note was found on the body that stated: "this is what happens when Americans do not pay their ransoms." The note was in Japanese. This effrontery cannot go unpunished, but the United States is not yet ready to go to war. It is up to you to find who was responsible and bring him to justice, quietly.

We are now Nine."

Sedret Agent "X" pulled out a match and burned the letter. It seems he had more than one reason to go to Southeast Asia.

"Lucky" Louie LePage was working on his baby. It was a genuine Sopwith Camel Fighter straight from the fields of France. Lucky Louie was a barnstormer in the 151st British Camel Squadron. Even though he was French, he was invited into the squadron for his knowledge of the French countryside and his inexplicable skills as a fighter pilot. There, he befriended the man now known as Sedret Agent "X".

It was Sedret Agent "X" who arranged for Lucky to live in America. He set Lucky up with a new life that would allow him to fly whenever he wanted, and plenty of land to fly over. The only thing Lucky had to worry about was maintaining contact with the Colonial Research foundation. He was yet another operative that "X" maintained to help complete his missions, and he had to be up to date with the current passwords.

As he turned the final nut in place on the wheel house, a man walked into the bay.

"Can I help you?" Lucky asked with a rich, deep Norman accent.

"The Osprey hunts the river," the stranger said.

"Only when the fish are jumping," Lucky replied, then held out his hand.

Sedret Agent "X" clasped Lucky's hand warmly.

"You look like a Spaniard today," Lucky said in French. "It has been awhile since you have visited me, my friend."

"Too much to do," "X" answered in equally perfect French. "You know how it is."

"Yes," Lucky mused. "Yes, I do." He remembered flying those missions over the Belgian front, his American friend protecting his flank. He remembered the dedication "X" had to the mission and the sense of duty he imparted on the whole flight.

"Can you get me to Panama," said "X". "Fast."

Lucky pointed to his plane. "She is the fastest of her kind. The best of her era. Of course I can. We'll have to make a few stops along the way, but we'll get there, worry you not."

"That's just what I wanted to hear."

Sedret Agent "X" kept a secret refueling station at the ready on a small, unknown Caribbean island for just such an occasion. The Sopwith Camel Fighter made several stops in the States to refuel. The last one was in the middle of the Everglades where "X" had to rustle up some navigational maps to explain to Lucky where his island was. From there it was a quick flight over the Panama Canal.

"X"prepared himself for a jump. It was risky, jumping into the middle of a jungle, but he had to make sure nobody saw his descent or the plane flying over international airspace.

"I really don't think this is a good idea!" Lucky yelled out, yet again, over the noise of the winding engine.

"It's the best way in," "X" yelled back.

"Are you absolutely sure?" Lucky screamed.

"X"gave him the silent signal. Enough was enough. He would brook no more argument. Lucky knew what that meant and just shook his head. Once Sedret Agent "X" got a crazy idea in his head, nothing could talk him out of it.

CHAPTER THREE

With the maw of the jungle below, "X" climbed out of the gunner seat and with a yell, dove straight down. Lucky veered off back to the ocean as "X" flew through the air. The rushing wind flapped at the fake putty on his face, coming dangerously close to ruining his disguise. He would have to double check it when he landed.

The trees rushed up at him, their leafy boughs looking like a false web of security beneath him. At what seemed the last second, "X" pulled the rip cord on his parachute. He rocketed back up over the treetops, but not high enough to be easily spotted. At least, he hoped so.

Falling through the canopy, "X" had to cover his face to protect his disguise. The harmless looking leaves and branches seemed to reach out to tear and claw at him. They left tiny little scratches covering his forearms and miniscule rips in the jumpsuit.

"X"was pulled up short of the ground when the chute caught on some branches. The force of stopping caused his head to lurch harshly and he almost passed out from the strain. Working quickly, he pulled out his knife and cut the straps holding him to the chute. He landed on the soft jungle floor and rested for a few minutes, allowing the world to stop spinning in his head and the blood to rush back to the rest of his body.

Doffing the jumpsuit, "X" began weaving his way through the foliage. He moved through the underbrush with speed and precision, avoiding the roots that tripped inexperienced travelers and staying low to bypass hanging hazards like branches and creatures. Sometimes, poisonous insects hang on low lying branches and attach themselves unaware to passersby. This could have dire consequences for the careless.

A few hours of rigorous travel brought "X" to where the jungle ended and civilization began. He noticed the beginnings of the ramshackle huts that made up the shanty town where many low grade, low pay workers lived. Many of these were Panamanian natives who were being exploited by the contractors tasked with making improvements to the canal.

"X"took out his putty and makeup kit. He flipped open the mirror to check his disguise as a Latino ship worker. After a few adjustments, the façade was perfect.

There is a certain art to blending into a crowd, and none were better at it than Sedret Agent "X". One would think that coming out of the jungle with a backpack on and dressed like a sailor would attract attention amongst the local populace. But "X" had a way of moving so subtly like his disguise, blending so perfectly in not only looks, but mannerisms and emotions as well, that he couldn't be noticed by even the most alert native observer.

Moving through the crowds, "X" found the local watering hole. He sidled up to the bar and ordered a drink. When the place began to fill with the local workers getting off shift, he listened in on their conversations. He had to listen closely to their words. Their dialect was distinctly different from the Spanish he learned in both Spain and Mexico.

Finally, he heard something useful. Work was opening up due to a proposed major improvement to the canal. A new set of locks was to be built large enough to transport the larger U.S. warships now under construction. If "X" could get in on this work detail, he would be in position to know exactly when the Sacred Heron came through the canal on its way to Southeast Asia.

It was then, that opportunity presented itself. One of the larger workers began bullying another. It was obvious that the others feared this man and didn't want to interfere through sheer physical intimidation. "X" could tell by their body language that they wished they could do something, but that it seemed hopeless to them.

The bully had the smaller man planted face first in a pool of spilled whiskey on the table. He had a smile on his face like he was enjoying this display of his mastery over the smaller man.

"You think you're smarter than me?" the bully said. "You think your honeyed words can get me to mind my own business?" He lifted the smaller man's head off the table with a fist full of hair. "If I want to touch your woman, I'll do so. And there isn't a damn thing you can do about it." He growled in the smaller man's ear.

"Why don't you leave him alone," "X" said loudly, so the whole bar could hear. A hush fell over the crowd. The big man turned slowly to look at "X" who used his body language to deliberately look smaller than he really was.

"What's this?" the bully said. "You have something to say for the little maggot?"

"No," said "X". "I just want you to leave him alone or else I'll have to teach you some manners."

All eyes went wide with shock. Nobody ever talked to the bully this way.

The bully laughed out loud in a show of bravado. "Walk away now, mister, and you'll live to see another day."

"You stink like a sweaty mule," "X" taunted.

Anger flashed in the bully's eyes and he roared as he charged the ready "X". "X" knew he couldn't stand toe to toe with this man, but he could see his movements as if he were in slow motion. He side-stepped the big man and brought him down face first with a simple leg sweep. At the same time he grabbed the man's wrist and twisted hard, bringing his arm behind his back and landing on top of him on the floor. The bully screamed as "X" held him in a wrist lock that was very painful. The big man tried to struggle but this only brought on further bouts of agony, so he was forced to stay very still.

"What do you want?" the bully cried.

"I want you to leave and never come back," "X" said.

"Never!"

The whole room flinched at the snap of a broken arm. The bully screamed again.

"I can do worse," "X" said.

"Okay, okay! I'll leave!"

"X" let the bully up and, with a last glower at the patrons, he ran out the door. The room erupted with a cheer as people started patting "X" on the back and offered to buy him drinks.

"X"was offered work right away, which he took in order to ingratiate himself further with the locals. After a few weeks he found out the information he was waiting for. The Sacred Heron would soon be passing through the Gatun Locks.

CHAPTER FOUR

Watching and waiting. These were two of the most important things to learn how to do when becoming a spy. None were better at it than Sedret Agent "X". Everyday he sweated and slaved in the heat while moving rocks and dirt in a wheelbarrow to help with the excavation. At night he went to the various drinking establishments, most of them just somebody's home cleared out to make room for patrons. These places were surprisingly upbeat. Many of these workers were family. They worked together, lived together and played together. Through his various contacts with many different workers, "X" was invited to many homes. His Panamanian accent had become very fluent over this time.

One night, he was invited to a more regular tavern that had a spectacular view of the canal. From there, out on the porch, "X" caught sight of his quarry at last. The Sacred Heron was berthed at one of the many docks on Lake Gatun. He was too far away to determine any movement on the ship, but at least it had docked instead of going straight through, probably to allow the sailors some down time.

"How do you do it?" a voice said behind him. It was the voice of Pedro Garcia, the owner of this house. He was also one of the gang bosses down at the excavation.

"What would that be?" "X" asked.

"You work harder than any man," Pedro explained. "Like a demon possessed. I know your supervisor. He does not make you work like that. You do it on your own. Why?"

"I look on it as a challenge," "X" explained. "Everything I do, I do to the best of my ability. Otherwise, it's not worth doing to me."

"You are a funny man. Yet to me, it seems as if you are a thousand miles away. And maybe soon, you will be," Pedro said. "I think it would be better for everyone if this were true."

"X"looked hard at the man. Pedro was no fool. He knew "X" wasn't here to work the canal. He had overstayed his welcome.

"You are right, my friend," "X" replied. "But I would appreciate it if no one knew."

"No problem, my friend," said Pedro. "I would not want to spoil any surprises."

"Thank you," "X" held out his hand to shake. "Someday, I hope to be able to show you my appreciation."

"That's not necessary."

"X"left it at that, but to him, it was very necessary indeed. No doubt, Elisha Pond would be making a donation in the future to certain individuals in Panama.

"Pedro," "X" said, quite serious now. "If you ever are asked the question, 'how far does the heron fly?' you must answer, 'as far east as it can go.' Do you understand?"

"Yes," Pedro answered in English. "I believe I do."

Later that night "X" made his way down to the docks with all of his gear. He found an advantageous hiding spot that allowed him to see and hear everything happening on the Sacred Heron. The people he saw moving around on the boat confirmed one of his suspicions. They were Japanese. The simple theft in a New York museum was for an international reason, which meant it had something to do with Japanese imperialism toward Southeast Asia, specifically Cambodia. "X" had to get on that boat.

Sedret Agent "X" saw what he needed. A lone sailor was making his way off the boat and walking down the docks toward him. "X" got a good long look at the sailor's face, memorizing his features. Once the sailor was past him, "X" discreetly followed at a distance.

The sailor led him to a seedy watering hole that consisted of all locals. He found a corner spot and sat by himself after ordering a whiskey using gestures and pointing at the bottle he wanted. The sailor laid down American money which the bar tender was quite used to seeing.

"X" sat at the bar and ordered a drink. He let it sit there while he studied his quarry. He noticed how the man seemed to be a loner. The sailor took stock in his surroundings but was easily distracted by a pretty woman. He would stare at them until someone else blocked the view or she took notice, at which point he would continue his scan of the room. All these traits worked in "X"'s favor. They were easy to emulate and kept him away from others with good excuse so he could do other things.

"X" stood up and walked over to the sailor.

"Mind if I join you," he said in perfect Japanese.

To say the sailor was surprised is too mild. He nearly jumped out of his chair in shock, almost tipping his glass over.

"Who are you," he asked.

"I used to work in the Philippines," "X" said by way of explanation. "Got to know your kind well."

The sailor sat down, a bit more relaxed, but still wary.

"What's your name," "X" asked.

"My name is Osamu Motonobu," he said, almost defiantly. "And you are?"

"I am Feli "X" Caban," "X" gave his alias. "I am pleased to make your acquaintance. I work for the Christ-damned Americans. They try to break my back and they pay me like dirt. They treat us no better than cockroaches."

Osamu just shook his head, sympathetic.

"What is it you do?" "X" asked. He guessed this man's real name wasn't Motonobu. Motonobu was a noble name from an ancient family. This man did not have the manner of nobility about him. That also suited "X" just fine.

"I?" Osamu barked. He seemed ashamed, but in the angry manner of his people. "I am a cook. Nothing more. A simple cook. I too, am treated like your cockroaches."

"Understood," "X" said. "When do you leave?"

"Dawn," Osamu answered.

"X"finished his drink and then got up to leave. "It was a pleasure meeting you Osamu. Good luck in your journeys." He bowed in the Japanese tradition. Osamu got up and returned the gesture.

"X"left the establishment and immediately hid in the dark recesses of the building. He only waited about fifteen minutes before Osamu left the bar. He followed him stealthily until he passed by a darkened area out of earshot. He then ran up behind Osamu and whispered him name.

"What?" Osamu turned around.

Just then a puff of white smoke was blown into his face and Osamu dropped to the ground, unconscious.

"X"lifted the body and carried him to his quarters. There, he got out his make-up kit and began mixing the special putty he developed to make his disguises so realistic. He removed the face of Feli "X"Caban and started applying a new face, that of Osamu Motonobu.

He then went back to Pedro Garcia's house. The party was over by the time he got there. He knocked on the door and waited for an answer. Pedro opened it himself, a long machete in his hand.

"What do you want?" he said, menacingly.

"How far does the Heron fly?" "X" said in Spanish.

Pedro was surprised. He couldn't believe this Japanese man would ask this. But it was true. Right before him. So he answered.

"As far east as it can go," he said, haltingly.

"X"smiled. "Yes, my friend. It is me. There is a man in my hut. He will not wake until morning. He looks just like I do now. Please take care of him once he figures out his boat has left without him. He may be a bit hostile at first, so be careful. Can you do this?"

"Yes," Pedro said. "I understand."

"You will be well rewarded, my friend," "X" said.

"That is not necessary."

"Maybe, but it will happen."

Sedret Agent "X" boarded the Sacred Heron just before it was ready to lift the plank and head out into the canal. He was reprimanded for being late by a superior officer named Kimo. "X" was familiar with most Japanese ships, so he found the kitchen without trouble. He immediately set about preparing a breakfast for about thirty men. It wasn't hard to figure out the usual fare these sailors were used to. Most of the larder was standard food stuffs, easy to stock, easy to make.

The boat smelled like a combination of sweat and oil and refuse. It permeated everything, even the food. "X" would have to get used to this life again. It wasn't an easy adjustment.

By the time he got all his work done and had a few minutes to relax, the Sacred Heron was passing by the Bridge of the Americas and into the Pacific Ocean. Soon, there would be nothing for him to do but ride out the journey, interact with others as little as possible, and avoid discovery.

The first few days were easy. Most of the sailors had plenty of work to do and there wasn't any time for social interaction. Eventually though, life of the high seas brings on a routine of boredom, which forces sailors to find others way to occupy their time. This usually leads to games of chance and skill that can have relatively high stakes for the losers, whether that was money or physical injury.

"X"was usually able to gauge other sailors' reactions to his presence as Osamu before they even noticed him, and thereby act in a manner appropriate to his façade. One time though, a sailor accosted him in the kitchen.

"What's the problem with these noodles lately!" the sailor said, slamming the door open. "I am sick of getting this soggy crap from you Osamu! You've been feeding us this slop ever since we left Panama. Why?"

"X"wasn't sure how to react. Had he been cooking them wrong? Should he be belligerent, apologetic, or plead ignorance? He hadn't had enough time to study his subject in the right setting. He went with apologetic.

"A thousand pardons, sir," he said. "I will try to do better next time."

This actually brought the sailor up short. An apology was the wrong tactic. This sailor was probably looking for an argument from a normally defensive Osamu.

"What?" he started to ask.

Suddenly, the warning horns began to sound throughout the ship. Men began screaming out "storm! Storm ahead! Tie everything down! There's a storm coming!"

The sailor promptly forgot about Osamu and ran out of the kitchen to prepare for the worst.

The storm came out of the west, unexpected and unseen. The ship rode up and down waves twice its size, tossing sailors over the deck with huge squalls of water. Fortunately, most of these men were experienced and knew enough to tie themselves off. If a wall of water tried to drag a sailor over the rails, his lifeline would keep him around.

"X"went topside to see if he could help. The rain came down so hard it stung. He made his way over to the command deck where he saw Commander Kimo shouting out orders over the din. "X" could barely hear him, but it sounded like there was trouble with securing all the items on deck.

Suddenly, a deluge of water swamped the command deck. "X" closed his eyes and held his breath, hanging on for dear life to one of the railings. The force of the water strained his muscles almost to their considerable limit. Just when he thought he'd have to let go and fly into the sea, the ship righted and the water fled. He was left gasping for breath and hauling himself to his feet.

With his head clear he looked around the deck. He saw Commander Kimo on the floor, face down in a pool of water. "X" ran over to the man and quickly flipped him over, getting his face into the air. He wasn't breathing. "X" tried pumping the water out of the man's lungs by performing compressions and giving air to him. Eventually, the man coughed up a splash of water and began intermittently breathing again.

Kimo looked up at who he thought was Osamu the cook and nodded his head in thanks. They waited out the rest of the storm tied down securely to the deck and lucky to be alive.

Later, Sedret Agent "X" was called up to the commander's office. He entered the sparse suite. It merely contained a desk, two chairs, a foot locker, and a steel filing cabinet.

Kimo indicated he should sit down. He pulled out a decanter of liquor and two glasses and poured them both a drink. He was meticulous in his movements, carefully placing the stopper back into the bottle.

"Osamu," he slowly pronounced his name. "Most of the men will believe I've called you up here to simply thank you for saving my life."

"X"nodded studying the officer, noticing that he hasn't touched or looked at the glass of brandy in front of him.

"They would be incorrect," Kimo continued. "My life, and the life of all the men on board this vessel are not important. Only the mission is important. Whatever we must do to complete the mission, we will do at any cost."

Kimo nodded his head toward the glasses, indicating they could drink now. Kimo took a small, conservative sip out of his glass and "X" echoed the action. He knew enough not to say anything unless prompted.

"Part of that mission is to ensure the survival of the officers in charge, in order to ensure mission control and cohesiveness. You have succeeded admirably in this, by saving my life. For that heroic service, I have deemed it necessary to offer you a higher position. Unfortunately, we have nobody on board who can handle the kitchen duties with the efficiency you have displayed. Therefore, I must keep you there, though your pay grade will be better. Is this suitable to you?"

"Yes," "X" said. He was actually relieved. Being in the kitchen served his disguise.

"Do you know what that mission is?" Kimo asked.

"No," "X" answered, hoping for clarity.

"It was to obtain this," the commander reached into another drawer and pulled out the statue head of Jayavarman VII. "Now we have to bring it to Singapore and deliver it to another officer. Do you know why this item was important enough to sail over half the world for? To risk an international incident to obtain?"

"No." "X" listened intently.

"Neither do I," Kimo said, deflated. "I don't understand this. It's an artifact of a lesser peoples. Why should the great nation of Japan be interested in such a thing?"

"X"cursed inwardly. Kimo's superiors wisely sent their man on a mission without telling him the true purpose. "X" understood the reasoning, respected it even, but it didn't help his cause. If he knew for sure that throwing this head into the ocean would put a stop to whatever the Japanese were planning, he would do it in a minute, no matter his current situation or the consequences such and action would bring down on him. But it could be a wasted effort, and might avail him nothing. He would have to wait at least until Singapore and see what happens there.

"May I look at it?" "X" asked.

Kimo studied him. "By all means."

"X"picked up the bust. He flipped it over in his hands. It was hefty. He could feel the age of the stone. The smoothness of time worn rock left a sensation on the fingertips unlike modern works. He found the vents in the neck and nostrils, almost like tubes, as well as pinholes in the inner ears. He felt certain they were connected on the inside, somehow.

He shrugged nonchalantly and put the head down.

"Could you discern a reason for such a thing?" Kimo asked.

"Not me, sir", "X" said. "I'm just a cook."

CHAPTER FIVE

The rest of the journey to Singapore was fairly uneventful. Sedret Agent "X" perfected the culinary art of mass noodle and rice production while still keeping as low a profile as possible. His mastery of the Japanese language improved immeasurably with over a month of practice.

The ship pulled into the busy port of Singapore, masquerading as a merchant vessel. Once all the customs were straightened out, Commander Kimo allowed his men some shore leave. "X" took this opportunity to slip away into the crowds and establish a new identity. With all his disguise equipment and weapons neatly arranged in his backpack, "X" left the Sacred Heron for good.

He found a safe house to swap his disguise to that of a Malaysian fisherman, unassuming and easy to blend in. These safe houses were ones he had established years ago traveling throughout the Southeast. Those were simpler times, he reflected. Back then, he didn't have to worry about security and enemies. It was a time of learning and honing his skills. Sometimes he missed those days. Sometimes he thought he should just take Betty and disappear with her into the safer, saner places of the world. But his stringent code and sense of duty wouldn't allow for that, and it seemed to him that those safe places in the world were disappearing all too fast, being devoured by the power mad hungry machine called the human race.

While his thoughts ran away on him, Sedret Agent "X" found a place to keep watch on the Sacred Heron. After a few hours, he spied Commander Kimo leaving the boat with a trusted right hand man and a package in hand. "X" took note of their direction and saw they were headed straight to the Japanese foreign embassy. He left his post and made his way there through back streets only he and the natives were familiar with.

"X"considered changing his disguise to that of Ho Ling. He knew for a fact that there were several spies of the Mint Tong Brotherhood inside the embassy, of which Ho Ling was a member. That way he could see first hand where the package that Kimo carried would end up. Unfortunately, he had no plausible explanation for Ho Ling's presence. The rest of the Brotherhood knew Ho Ling worked mainly in America and China. No, Ho Ling's appearance would only complicate things. Best

"I'm just a cook."

to keep it simple for now.

He kept outside watch on the embassy. He knew the workings of it, the shift changes and the schedules of incoming clientele as well as lowly maintenance personnel. He watched as Kimo went inside with the package under his arms and then exited not half an hour later with nothing. Kimo was out of the picture now. He had to get in closer.

He moved through the embassy grounds like a shadow, keeping out of sight. The guards at the front door were alert, so he made his way in from the side, flanking the entrance to look for a different way in. A servants' door was nestled in the recesses of the overhanging roof, covered in darkness. He sidled up to it and began picking the lock with the tools from his backpack.

Suddenly, the scent of jasmine wafted through the air. "X" quickly stopped his breath from sucking in and at the same time dropped his lock picks. He pretended that he felt calm, relaxed, even drowsy.

When the blow came, "X" was ready for it. He quickly blocked it with a snatching grab and dragged the caught wrist toward him. He slung a hard elbow strike into his assailant's chin, following through and forcing his head up against the hard stone wall. The blow knocked the gas mask right off his assailant's face, who crumbled to the ground, unconscious.

"X" ripped the gas mask off his assailant and adjusted it over his own face, clearing the vents and checking the seal before he allowed himself to breath again. He took a moment to steady his breathing before studying his attacker's face and attire. He was a Japanese ninja. The question was, why was he using this rare and secret Cambodian mixture to neutralize opponents? And where was he getting his supply?

"X" finished the lock pick job on the door and dragged the man inside with him. He was in some kind of food pantry storage area. He stripped down the man's attire and proceeded to change his disguise to that of a Japanese ninja. Fortunately, they usually wore attire that covered everything but their eyes, so all he had to do was make his eyes look like his assailants.

When he was ready, he gave his assailant a shot. It was a special chemical he developed that would keep the body in a semi-state of hibernation for a few days. By the time this man awoke, no worse for wear, "X" would be long gone.

Even with this disguise, "X" would have to stay out of sight. He didn't want to take the chance of interaction, not having had the chance to study the subject of his disguise he didn't want anything he said or did to raise suspicion. Also, he didn't want to be conscripted into some other task that a ninja would be required to do.

Keeping to the shadows in the weakly lit halls of the embassy, "X" eventually found an office where he heard voices speaking in normal conversational tones. He overheard two men discussing an upcoming journey. "X" could tell by their vocal cadence and manners that one was a diplomat and the other a military man.

The military man spoke with impatience, "I must leave immediately. Those are my orders."

"But, why?" said the diplomat. "It doesn't make any sense that you have to go traipsing through the jungle because of some stupid statuette."

"I know that!" snapped the military man. "But my orders are clear. You know General Oyakata brooks no questions from his officers."

"Very well," said the diplomat. "When does he expect to launch the attack on Cambodia?"

"That is on a need to know basis," said the military man. "But what I do know is it starts from a jungle temple called Prasat Neak Pean."

"Whatever," the diplomat whined. "I just hope it isn't the impetus to get the Americans involved in our affairs."

"Enough," the military man finished. "Farewell, my friend."

"X" had heard enough. He turned down the hallway to leave. He was brought up short by three other ninjas rounding the corner. They seemed a little surprised at his presence.

"Dragon," one of them said quietly.

When "X" didn't give the expected response they exploded into action, attacking in unison.

"X" didn't waste any time. He grabbed a smoke bomb and threw it hard at their feet. It exploded and created an instant smoke screen that obscured all vision in the immediate vicinity. "X" still had to dodge a few hastily thrown punches as the ninjas flayed wildly through the fog, trying to hit something. "X" tumbled forward through their ranks, hoping the move at them instead of away would throw them off guard. It worked. He came through the smoke and bolted down the hallway. He would normally try to take them out, but he wasn't here to fight. He needed to get away and find a plane.

"X" made it out of the compound and disappeared back into the city streets.

Sedret Agent "X" was an accomplished pilot. He had flown many missions during the war over the French and German countryside. Flying a Japanese fighter plane was a completely new experience though. The controls were in different places and the technology was updated from what he was used to. Still, after a few mishaps he managed to right the shaky take off and make headway into a cloudy sky.

Getting one of these planes was no easy task either. After his exploits at the embassy, "X" found that there were operatives of the Japanese government scouring the city for him. He easily avoided them by changing his disguise back to that of a Malaysian fisherman. He then scouted out the few small airstrips on the island. He found one supposedly owned by a wealthy Japanese businessman. "X" easily saw through this thin veneer of legitimacy and discovered the fighter plane under a tarp in a warehouse. He also scouted out soldiers inside that he had to avoid.

Fortunately, he didn't dispose of the ninja suit he had taken earlier. Inside that suit he found another vial of the very gas the previous owner had used to try and take him out. He was aware, upon further study, that the gas had a tendency to sink in air. With this in mind, he climbed to the top of the warehouse using the ninja's tool kit, a claw shaped grappling hook and thin silk woven rope. From the ceiling vent he released the gas into the interior atmosphere of the warehouse. He caught a whiff of that familiar jasmine scent just before he put on his gas mask which told him the gas was successfully released.

Within minutes the soldiers inside walked around in a glazed, content stupor. "X" climbed down through a skylight and not one of the soldiers bothered to look up at him. He soon had the tarp off the plane and the engines running before any of them glanced in his direction. When they did, they gave a non-committal shrug and went back to staring at whatever daydreams invaded their minds.

Problems arose when two soldiers from another room in the warehouse came in to check on the noise. These soldiers were probably the officers in charge of the detail. They took in the situation and acted quickly, firing their guns on the plane as it began rolling towards the bay doors. "X" gunned the gas and prayed the plane would hold together. He hoped the doors were as flimsy as they seemed from the outside.

Bullets flew past him as the plane smashed through the doors, sending them flying back in crinkling sheets of corrugated scrap. The plane's engine skipped a beat but kept on chugging, eventually lifting into the air as "X" pulled back on the throttle. The plane dodged and wove the air currents as "X" familiarized himself with the controls and righted his course north to the southern shores of Siam.

Two-thirds of the way there, Sedret Agent "X" noticed his fuel was getting low. He estimated he wouldn't make it and he was stuck out over the Gulf. His best bet was to climb as high as he could and glide the plane as far as it would go. He managed to glide on air currents until the shores of Siam were in sight, although still not close enough for comfort.

With no other recourse available to him, "X" climbed out of the cockpit, tested the straps of his parachute and abandoned the doomed aircraft. His chute opened above him as he watched the plane hit the water nose first and quickly sink out of sight.

He touched down upon the rolling waves, taking care to immediately cut the lines tying him to his parachute. It was difficult enough swimming in the sea without having the extra complications of tangling parachute lines. After a short rest where he floated on his back to steady his breathing, he set out swimming toward the distant shore. Fortunately, the sea was calm and he was able to make good time without taking in too much water from swells.

A few hours later he crawled, exhausted, up onto a sandy beach. A Siamese fisherman watched his progress contentedly, as if watching a hermit crab struggle against the tide. When "X" finally stopped in a shaded, dry place, he closed his eyes for a few hours rest.

Sedret Agent "X" opened his eyes to dim light. It was night. The salty ocean air tainted his tongue senseless. He heard the endless crash of waves on the shore. Below that, the faint sound of crackling wood alerted him to a fire. Covering him was a blanket. He looked across the fire to spot two figures outlined in a ruddy glow.

He rose and walked over to them, stumbling a little as the soreness from his exertions seeped in. As he approached, the warmth of the fire lent strength to his limbs. He noticed that one of the figures was the fisherman he saw earlier. The other he figured to be his wife as they were huddled together.

"Thank you for the blanket," he said in broken Siamese.

The fisherman, lines crossing his weather beaten face, nodded solemnly. He indicated that "X" should sit. "X" did so gladly as he doffed his backpack and laid it next to the fire to ensure it dried out properly. He wasn't worried about the contents, as everything was in waterproof containers, but he didn't want the bag itself rotting.

The fisherman suddenly spoke. "The last white man who washed up on these shores was dead."

It was then that "X" realized his disguise must have dissolved during his long swim in the ocean. His special putty didn't really hold up that well to long exposure in salt water. It wasn't usually a problem. These two simple folk were seeing his real face, something nobody ever sees back in the States. There was nothing to be done about it now except to be careful what information he gave away. One never could tell when information casually given would come back to haunt you.

"Who was it?" he asked, innocently.

The couple shrugged. They called the authorities and let them deal with it. Like any folks who made a simple living without the complications of politics, they didn't want to get involved with anything that might compromise their way of life.

"What is the best way to get to Cambodia from here?" "X" asked.

"So you are a Frenchman?" the fisherman asked back.

"Yes," "X" lied. "Why?"

"Lots of Frenchmen pass by here. There is a good road through here that leads to Battambang. Plus, many Frenchmen try to smuggle out precious stones through here. Some get caught. Others don't. We don't get involved." The fisherman was nearly chanting this, like a mantra. He's stated it a thousand times before.

After he gave the directions, "X" thanked him and began the long journey to the Cambodian countryside.

During the journey, Sedret Agent "X" changed his disguise to that of a rice farmer from the Battambang area. Using his specially designed putty, and his incredible memory, he made himself into a peasant with the features of that specific place. He stopped in a village and obtained the proper clothing that would allow him to blend in seamlessly. It was drab, loose and nondescript. He wrapped his backpack with old burlap cloth. Only the nobility or the military were expected to dress with any kind of flare. The peasants of the area would only dress up during festivals and holidays. It had been over a decade since his last visit there, but he knew from experience that changes in lifestyle and demographic were exceedingly rare in this part of the world.

The French guards at the border let him through without too much trouble. When asked any questions, "X" babbled in the Khmer language, gesturing wildly and speaking about grains, seeds and bad weather. Most Frenchmen never bothered to learn the language of their colonies. These guards were no different and soon grew exasperated at what they considered silly native antics.

Once through the border, "X" looked closely at the villages he passed by. He saw that nothing had changed. He had heard back in the States that some of the urban Khmer elite were making nationalistic overtures to the French. They condemned French policies and corruption, especially in these rural areas he was traveling through now. "X" knew that the French hadn't made any plans to improve literacy amongst the commoners here. Efforts along those lines had given them too much trouble with nationalism in Vietnam and they didn't want the same hassle in Cambodia.

The same couldn't be said for the French restoration of ancient Khmer ruins. The French began large restoration projects on Angkor Wat and other historical sites like it. They were hoping to use these projects as a revenue source for both tourism and artifact sales to museums. "X" now realized that the very artifact he chased to start this venture was probably one of them. He only had to find out what the Japanese were using it for, and where Prasat Neak Pean was.

Finally arriving at Battambang, "X" took this opportunity to get some rest. He rented out a room from a cloth merchant, paying the man extra to keep silent. It would raise suspicion for a rice farmer to be able to pay for a room. He used French currency so the merchant would have an easier time bribing export officials.

The next morning, "X" examined some maps of the area in the merchant's office. He flipped through the pages, some just mere scribbles on torn sheets, but was frustrated by what he couldn't find.

"Where is Prasat Neak Pean?" he finally asked the merchant.

"Lost," the merchant said. "Until a couple of years ago that is. None of those maps are updated. The French discovered the place and they don't even let us know where it is. It belongs to us, but like everything else, they take and take."

"Do you know any Cambodians who know where it is?" "X" asked.

"Yes," the merchant answered. "There are some local guides around."

"Could you introduce me?" "X" asked.

The merchant nodded and stepped out. Not a minute later, he walked back in with a boy of about ten years of age.

"What's this?" "X" asked, surprised.

"Best guide in the world," the merchant said, smiling.

It was a good thing "X" had his new guide. The boy's name was Kimsoth Im. He was familiar with the jungle because he was an orphan. His parents died during a demonstration in Phnom Penh protesting colonial policies toward lack of schooling. When the protest got out of hand, rioting ensued and both of his parents were struck with stray bullets. Kimsoth fled to the jungle to escape both the rioting and any authorities that would have put him in an orphanage. He survived on both wit and luck, traveling all the way to Battambang. Half-starved, he ended up on the merchant's stoop. The merchant took pity on him and gave him a job.

Without Kimsoth, "X" would have lost his way long ago. The jungle undergrowth was a tangle of vines and brush that was unforgiving to the uninitiated. Kimsoth navigated this maze of foliage with the instinct and wisdom of a natural predator.

"This doesn't seem like a normal path," "X" commented.

"It's not," Kimsoth replied. "You don't want to be seen. Correct?"

"Yes," "X" answered. "How did you know?"

"Why would a Cambodian want to go to a place where Japanese are, unless he went there secretly?"

"You assumed I knew there was Japanese there, instead of French."

"Yes," the boy said. "You must have a reason. Although you look it, you do not act like Cambodian."

"You're a smart kid."

The boy spoke very softly, as if he didn't want to disturb the jungle. He was very good at what he did. "X" would have to make him a more permanent offer of employment once this was done. He was always on the lookout for good people to add to his network.

"Have you ever seen the crane flower?" he asked the boy.

"We have passed several already," Kimsoth said, matter-of-factly.

"Show me," "X" said.

Kimsoth searched around in the underbrush for a few minutes. When he finished, he showed "X" an oddly shaped mushroom that grew nearly flat to the ground under thick foliage.

"That looks nothing like a crane or a flower," "X" commented.

"It's what we tell foreigners so they think it's too rare to find," Kimsoth explained. "If you look close, you can see it's shaped just like a crane's foot, and not the crane itself."

"Amazing," "X" said. He was pleased that some things in life still managed to fascinate him.

After a few hours of rigorous travel, they came to an opening in the jungle canopy. Staying hidden in the brush, "X" let his eyes and mind revel in the beautiful sight of the ruins of Prasat Neak Pean.

CHAPTER SIX

Sedret Agent "X" was looking at a large square pool with four smaller square pools arranged on each axis of the larger one. In the center of the large central pool was a circular island made of stone. The stone was carved in the relief of two snake-like creatures with intertwined tails that surrounded the island, which also gave this place its name; Intertwined Naga. He spotted ornamental spouts in the pavilions at each axis of the pool, indicating that water once flowed from the central pool into the four peripheral ones.

He took his time examining the intricate line work in the stone. It had definite influences of Hinduism yet was quite distinct in its Southeast Asian iconography. From his earlier travels "X" had learned that some of the myths of the Khmer people say that they were descended from the union of a reptilian race and an Indian Brahmana. The significant numerology and dualism of the statues before him bore such evidence in the beliefs. He was awed that this grand piece of art was created over seven hundred years ago.

Contrasting the beauty of the scene was the presence of Japanese soldiers. Worse, beyond the ruins was the sound of construction.

"Kimsoth," "X" whispered. "Where are those sounds coming from?"

"Just beyond those trees there," he answered, pointing to the tree line beyond the pools.

"Good," "X" said. "I want you to go back home now. I can handle it from here."

"No," Kimsoth said. "I want to help."

"Look, you're a good kid, and probably a lot tougher than most folks, but I'm not putting you in danger."

"I've been in danger my whole life."

That was probably true, but that didn't matter to "X". "I need you to make sure that merchant friend of ours stays out of trouble. I'm going to need you both in the future. I insist you go back to him now." "X"'s tone brooked no argument. The boy nodded and disappeared back into the jungle so completely it was like he was never there. I must learn how to do that, "X" thought.

"X"focused on the guards next. They were lax, not expecting trouble from a normally docile populace. Loading a sleeping gas pellet into his specially designed gun, he moved with silent precision into range to fire without being seen. Soon the unsuspecting guards were unconscious on the jungle floor.

"X"figured the best way to find out what was going on was to infiltrate the site as one of these guards. He set about hiding the sleeping bodies and dressing in one of their uniforms. He put his own pack inside the soldier's to hide his own equipment. He used his special putty and a mirror to make himself over in the image of one of the soldiers.

Fortunately, he only had to wait about an hour for the shift change. Two new soldiers came marching down a path that skirted the edge of the pool. They greeted him in the traditional military Japanese manner and he replied back similarly.

"Where is Takeo?" one of the soldiers asked.

"He took off early," "X" lied. "He said his stomach was bothering him."

The soldier scoffed. "These new recruits have no honor."

"True," "X" said. "But then, there is nothing out here to guard against."

"Right," the soldier said, looking askance at "X". "X" hoped his voice wasn't to different from what this soldier remembered. "Well, report back. And make sure the new one does so as well."

"Yes, sir."

"X"marched quickly down the path toward the construction site. When he got there he saw about fifty Japanese men wandering around a newly built foundation. Some were working on various tasks of general maintenance but most were sitting around either playing cards, dice or other activities. There was dormant machinery, trucks and cranes, parked off to the side.

"X"casually walked up to one of the civilian workers. "Still waiting around?"

"Yes," he said. "Not for long though. I heard the blueprint will arrive tonight."

"Blueprint?" "X" asked. "For what?"

The worker looked at him strangely. "Where have you been?"

"Oh," "X" tried to look sheepish. "Too much jungle work, you know."

"Yes, I guess," the worker sympathized. "Well, it's for the head, of course."

"Right," "X" could see it now. The foundation was built in a way that would allow a narrowing in the center, sort of a neck for a giant head. This reminded "X" of the statue bust stolen from the museum back in New York. The one he held in his hands on The Sacred Heron. They were basing this new construction on that bust. He could only assume they were to construct the same exact passages on the inside as well.

"X"thanked the worker and went toward the foundation. At the back side of the construction he saw five men going down some steps into the ground. They were carrying bulging cloth bags and wearing gas masks. "X" waited until they were out of sight and then walked discreetly up to the steps. On the ground, he noticed spilled Kapok seeds. He took his own gas mask out of his pack and walked warily down into the darkened hole.

Inside, he found himself in a stone hallway that curved as if it was built in a circular fashion. He walked slowly down the hallway, keeping in the shadows and moving silently. After walking about fifty feet he heard muffled sounds ahead. People were moving objects around and trying to speak through the obstacle of a gas mask. "X" couldn't make out what they were saying.

The scent of jasmine intruded on his thoughts. Why was he smelling that now?

And then, he just didn't care anymore. He just wanted to sit down. Relax. Why was he going to all this trouble? It made no sense.

No!

He shook his head to clear it.

Fight it!

His mask! It must not have sealed properly. The putty for his disguise must have distorted his features enough to compromise the seal and now he was breathing in some kind of gas.

But it was so easy to just breathe, in and out, in and out. Let it wash over him.

NO! He dug his hands up under the mask and tore at the putty of his disguise, ripping away the sticky substance from all around his forehead, temples, cheeks and chin. He worked frantically to replace the mask and properly fit the seal again.

Why bother? Just relax. Everything will be fine.

Sedret Agent "X" sat against the wall in bliss. Finally, he could forget the worlds' problems. America would get on just fine without him. Betty...Betty...

CHAPTER SEVEN

A splash of water woke him up with a jolt. He was tied to a chair in an enclosed chamber. It was small, only about seven feet on a side. Through the blur of his vision, he saw a soldier holding a now empty bucket. The man had a rifle strapped across his shoulder and an officer's katana in a scabbard at his belt.

The soldier dropped the bucket and walked in front of him. He slapped his face hard. Sedret Agent "X" felt the sting of that slap and it snapped him out of the fog his mind had been in. It was a sting to his pride that he had been captured thus.

When the soldier noticed "X"'s reaction, he knocked on the solid oak door. The door opened with a whoosh and in stepped a man wearing a gas mask and holding his pack that had all his supplies in it. The new person held the rank of general in the Japanese army. The other officer quickly closed the door again, which popped as if with a seal of some kind. The general removed his mask.

"Greetings, spy," he said in Japanese. "My name is General Oyakata. I would like to know yours, though I doubt you'll give it to me so willingly."

"X"stayed silent, seemingly inattentive.

"You've penetrated our new edifice. You've seen what we are trying to accomplish here. You do realize you will have to die. It's only a matter of time, and a matter of how painlessly this occurs."

With a wild yell the general suddenly drew forth in one smooth motion his own katana and swung it directly at "X"'s neck. He stopped it just short of cutting the skin. "X" didn't flinch for two reasons. He didn't want to give him the satisfaction and flinching the wrong way may actually cause the man to maim or kill him by accident.

"As you see," said the general. "I can and will kill you at my whim." He sheathed the sword as quickly as he drew it. "Now, you must be an American. You Americans are becoming pests with your backwards government and ignoble mercantile practices. Unfortunately, you've become too big to just brush aside like the insects whose country we occupy at present. No. Once we secure the east, I'm quite sure we'll have a fight on our hands with your precious United States."

The general nodded to the officer. The officer struck "X" hard across the right cheek. The pain was immense but "X" welcomed it. It allowed him to focus. A tooth came loose, so he worked it with his tongue to try and dislodge it.

"Tell us," the general said. "What is your mission here?"

"X"was silent. General Oyakata nodded again. Crack! The punch rocked him back in the chair. Perfect. The tooth came out.

Just then, a quick knock and the door to the room was opened and closed quickly. In stepped another officer who removed his mask and then handed Oyakata a box. As they spoke formal greetings, "X" recognized the officer's voice from Singapore. He was the military man speaking to the diplomat behind closed doors at the embassy.

Oyakata pulled the bust of Jayavarman VII out of the box. "Yes. We now have the final piece to complete our weapon." He showed the bust to "X", taunting him. "This ugly little man was quite ingenious. He designed a distribution system for the sleeping crane gas that you were so unfortunate to breathe in. He put these statues of himself in all the local temples. Each of these statues had a storage vat in the bottom and a comple "X"lever system in the back. When worked correctly, the gas would vent out through the nostril and ear canals. The statues were positioned next to vents throughout the structure and the gas would permeate the whole temple complex. It seems this ancient ruler of Angkor Wat liked his populace to be docile, especially when praying. I thought this was a good idea. Except I'm going to take it further. I'm going to build this comple "X"big enough to put all of Cambodia asleep. I've even modified the vent system to ensure the heavy gas goes high enough in the air to come down and cover thousands of square miles. We'll conquer Southeast Asia without wasting a single soldier's life. Then we'll move on to the next phase. With enough resources, we could secretly set up one of these statues even in your vaunted America."

"You'll never pull it off," "X" finally spoke. Throughout the beating, he was secretly working the ropes behind his back, stretching them out slowly in order to la "X"their hold on his wrists. He managed to work one hand free by the time he asked his question.

"So you do speak," Oyakata said. "And very fluent Japanese as well." "How would you get such resources?" "X" played ignorant.

The general laughed. "You Americans are soft. I capture your rich capitalists. Their sons. Their daughters. They give me whatever I need."

"All of them?" "X" asked.

"No," the general admitted. "There was one who did not comply. He was different. It was difficult to pin down any relations to him and threats to his life seemed to have no effect. He was killed for his false ideals."

That was what "X" was waiting for. Now he knew who killed one of his benefactors. Though he never knew the man's identity, and that man never knew him, he still felt a certain sense of loss. They were both like minded in their pursuit of justice and in the protection of the American dream through secret channels. It was as ephemeral a connection as one was likely to have, but a connection none-the-less. "X" was saddened that such a man who was willing to use his wealth for such a great cause was no longer in this world.

"Sometimes," "X" said. "One is all it takes."

"X"leapt into action. His hands suddenly came loose of their bonds and he struck both the general and his officer hard in the throat with a double ridge hand strike. At the same time he spit his tooth right into the eye of the military man from Singapore. The two officers fell to the ground choking as the third grabbed his eye in pain and surprise. "X" took that opportunity to grab the gas mask from his belt and throw it on as he opened the door to the sealed room. Holding the mask firm against his face, he made a mad dash down the stone hallway.

Back in the room, with the door seal broken, the invisible gas already began to have an effect on the three Japanese officers. Only General Oyakata managed to get his gas mask on soon enough to avoid succumbing to the jasmine-scented fumes. The other two officers couldn't be bothered to chase one renegade spy. What could just one man do, anyway?

"X" stumbled through the convoluted halls, trying to reason his way out of a literal maze. After a few dead ends, he was finally able to discern a slight slope in the grade of the hard packed dirt floor. He followed the incline upwards. He bypassed areas where he saw apparatus for crushing Kapok seeds and boiling the sleeping crane roots. He noted the positioning in comparison to what he thought was the outside wall. Finally, he came to a portion that looked familiar. This was where he had passed out earlier from the sleeping crane gas, where his determination to protect America had failed him. He would not let that happen again.

He found the stairs he had originally descended and sprinted up them two at a time. Once outside, he looked around and spotted one of the construction vehicles idling, a large, front end loader. Keeping his mask on, to hide his identity as much as keeping himself safe from any aftereffects, he sprinted to the truck. The idle workers watched him with curious glances, unsure of his intentions.

As he began revving up the engine, all chaos broke loose.

General Oyakata emerged from the foundation screaming orders through his own mask to stop the intruder. "X" stomped on the gas and drove the loader at full speed, ramming the foundation so hard that the wall partially collapsed. "X" rammed the wall where he believed the apparatus for making the sleeping crane gas was. Bullets began to hum past "X" as glass shattered all around him in the cabin of the loader. "X" ignored the gunfire as he slammed the bucket of the loader down again and again off the weakened roof of the structure. The roof was only partially finished due to the fact that they were waiting for instructions to build the rest of it, so the loader had no problem demolishing what was there. The structure began to collapse into the maze of tunnels that were beneath it. "X" heard the satisfying crunch of machinery below.

"X" was suddenly slammed into from the side and knocked right out of the loader cabin. He rolled to the side and brought up a stray brick just in time to block the downward stroke of a razor sharp katana. Oyakata stood over him, rage visible through the hazy steam of his gas mask. He meant to cut down "X" here and now.

"X" kicked out at the knee of the general, knocking him back a couple meters. This bought him just enough time to get to his feet.

Oyakata attacked relentlessly, swinging his sword in perfect, practiced strokes. The man was a very good swordsman, and "X" had to put every ounce of concentration into avoiding either a loss of limb or instant death. Fortunately for "X", Oyakata adhered strictly to the sword form, everything precise and measured. This allowed "X" to begin to predict what was coming and avoid it. Finally, when he knew a side stroke was swishing toward him from the right, "X" leapt high in the air and drove his heel right under Oyakata's chin, knocking the gas mask clean off. He let the weight of his body drive him forward, knocking the general to the ground and landing on top of his chest. He quickly drove his palm right between the general's eyes, slamming his head into the ground and knocking him out cold.

Another soldier, muffled shout filtering through his gas mask, was charging straight at "X". "X" didn't have time to move. Just as the man was about to reach him, a sling stone caromed off the side of his head, and the soldier crumpled to the ground. "X" looked around to see who threw the stone, but only saw rustled bushes at the edge of the jungle.

In no immediate danger, "X" took in his surroundings. The clearing was littered with loitering men. Most were lying down to go to sleep. Under the influence of the newly released sleeping crane gas, they did whatever made them most comfortable.

He took another trip into the now ruined underground foundation. There, he retrieved the object that started his quest– the head of Jayavarman VII.

"You have caused me a lot of trouble, my friend." "X" also retrieved his pack of equipment, casually tossed in the corner of the cell, and made his way back outside.

Heading back into the jungle, "X" was brought up short by the sudden appearance of Kimsoth.

"Kid," "X" said. "You're about the only person in the world who can surprise me like that."

Kimsoth just shrugged. He was holding a stick that was slotted at the end. In the slot there was some sort of incense burning. It was then that "X" realized Kimsoth had no gas mask on.

"How are you able to avoid the effects of the sleeping crane gas?" he asked.

"Simple," Kimsoth answered. "Other fragrance from this root keep back fragrance from that root."

"X" smiled. Sometimes the most obvious solutions are the last ones to be grasped. He removed the gas mask and breathed in the perfume like fragrance of the incense.

"How would you like to be part of a secret network of agents?" "X" asked.

"Sure," Kimsoth replied.

"X"took out the bust of Jayavarman VII. "I need you to hide this in the jungle where nobody will ever find it again. Can you do that?"

"Sure," Kimsoth said again.

"X"smiled wider. During the journey through the jungle he went over all the signals he would need to use with Kimsoth if ever he would have to call on his services again. Kimsoth absorbed everything he said with simple nods and quiet demonstrations of his skills. He could get used to working with a contact who didn't talk so much.

EPILOGUE

Weeks later, Betty Dale was busy typing up another hot story, punching the keys with an unexpected ferocity from such dainty hands. She was so absorbed in her work that she failed to notice a man sitting patiently on the edge of her desk.

"Ease up, doll," said A.J. Martin, or as she also knew him, Sedret Agent "X". "You're going to poke a hole right through the desk."

"Oh!" Betty exclaimed. She hopped up and threw her arms around him.

"X"looked around, abashed, and said quietly, "Ease up on the display, Ms. Dale."

Betty backed off. "Sorry," she began and then thought better of it. She looked around the office and said in a more formal voice. "I just wanted to congratulate you on your story getting nominated for a Pulitzer."

"Why, thank you Ms. Dale," "X" said. "I couldn't have done without your help and keen investigative skills." "X" winked at her. "X" knew that it was all Betty's story that she wrote for him while he was out of the country. It bothered him that he would have to take credit for it and he swore to himself that he'd make it up to her somehow. Betty, for her part, never complained.

They walked outside the building together so they could talk more freely.

"So," Betty began. "Everything went well?"

"As much as it could have," "X" said. "I had French officials round up all the Japanese and deport them. All the locals now believe the area to be haunted with sleeping spirits, which is just as well. Hopefully, it will keep prying eyes away." "X" became more thoughtful then. "I worry about what's coming. The rest of the world is not so content to let our great nation continue on as it is. I fear things on the international front will get worse before they get better."

Betty sighed. She'd heard this speech before. One thing she knew it meant was that they couldn't be together like a normal couple. No matter how much she loved him, his duty to his country, and hers as well, would come first.

Wilfred O'Malley stared at the spot in the museum that represented his failure on the job. It was an empty pedestal that used to hold the bust of some ancient Eastern king. He often stopped here during his rounds, wondering why he still had a job. Whenever he asked his boss about it, he was told succinctly to mind his own business.

O'Malley shrugged and double checked the nose plugs he constantly wore on the job. He would never be caught off guard again. Wilfred O'Malley was ready for anything. Which is why he was so surprised when a high pitched whistle caused him so much pain in his ears that he blacked out...

Sedret Agent "X" checked in at the safety deposit bo "X"that he kept at the First National Bank. When he first returned from the Orient, he had left his full report about his findings, including his speculations on how and why one of his ten benefactors was killed. Now he received a note in return which read:

"Agent "X",

Excellent news. Justice has been served. We thank you.
We have made inquiries while you were away.

"Ease up, Doll. You're going to poke a hole right through the desk."

This has led to future support from another.

We are now ten again."

 "X"burned the letter as was customary. His mission done, it was time
to prepare for any other missions that may come his way.

Once he got back to his black sedan, he checked in with Harvey bates over the
radio receiver.

"Anything to report Harvey?" he asked.

"You bet, boss. Something going down at the museum again."

"I'm on my way," "X" signed off. He put on the disguise of ace reporter A. J.
Martin once again.

The End

RESEARCH IS FUN

Research is fun. I get a kick out of it, especially when it comes to history and foreign civilizations. My first step to researching Sedret Agent "X" was, of course, the Agent "X" Data File presented in volume one of this series. The first thing I read stuck in my mind, "as a young man he spent many years in the Far East and learned many Oriental languages." That's awesome. Then I read he served in WWI and traveled extensively from Russia to Mongolia to Mexico. He also flew in France. This guy gets around!

Moving on, I read all the excellent stories in volume one. I was introduced to Betty Dale, probably my favorite character, and all the other great characters that inhabit "X"'s universe. I noticed that in every story, each character had their place to move the story along and to either help or hinder "X" in various ways. Each story introduced new, fascinating characters that lived and breathed in "X"'s world. I thought, yes, I want to create characters like that. How do I make them different from what went on before?

In all these stories, "X" had all this knowledge of the world. Yet, he was always stateside. That's it! "X" needs to get out of the country! He needs to show off all that international clout, all the proficiency he gained with foreign cultures over the years. This also gave me a chance to create some truly unique characters, even with "X" himself. I wanted to really test his ability to become somebody else. Although he always keeps the mission in mind, "X" has to really dig deep into a different thought process, with different mannerisms and life goals in order to pull off what he needed to. I thought that would be a good challenge for him.

I live in a city with a large Cambodian population. Because I've come across various aspects of their culture and heritage, I've always wanted to write a story that included some of that in it. I think part of my fascination with their history stems from the fact that there isn't much widely known information about it. Japan has its Samurai and Ninja and Pearl Harbor and imported cars. China has its dynasties and kung-fu and paper and fireworks and Mao. Even Vietnam dominated the news for half of the 20th century.

What does Cambodia have? During the Middle Ages, when Knights were running around France arguing with each other and Islam, the Khmer people carved out a sizable Kingdom in most of Southeast Asia now called, in modern terms, the Kingdom of Angkor. They built great Buddhist temples like Angkor Wat, and thousands of other religious sites, some based in Hinduism and some an amalgamation of the two religions, litter the countryside. I can only imagine that discovering some of these places would be like roaming a dungeon in a game of Dungeons and Dragons. Research is fun.

Of course, I had to get "X" there. I couldn't just start out with " "X"arrives in Cambodia." As we all know, the point of getting somewhere is to take the journey.

So then I had to do more research. What kind of planes did they fly in the Camel Squadron? How would a boat go to Cambodia? What stage was the Panama Canal at in the 1930s? What was possible back then? What could I make up? All these questions had to be answered before I could start my story.

Okay, that last sentence is a lie. When Ron Fortier asked me if I was interested in writing a story, I said "sure, I'm interested." The next day I started writing it with what I knew about Cambodia already on my mind. It was only after that initial rush of three or four pages that I actually confirmed with Ron via e-mail that, yes, I was going to write a Sedret Agent "X" story. Why? Because writing is fun.

So I wrote some more and then stopped because I can only sit at a keyboard for so long before it starts to feel like work. Then I did some of that research I talked about earlier. Then that started to feel like work, so I did some more writing. Then I read some comics, because that's always fun, until you do too much of that as well. This process went on for a couple of months. (During this time I had to keep in mind that I'm not writing a research paper. I'm writing a fun pulp story about a heroic secret agent. I've got to make up cool stuff! So there's a lot of stuff in there that is definitely not historically accurate. This was to make it fun for you, the reader, as well. I hope I succeeded.)

Eventually I finished, all funned out. I sent it on to Ron with the usual doubts running through my head.

Ron said he loved it.

That was fun.

Thanks, Ron.

H. JARROD COURTEMANCHE—I was a late bloomer. Math was my best subject in high school. I ended up becoming a water treatment specialist and chemical lab tech and eventual quality manager. This is all stuff with a math background. I always had the imagination. I just never applied myself to figuring out how the words went together until much later in life. I started college in my late twenties. I was taken aside by an extraordinary literary professor who proceeded to teach me more about grammar and sentence structure in one hour than I had managed to figure out in the previous twenty years. Since then, the writing bug has grabbed me at various times and I've put out a few independent things. (Independent = still have full time job and still scraping by. Some of you know what I mean.) I graduated magna cum laude from UMASS/Lowell in my late thirties with a Liberal Arts degree focusing on history and English.

One of the many things in this life I'm most proud of is Mindbeside Studios. This is a local collaborative film-making group consisting of myself, my brother, and a few other film making friends. We have made four films, one feature and three short films. I've written all four and directed the latest two. Check us out at: mindbeside.com.

I've also self-published a book of short stories in the fantasy genre (though there is one early twentieth century detective tale in there for you pulp-minded fans.) It is called "The Other Side of Imagination" and is available at: i-proclaimbookstore. com.

I also write comic book reviews every week for a local comic book store. Check them out at: larryscomcs.net, and click on the word, comics, and then the reviews box.

I also do podcasts, make music, dungeon master, write other stuff, and generally dip my hand in whatever creative well comes along. I'm a veteran of the U.S. Airforce and the proud father of two boys.

Chapter One

Secret Agent "X" ran for his life.

He lost his footing for a moment, his shoes skidding in the loose roof gravel. Pausing to regain his balance saved his life as a bullet sizzled by his right ear, the lancing hiss loud over the thunderous roar of the rain. A second shot spanged off the air vent to his left, sending the metal cylinder spinning crazily.

Up ahead, partially obscured by the steel rods of rain clamoring down all around him on this chilly Los Angeles night, the Agent spied his quarry as the man ducked under a wash line festooned with sodden garments their owner had neglected to retrieve before the storm broke.

Agent "X" doubled his efforts to close the gap. No more pistol shots reached him and the faint voices of his pursuers dwindled for the moment.

There was the man he sought! "X" watched him leap frantically across the narrow gap to the adjoining tenement, saw the man sprawl on the slick tarpaper.

The voices behind the Agent rose once more. The Agent's legs pumped with effort as he ran, in seconds he was sailing across the same gap his quarry had spanned. He landed deftly, hardly seeming to break stride.

The man Secret Agent "X" chased was almost at the far edge of the roof. "X" saw the man turn and disappear over the side.

The fire escape!

The Agent knew he'd lose his prey if the man managed to reach the street.

He could not let that happen.

"X" reached the roof edge too quickly and had to skid to a stop, his shins striking the tin roof edge. He almost pitched headlong off the tenement but the metal looped handrail of the fire escape broke his fall. The metal was cold and slick against his palms as the Agent hurled himself over the edge and began what could best be described as a controlled fall down the fire escape.

He spied the dark, hatless head of the man he chased through the iron lattice landing below. The man was two levels beneath the Agent.

"X" continued his plunge.

The man slipped on the wet iron and fell awkwardly against the base of the ladder.

"X" used the misstep to close the gap.

The voices the Agent had heard behind him now sounded loudly only this time they echoed from above. These shouts were soon replaced by hot lead stabbing down at him. Ricochets off the iron set off explosions of sparks like miniature fireworks all around him.

The Agent made the landing vibrate when his shoes struck. His prey was at the top of the next ladder down, placing his feet with as much care as his desperation would allow.

Secret Agent "X" lunged for the man.

They grappled, barely maintaining their balance on the swaying ladder, which was twelve feet off the ground.

"X" threw a glance downward and saw the dumpster below. The lid was up and cardboard glistened wetly, rainwater cascading down the soaked matter.

A volley of shots from above rained down on them. One bullet clipped the pinky finger of the man "X" fought and he instinctively jerked his hand off the rung. The man's balance was lost and he could not prevent himself from tumbling into the dumpster.

The Agent had no choice but to follow. "X" picked a spot that would most likely break his fall and let go of the ladder. Agent "X" heard a groan as he landed and, for a moment, thought he might have landed on his combatant. But his shoes merely shredded the weak cardboard and pungent offal.

"X" regained his feet and pawed through the garbage to find his man. Shoving aside a rusty coalscuttle, he revealed the man's face.

The man's features were twisted in a rictus of pain and blood flecked his lips.

The Agent soon determined the cause.

Apparently the man had fallen on the broken frame of a bicycle and the sharp shaft of tempered steel had javelined through the man's chest. He was mere seconds from oblivion.

Shouts reached "X" where he stood. The sound of ringing footsteps pounded down from above like a horde of avenging angels descending to claim the soul of the dying man. The Agent leaned over the man and had to shout to be heard over the rain and clamor from above.

"Who do you work for?" "X" demanded. "Before it's too late, tell me!"

The man's eyes rolled up to lock on the Agent's glaring orbs. "X" shook the man, but all the dying man could do was open his large mouth like a gaping fish.

"Who sent you?" The Agent tried again to draw information from the man.

The Agent's pursuers were directly above them now. One tried a shot through the grilled landing but it went wide. A blurted curse put an end to any further volleys as it was impossible to draw a bead through the narrow gaps between the iron flooring. It was no matter to them. They had their prey trapped in the dumpster a rod below them. The chase was over.

But Secret Agent "X" thought otherwise. He shook the dying man again and this time his lips seemed to be attempting to form words.

"X" bent low over the man.

With his last dying gasp, the man whispered weakly, "Six… million… eyes…"

And with that he was dead.

The Agent did not hesitate to ponder this cryptic epitaph. Instead he released the man and vaulted out of the dumpster just as the first of his pursuers dropped down into the metal canister.

"Halt!" one voice called out to the fleeing Agent. "We've got you! There's nowhere to run!"

Bullets followed on the heels of the words and hot lead dug grooves in the concrete alley floor. But "X" kept running.

He reached the mouth of the alley and swung around the corner, startling a pair of night strollers and drawing the attention of a saloon crowd as he barreled past the large, glass window. He headed east away from the parked autos of his pursuers in front of the building where the chase had begun.

"X" shot a look over one shoulder and saw the first of his hunters becoming entangled with the bar crowd that had emerged to gawk at the Agent's fleeing form.

Then Secret Agent "X" was swallowed by the night.

Chapter Two

A man stared after X's fleeing form, his eyes blazing with the thrill of the hunt. Gun dangling at his side, he had casually stepped aside as his men fought to extricate themselves from the milling throng. The man was of medium height with a head too large for his slim, athletic frame. His rust-red curls were matted to his head, and if not for the lowered brow and hard set to his lips, the man might have been called boyish in appearance. The men with him knew him as Joseph Kovacs, but that was only one of his many identities.

His men dodged questions from the bar patrons as they tried to draw away form the crowd. Sirens could be heard drawing closer. The police would soon arrive and there would be questions that could not be avoided. The redheaded man could not afford the delay. There was too much as stake to lose time trifling with the police.

"That's it, Mr. Kovacs," his subordinate announced. "We've lost him sure now."

Joe Kovacs pulled his eyes away where Agent "X" had last been visible and locked onto the face of the speaker. "I would have to agree, Edwards. Let's get back to the car."

The two men withdrew from the crowd. Their auto was parked in front of the neighboring building. Rain drummed on the roof of the yellow Packard while Kovacs yanked open the door and dropped down onto the passenger seat. He left the door open and Dave Edwards stood in the opening, the wet door against one hip.

"Calling base," Kovacs barked into the handset.

"This is base."

"We've lost the target for the moment."

"How long to reacquire?"

The redhead looked up out the streaked windshield and considered before replying.

"Hours? Days? It is difficult to say."

"We need the target in custody," the disembodied voice spoke chidingly.

"I am well aware of that. I'll find him."

Police sirens wailed up the next block. Kovacs caught the eye of his subordinate who had also heard the sirens. He addressed the man, "Anyone hurt?"

"Just Moore," Edwards replied, shaking his head slowly. "He tumbled down those damn stairs, busted his leg up pretty good. He's lucky he didn't break his fool head."

"Post a couple of men in the crowd," Kovacs said, decisively. "Stay with them and make sure the cops stay clear of that dumpster. Tell the boys to keep their ears open, too. Get the rest ready to move. I'm clearing out."

Edwards nodded and was gone from the open door intent on what he had to do.

Over the sound of the rain, Kovacs spoke into the radio mike. "I'll bring him in or knock him down, sir. That is a promise."

There was a pause. "Understood. You have done well up until now."

"Thank you, sir."

"You are welcome, Secret Agent Y. K-9 signing off."

Chapter Three

Secret Agent "X" glided into the hotel room. This base was one of many scattered all over the globe for his use in his never-ending crusade against crime. With Jim Hobard behind bars, and the intricate network "X" had created to wage war on crime now scattered and in hiding, the Secret Agent had selected an address he had not frequented in several years and had spent forty-five minutes making his circuitous way there.

Still he was cautious as he entered. He did not turn on the light, relying on his photographic memory to project a map for the scrutiny of his mind's eye. Door closed behind, he stood in the stygian darkness and listened. Time was not yet his enemy. He had more than an hour before he was expected at the restaurant.

"X" stepped gingerly into the room. All was as he remembered it save for the musty odor of disuse. Upon easing the door open, he used the lobby lights to show him that the dust on the floor inside the door was uniform, unmarred by the footprints of an intruder and he knew that the windows remained locked from the inside. A burglar would have had to shatter the glass to gain entry and the Agent would hear the rain still thundering down outside. There was no hint of danger. He stepped deeper into the room and his heel clicked loudly on the hardwood floor.

Instantly, the Agent dove to one side. There was a rush of air six inches from his left ear as something whooshed by to smack loudly into the standing lamp in the hall. The lamp fell with a crash.

"X" used the momentum of his dive to propel him into a tuck and roll that would have put an Olympic gymnast to shame. He curled deftly to his feet and turned to face his opponent.

The distance gave the Secret Agent the chance to end the altercation quickly. His opponent was of a large, hulking stature, which "X" assumed would make the man cumbersome. So "X" whipped out his gas gun and pointed it at his foe.

But the man surprised the Agent by lunging forward and launching a powerful kick which numbed X's hand and sent the gas gun spinning off into the darkness. The man followed the kick with a right cross that "X" blocked.

The Agent sent a stinging jab into the man's face, then danced away. The man grunted then charged bull-like into the combination of punches "X" had set up prior to inducing the man's rush.

However these blows could not halt the large bulk of the man and he collided with X. They tumbled together over the chesterfield and shattered the coffee table. The Agent delivered an elbow to the man's stomach and another piston-like jab to the jaw before extricating himself.

The man, slightly stunned by this assault, was slow rising to his feet.

Secret Agent "X" took advantage of this and kicked the man soundly in the ribs. He then seized the man's collar and pummeled his head with terrific punches. The man reared back against the sofa, dazed.

The Agent searched his groggy foe and found an empty shoulder rig. This told "X" that the man had attempted to brain him with a pistol butt and wanted the Agent alive. His attacker was harmless for the moment so "X" removed a small flashlight from a vest pocket and shone it discreetly around the room. He did not turn the lights on in case his foe had men outside watching the room.

"X" spotted the fallen revolver and pocketed it. Then he briefly examined the clear patches of floor made by the man's footprints when he had taken long steps into the room so that the dust on the floor in the entrance would remain undisturbed. Had the Agent's heel not clacked loudly against one of the dust free footprints, his attacker might have succeeded in getting the better of the Agent. "X" retrieved the gas gun and returned to the moaning man who was starting to come around.

"How did you find me?" "X" demanded with considerable ire.

"Six million eyes," the man smiled through split lips. Then he brought his teeth together sharply.

The Agent made as if to prevent this action for he recognized its purpose. There was nothing he could do.

When the man's teeth clicked together a capped back molar shattered and deadly poison oozed into his system. He convulsed and was dead in two seconds, the twisted smile now a frozen rictus taunting X.

The Agent leaned back on his haunches while the implications of what he'd just witnessed became evident to him. He dug a hand into the inside pocket of the man's coat and withdrew a wallet stuffed with currency. A further inspection turned up a handkerchief, a half-eaten roll of breath mints and a hotel key. "X" laid these items aside save for the wallet.

Quick scrutiny of the wallet confirmed X's suspicion.

The corpse's name was David Edwards and he worked for the same Intelligence Division as Secret Agent X.

At least "X" used to work for the Intelligence Division.

The Agent cupped his chin in thought as he stared at the man's frozen features. None of what had transpired in the nondescript flat made any sense.

Then again, "X" mused, very little of the last ten days did.

He picked up the key and idly examined it before thrusting it into a pocket.

A sudden thought had occurred to him. If the Intelligence Division had tracked him to the flat, they might have put men on Betty Dale who "X" was on his way to meet.

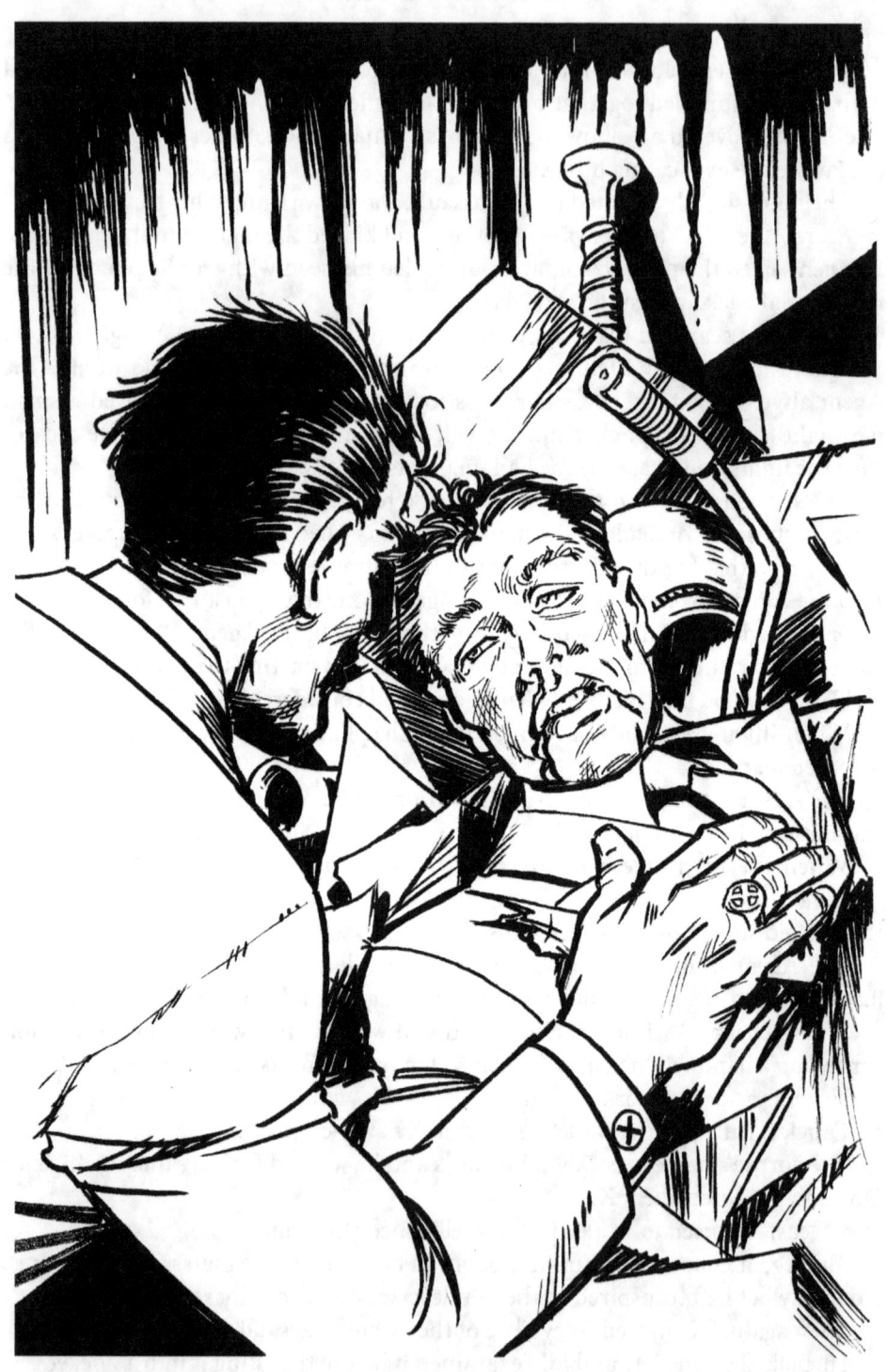

"Six million eyes..."

"She could be in danger at this very moment," the Agent said aloud as if addressing the corpse before him.

He sprang into action.

"X" washed hurriedly and donned fresh clothes, transferring the hotel key into one pocket. Then he applied a facial disguise unknown to all those who knew him. With one last check of his appearance, he sidled to the window and scanned the street below. There was no sign of operatives. The way was clear. "X" slicked back his hair with one palm and left the flat to merge with the shadows.

Chapter Four

R afael's had catered exclusively to the swank crowd during the Roaring Twenties but the last few years had worn heavy on the eatery and in a time of economic upheaval a paying customer was not someone you turned away because you didn't like the cut of his suit. On this night, a good-sized crowd worked through Rafael's menu with all the subdued gaiety a Wednesday could manufacture. Although the establishment could not afford to be as fussy as in pervious years, folks anxious for a meal before hitting the town could still reserve tables at the restaurant. This tended to be in the rear of the joint so potential customers with more dreams than coins in their pockets would not be dissuaded from entering by the sight of tables reserved for the well-heeled.

In one of these red leather booths in a dark corner of the room, a single man sat, eyes furtively scanning the crowd. The restaurant was fairly busy and a din of chatter predominated.

A waitress dressed in the feminine version of the formal tuxedo approached the dim table.

"Good evening, sir," she said with obsequious courtesy. "May I get you something from the bar?"

The patron eyed the waitress a moment before ordering a Manhattan on the rocks. She returned a minute later and paused in the act of setting the drink down.

The man, in her absence, had unscrewed the top of the saltshaker, poured a quantity of the crystals onto the table and smoothed them out with his palm.

Into the salt he had traced a clearly defined letter X.

"It is you!" the waitress hissed, setting the drink down. "As you never drink, I was confused at first."

"Hello, Betty," "X" said, warmly. He picked up his menu and made a show of looking over the dishes. "Formal wear suits you."

Betty Dale mimed pointing out the day's specials as she replied, "I kind of like this cloak and dagger stuff. Maybe as a sideline."

Dale was the crime reporter for the Herald and the love of the Agent's life.

"X" grinned knowingly. "Did you get the information I requested?"

He asked this while tipping the menu inquiringly, then looked up at Betty as though waiting to hear a description of an indicated dish.

Dale's eyes flashed. "I sure did." "X" raised his eyebrows expectantly and she went on. "You were right about the name: Seymour Godfrey. But it can't be the same man."

"Why not?"

"Because this Seymour Godfrey drives a forklift at the Sweet Chariot Sugar plant."

"Sugar?"

Dale nodded. "And that's all there is about him. A couple of arrests for minor infractions when he was a boy, but that's all. Did you find out anything from him?"

"The man is dead," "X" said. "He fell off a fire escape. Do you have an address?"

"Wait. If we're going to continue this waitress/diner game, you should order. I've been here too long while you fooled with the menu."

Secret Agent "X" named a dish at random and Betty sashayed to the kitchen to put in the order, then went off to see to another table. The Agent had ordered a cold chicken sandwich as this would be easy to prepare. Betty returned a minute later with a dinner plate in hand.

"The address is 1985 Braun Avenue, apartment 12."

When she was finished, a worried look marred her breathtaking features. "Are you all right?" she asked. "You have a haunted look about you. All this sneaking around…"

"Right now, it is necessary. I — "

The squeal of rubber tires on wet pavement sounded outside. Doors slammed.

"Betty, did you tell anyone about coming here? We're you followed?"

"No, I've been hiding since this all started. I — "

"Did you explain yourself to the waitress you replaced or did she take the money with no fuss."

"Not a word. The poor woman was happy to miss the shift. She called home right away to her babysitter — "

Women exclaimed in surprise and male voices demanded explanation for having their meals interrupted. The tromp of heavy boots sounded on the wood floor, coming closer.

"Betty," the Agent blurted. "Run!"

"X" slid out of the booth. He strode boldly towards the tall, burly detective pushing his way through the patrons. The Agent stood before the cop with hands on hips, blocking the way.

"I say," He began pompously. "What is the meaning of this interruption? I demand an answer!"

"Don't worry, we'll get to you!" The big detective thrust the Agent to one side and stalked towards Betty Dale whose escape had been inadvertently blocked by the kitchen staff and waitresses jammed in the doorway to watch the proceedings.

"You!" the cop barked. "In the crowd there, trying to skate out the back." Dale turned slowly as the detective went on. "Yeah, you, Blondie. You're coming with us."

The Agent, trapped in his role, could only watch helplessly as Dale was hauled roughly out of the throng. She fought every inch of the way, but to her credit did not so much as cast a glance at "X" who seethed silently at her mistreatment. His only consolation was that she was being taken in by the police and not the Intelligence Division or the secret group he sought.

However to be certain she was not too roughly handled, Secret Agent "X" followed the exiting policemen to the street. He watched as Betty was placed in a squad car. At the first sign that a canvassing of the restaurant patrons was about to begin, "X" faded away from the place. Streetcars and taxis passed as he walked away but he paid them no mind. As vital as it was that he reach his destination, he could not afford to be observed. On foot, clear of the busy thoroughfares, he had a chance of reaching Godfrey's apartment. He felt invisible eyes watching him from every window and recalled Seymour Godfrey's dying words in the dumpster.

The Agent's feeling of being watched only increased when he reached Braun Avenue. The building containing Godfrey's residence was ablaze. "X" stood on the opposite corner as firemen dashed here and there with thick, oily hoses in their fists. The sky was cast crimson by the soaring flames. Flames that consumed any answers Seymour Godfrey might have yielded.

"X" fingered the hotel key in his pocket.

He wasn't sunk yet.

Chapter Five

He gained entrance by the rear stairs of the Grandview Hotel. Ensuring he was unobserved, he made his way up to the twentieth floor. At this late hour there was no maid service and the guests were asleep thus a deserted hallway was all the Agent saw before him as he cracked open the door leading from the stairs.

"X" moved like a wraith up the empty corridor, his shoes whisper-quiet on the carpet. He reached suite 2369 near the rear of the building, close to the fire door. The key "X" had obtained from David Edwards slid smoothly into the lock. A quick turn and Agent "X" was inside.

He eased the door shut and flicked on the light.

The room was not lavish but bore some hallmarks of sophistication. So much so that the Agent had to wonder how Edwards could afford such expensive quarters on a government salary.

"X" prowled around the room. The bed was made, there was nothing under it. The closet yielded a couple of changes of clothing with empty pockets. That morning's newspaper was on the nightstand undisturbed. The astray had been recently emptied, as had the wastebaskets.

The Agent was undaunted in his search for something had caught his eye upon entering the unit: a cluster of items on the small writing desk which Edwards had moved from its original spot at the foot of the bed if the indentations in the carpet were any clue. The desk had been moved out of sight from the window into a shadowed corner. "X" had not investigated the items straight off as he did not want to overlook any small detail or clue he might find scattered about the room.

His search of the room completed, he turned his attention to the desk. Without handling anything, he studied the set-up. There was a telephone, a loudspeaker as well as what appeared to be a small televisor reception set. The Agent was familiar with the concepts behind television but every model he'd seen had been massive floor units not the compact screen before him now. The cabinet stood about a foot in height with a viewing screen some six inches in width. He scrutinized the spider's web of wires and cables tangling out of the back of the telephone, speaker and televisor. Each had two cables, one running to the large covered item, and a second that disappeared down behind the table where it met the wall.

"X" crouched down to peer beneath the desk.

A rectangular black box squatted under the table and the cables from the devices all ran into it. The Agent's keen eyes traced along each of the wire connections in an attempt to fathom their meaning. He could not even hazard a guess as to their function and returned to his study of the devices on the desk.

As astounding as the televisor screen was, it was the central, covered object around which these other devices had been arranged that captured the Agent's attention. He switched on the standing lamp next to the desk, then with one long-fingered, tapering hand removed the canvas cover from the central device. This action had a reverse effect on the Agent. For what was revealed by his action served only to cloud the mystery, not clarify it.

At first glance the strange device resembled a bicycle wheel atop a triangular base. The Agent placed his two thumbs together and stretched his fingers out to measure the circumference of the circular screen. The tips of his little fingers touched the smooth shell on either side of the device. The circular screen was divided into five sections, the spokes sparking X's comparison to a bike wheel. The bottom two sections bore the symbols of a microphone and a phonograph record. Above these were symbols of a radio and the televisor screen. Above these a drawing of a telephone had been etched. The panels bearing these icons were of a glassine material which shone dully in the dim light.

"X" studied the device with rapt wonder. He had never seen anything like it. He leaned over the machine, fingered the connecting wires. He touched the divided screen and discovered that the spokes separating the icon panels turned with his touch. He ran his hands along the base of smooth metal. His fingers encountered a switch. As his keen intellect could tell him nothing about the device, he turned the unit on.

A low hum shattered the silence of the room. The symbol wedges began to glow a faint yellow. "X" switched on the radio speaker and the televisor screen. He stared mutely at the devices as they came to life.

Suddenly the top wedge with its telephone icon glowed a deep vermilion. A heartbeat later the telephone beside the wheel jangled.

The Agent had not heard the voice of Edwards prior to the man's death only his grunts as they tussled. However it was possible there might be a way around this. The storm outside would make for poor telephone reception.

Secret Agent "X" lifted the receiver to his ear.

"Hello?" he whispered, hoping the lateness of the hour would justify his low tone and the crackling on the line would do the rest to hide his identity.

"State your code, Unit 6282."

"X" had no clue what to say. As he sat there, the spokes on the wheel before him turned and the wedge with the radio glowed along with the telephone section.

The insistent hum grew louder in the room. It seemed to be sounding at his feet now.

The phone line went dead.

The Agent looked down and saw a small light on the black box flare red. The light began blinking rapidly, its rhythm increasing as the pitch of the hum rose.

"X" pushed back in his chair, every nerve fiber alert. He stood up quickly. Thinking fast, he yanked out the connecting wires on all of the components. The hum rose to an ear-splitting whine. He seized up one of the pillows off the bed and shook the cover free. The Agent began ramming each of the components into the pillowcase.

The whine became a banshee's wail.

"X" lunged for the door, unlocked it and dove out into the corridor. His destination was the door to the service stairs.

But the precious, fleeting seconds were against him.

He barely managed four steps when the suite erupted in a fireball behind him. The blast seized him from behind and tossed him tumbling towards the service stairs Somehow he managed to retain his grip on the bulging pillowcase. He landed heavily on one shoulder, dazed, his ears ringing. But over the claxon ring, he heard muffled voices and the pistol-crack of deadbolts being drawn back.

In seconds the hallway would be filled with startled, sleepy-eyed guests.

He lurched to his feet, took a feeble step and collided with the stair door. "X" fumbled the door open and started down the steps. Despite his groggy state, he had to hurry. The blast had shaken the entire building. Every floor would be crammed with rattled guests out of bed to investigate.

The Agent reached the service exit undetected.

But he was not out of danger just yet. The explosion above had also blown out the windows of Edwards's room. This would awaken the whole neighborhood. Police, firefighters and ambulances were already on their way, "X" knew from the distant wail of sirens his still-ringing ears detected.

Wanted by the authorities, "X" needed to get to safety.

But how? Where?

Then he had it.

The Agent threw himself down and rolled around in the puddles of filth in the alley. Sadly, since the crash, hobos and destitute wanderers were all too common a sight on city streets all over the country. With his now disheveled appearance, the soiled pillowcase would be mistaken for the meager possessions of a poor tramp on the bum. Any late night pedestrians he encountered as he made his escape would avert their eyes.

He barely managed four steps when the suite erupted in a fireball behind him.

An impeccable mimic, the Agent transformed himself instantly into a shuffling hobo and moved away from the hotel clutching the pillowcase in both hands.

Chapter Six

The second business office "X" came to had a burnt out streetlight in front of it. "X" took a nonchalant look around, then leapt down the stairs to the sunken door. Setting the pillowcase down, he used a skeleton key on the lock. The tumblers sprang and the Agent hurled himself inside.

Moving in complete darkness, he strode past the receptionist's desk to the inner office. This door was unlocked and "X" glided stealthily into the room. He set the pillowcase down on the desk and fell into the vacant chair. The office appeared to be that of a small printer. Reams of paper were stacked on a tall filing cabinet, boxes of envelopes on the floor. The office, closed for the night, had an atmosphere tinged with the odor of printer's ink.

"X" took these details in as a matter of course. Upon catching his breath, he turned on the desk lamp and set to work. First he unpacked the components from the pillowcase. Relying on memory, he hooked them together, using the telephone on the desk. In seconds he had recreated the set up from Edwards's suite. As the speaker and televisor plugged into the larger unit, he assumed enough current would be drawn from the wall plug to power all three.

Once certain he had attached the telephone properly to the device, he sat before the ensembles a moment, his mind churning.

He switched on all of the components.

The spoke wheel cast the Agent's features in ghostly pallor while the radio speaker crackled to life.

Almost immediately the telephone jangled loudly in the confined space.

A wry grin tugged at X's lips. He was certain he had not packed any explosives along with the components when he fled Edwards's room. The telephone rang insistently. The devices on the desk were key to X's objectives. He had to find a way past the screening process that had resulted in an explosion the last time he'd attempted to bypass them. As there was no danger of this happening again, "X" steeled himself to attempt another bluff. With some measure of confidence he answered the phone.

However, instead of a rough, demanding voice, the handset was silent. Not even the voice of the operator sounded in his ear.

The Agent contemplated this queer development as his eyes ran over the strange collection of machines on the desk before his probing orbs came to rest on the standing, spoke wheel.

"What is this thing?" he whispered.

"Specify?"

Secret Agent "X" had forgotten the receiver pressed to his ear. He pulled it away from the side of his head and stared at it, then returned it to his ear.

"What?" he gasped.

"Televisor screen," came the immediate, cold reply.

The Agent had switched the screen on previously and the unit glowed dully. He waited but nothing happened.

"Televisor screen," the voice repeated.

Baffled, the Agent's eyes flicked over the items on the desk but no solution made itself apparent.

Then he had an idea.

Reaching up with his left hand, he turned the spokes on the wheel until one of them bisected the segment with the televisor icon.

The televisor unit flickered.

X's mouth dropped open as the image of a book page appeared on the tiny televisor screen. It was a page from the Oxford English dictionary containing words that began with the letter 'W'.

A voiced droned on the speaker:

"WHAT/ interrog.adjective. 1.asking for a choice from an indefinite number or for a statement of amount, number or kind. 2. colloq. = WHICH interrog.adj. how great or remarkable…"

It was all the Agent could do to hold onto the phone as he listened mutely to the voice reading out the long definition from the dictionary page projected on the televisor screen.

"Satisfactory?" the voice interrupted his train of thought.

"Yes," "X" croaked.

"Next query."

The analytical portion of Agent X's brain began processing this new, astounding information about the device. "X" surmised that the voice on the telephone had awaited a request for information and his harsh whisper of that singly-worded question, 'what', was an indication to the voice that he wished to see and hear the definition of that word.

"X" read the numbers of the top of the spoke wheel, then, choosing his next words carefully, he put the phone to his ear and spoke into it.

"What is unit 6282?"

"Unit 6282 does not exist."

Grasping the problem, namely that the voice believed Unit 6282 to have been destroyed in the explosion, "X" restated the question. "What was Unit 6282?"

"Unit 6282 was an electronic telescope."

"What is an electronic telescope?"

"An electronic telescope permits Information Architects to access the core from great distances via a connection to a telephone line."

Secret Agent "X" could not believe what he was hearing.

"Where is the core?"

"That information is restricted. Do you have the proper authorization code?"

"X" did not. However he was starting to get the hang of the device.

"Who constructed the core?" he asked.

"Information Architects."

"Is David Edwards an Information Architect?"

"David Edwards does not exist."

"X" realized whoever was running the core believed Edwards was killed in the blast they had initiated. "Was David Edwards an Information Architect?"

"Affirmative."

The desk lamp was beginning to dim. The electronic telescope was drawing an immense amount of power. It could overload the fuse at any second. "X" clutched the telephone receiver tightly in his fist.

"Who was Seymour Godfrey?"

"Seymour Godfrey was an Information Architect."

"Who conceived the core?" "X" demanded rapidly.

"Leopold Otlet."

"Who is Leopold Otlet?"

"Televisor screen."

"X" urged the device on as the light continued to dim in the small office. The televisor screen was also fading, the image of the dictionary page all but unreadable. And a peculiar hum seemed to be coming from the wall outlet as well. An overload was building. The Agent was sure of it.

Suddenly a photograph of a man replaced the image of the book page. The face on the screen possessed bulging, dark eyes staring out from under protruding brows, a slightly bulbous nose and high, gaunt cheekbones. A full snow-white beard rimmed his square jaw. A thin drift of equally white hair rimmed the sides of high, broad head.

The voice on the speaker, now clouded by interference, began to recite, *"Leopold Otlet was born in Brussels — "*

The bulb in the desk lamp exploded in a small spray of scalding hot glass fragments that scattered across the desk, several burned the Agent's left hand.

Secret Agent "X" switched off all of the devices, then leaned back in the chair to consider what he knew. The fact that Edwards was one of these Information Architects was of great importance to X. Since the whole thing had begun, it seemed that his adversaries were always one step ahead of him. He recalled the last words spoken by Seymour Godfrey before he succumbed to his injuries.

"Could it be?" "X" mused aloud. Then he snatched up the telephone and hissed into the mouthpiece. "Operator! Operator!"

"How may I help you?"

"Long distance," "X" blurted, putting a throb of urgency in his voice. "Connect me to the White House. I've solved the mystery of the electronic telescope. I tell you, I've solved the whole thing!"

"O-One moment, please."

"Hurry! I'll stay on the line."

The Agent laid the receiver on the desk blotter, then quickly re-packed the components into the pillowcase.

With the bundle under his arm, he eased out the rear exit of the Printers, pressed between the narrow passageway between the building and the one adjacent, and dashed across the street to the alley facing the small shop.

The alley was rank from a cluster of overflowing garbage cans. "X" crouched behind the foul-smelling cylinders and watched to see if his theory was correct. If he had guessed right, then any second now, police and federal agents would swarm around the Printing concern.

No sooner had the Agent formed this thought when the throbbing approach of automobile engines sounded in the still night. It appeared "X" had guessed correctly as to how the electronic telescope was being used.

However, what happened next, Secret Agent "X" could not have predicted.

The Agent could only stare in mute astonishment as an empty streetcar sluiced around the corner and slewed to a stop close to the Printing shop. The motorman hopped down and dashed towards the office. He was followed by a milkman who was out of his panel truck before it had skidded to a halt. A police car screeched to a stop. "X" noted that the siren was not blaring, nor were the roof lights spinning. The officer joined the growing crowd now fleshed out by a street sweeper, a taxi driver and an ambulance attendant. A half-dozen pedestrians sprinted to the group which now boasted a mailman and the driver of a newspaper delivery truck.

For one of the few times in his long fight against evil, Secret Agent "X" felt overwhelmed by the forces allied against him. His original theory was that Information Architects were monitoring telephone lines and that upon his broadcasting false news devastating to the enemy's cause, the call would be traced to the printing shop and other Information Architects, posing as police and agents of the government would swoop in to silence him.

But the men and women from all walks of life now gathered outside the office told him that Leopold Otlet had Information Architects scattered everywhere, watching, recording, transmitting a vast, surging stream of endless information to this core "X" had uncovered.

This explained how the various identities "X" had built up over the years had become compromised, forcing him to abandon them. This information, in the hands of Otlet, had next lead to the eventual arrest of his most trusted aids, which had spurred "X" to investigate the matter days ago.

If the people who had taken X's bait were a mere fraction of Otlet's Information Architects then the potential power they placed in his hands was staggering. With such a network, there was no limit to what Otlet could do.

Once again "X" heard Godfrey's dying word: "Six million eyes."

Yes, they were all over the city, the country! How many millions throughout the world? Or maybe Otlet hadn't gotten that far yet. Perhaps he could still be stopped.

Stars exploded in the Agent's head and he reeled from a blow, dropping the pillowcase. X tried to turn but a series of precise blows to pressure points on the back of his neck numbed key nerve centers and "X" fell in a heap, unconscious.

Joe Kovacs, Secret Agent Y, gazed down at the sprawled form, then motioned his men to load the body into the Packard. The men did so.

Kovacs sat in the front passenger seat and thumbed on the two-way radio.

"We've got him," he announced, simply.

There was no reply, nor did he expect one. He returned the handset to the dash cradle and motioned to the driver. The engine roared to life and the Packard sped away in a cloud of exhaust fumes.

Chapter Seven

The next sensation Secret Agent "X" was aware of was the feel of a cold breeze on his brow. The steady, throbbing hum of rubber on asphalt reached his jangling ears. Beefy shoulders pressed against him on either side. A cold, steel gun muzzle jabbed crudely into his ribs.

"X" opened his eyes and saw the grinning face of Kovacs leering back at him.

"Welcome back," Kovacs said. "We have a great deal to discuss and not a lot of time."

This brought throaty grunts from the men on either side of "X" in the back seat of the sedan. Kovacs leaned across the back of the front passenger seat, one arm draped over the top, the hand clutching a .45 carelessly pointed at the Agent.

"You have my attention," "X" said.

Kovacs winked good-naturedly at Agent "X" before saying, "You and I are going to get along." His expression turned serious. "Look, we're on the clock here so I won't mess around. The good ol' US of A has soured on you, friend. You know it and I know it. K-9 sicced me on you to bring you in and that's exactly what I'm going to do."

"Then why all the chatter? You've got a job to do, do it!"

Kovacs smiled again. "Yeah, I like you."

"X" looked away disgustedly. "Turn that record over, will you?"

The men beside the Agent laughed at that but an icy glare from Kovacs stifled their merriment. His fiery gaze returned to "X" and he cautioned, "Don't turn a deaf ear to the one guy who can help you."

"Help me go over on a treason rap," "X" added.

"There's a road that doesn't lead to Leavenworth."

X's eyes narrowed, "I'm listening."

Kovacs gazed turned inward as he contemplated his next move.

"I'm still listening," Agent "X" urged.

The eyes of Kovacs again fixed on the face of the Agent, the orbs probing the inscrutable features. "Way I see it, you've got two choices. Take the fall – and believe me, brother, I've seen the evidence against you and you haven't got a leg to stand on. You're through. Which leads us to the second option. Join up with the outfit that's going to run the whole show by '40."

"Leopold Otlet?"

Kovacs threw his head back and barked out a harsh laugh. "Act your age, will ya? Otlet's an old fool with blinders on."

"He created the electronic telescope, put together an army to use it the likes of which no one's ever seen. Pretty farsighted if you ask me."

"I didn't ask." Kovacs gestured idly with the gun. "The old guy's had his moments. I'll give him that. But, farsighted? You're stumbling around in the dark there, friend. He built the electronic telescope to drive the Nazis out of Belgium, then went soft in the head, fancies himself a shepherd for the world. Him and all his dizzy followers want to create paradise on earth with him pulling the strings."

"X" shifted in his seat, easing his shoulders slightly forward from the pressure of the men flanking him. "You still haven't said anything I want to hear, Secret Agent Y."

Kovacs's eyes widened at hearing his assigned ID mentioned. "You do your homework. I was moved up after you turned traitor and got cut out of the loop. And yet you still dug up enough to know who it was after you. That's good to hear. I can use a fellow like you. That's right, I'm taking over the show. Otlet wants to play God, well, I'm better suited for the role. When I do run things, there's going to be two groups on this ball of dirt; those with me and those against me. Brother, you do not want to be my enemy."

A cruel smile twisted the lips of Agent X. "From where I sit, I see a two-bit double-crosser with delusions of grandeur. If I work for anyone, it'll be for Otlet. At least he built something on his own and he's not some Johnny-come-lately."

The barrel of the .45 in Kovacs's fist flicked out and struck "X" on the side of the head. The Agent tried to roll with the blow but was hampered by the confines of the rear seat. Stars flashed before his eyes and he almost blacked out.

Kovacs had his hand raised as if to deliver another blow but restrained himself. "I'm a reasonable man and I guess there's some truth in what you say. Which is why you're still breathing. I belted you for mouthing off, not for what you said. And I suppose I'm indebted to you for getting that backstabbing Edwards out of the way. I don't encourage ambition in my people."

"X" glanced out the window and saw that the sedan had eased to the right to take the approaching exit. It was the exit for an airfield.

"We're almost where we need to be," Kovacs announced. "I need an answer from you. You want to join the winning team or do I have Lenny hear stop the car so the boys can march you out into the fields and put you out of your misery?"

"Boss," one of the men in the back spoke up when he spied the distant lights of the airfield. "When we get to 'Zona, can I — "

"Silence!" Kovacs roared.

Agent "X" showed no reaction to the man's blunder, but instead stared at the muzzle of Kovacs's .45 which was now rising to point squarely at him.

"Well, ex-Secret Agent X," Kovacs said. "Are you in or are you out?"

The Agent slowly raised his gaze from the gun to fix on the stony features of Secret Agent Y.

"Out!" "X" hissed.

Then he sprang into action. He threw up his right hand and chopped at Kovacs's arm. Caught by surprise, Y's gun hand was batted aside as he fired. The bullet plowed into the shoulder of the man to the right of Agent "X" as the startled driver sent the car skidding all over the road.

"X" launched himself at the man on his left, increasing the distance between him and the man Kovacs had shot. For the man still had a gun pressed against the Agent's ribs. The man fired as his body spasmed from the impact of searing lead. "X" felt as if he'd been hit in the side with a sledgehammer. Luckily the gun was only a .38 and the bulletproof clothing Agent "X" wore under his street clothes stopped the bullet from tearing into him. The impact of the slug against the near impenetrable barrier stove in one of the Agent's ribs however.

But that was the least of his worries.

Once the element of surprise was lost, "X" was a dead man.

Grappling with the man on his left, the Agent clutched at the door handle, turned it and flung the door wide. The road streaked by beneath them, the car roaring along at fifty miles an hour.

Seizing the man by the lapels of his overcoat, "X" shoved him out the door as Kovacs fired. The bullet missed "X" by inches and the door window exploded in a spray of lethal fragments. Clutching tightly to the man, "X" tumbled out along with the gunsel.

Using the frantic man as a crude human sled, "X" let the man's body take the initial impact as they hit the concrete. The man screamed but then went silent as the air was pounded from his lungs. They hit and slid in a jumble. "X" released the man and, using his gymnastic skills rolled over and over, letting his armored under garments absorb his momentum. His street clothes were quickly reduced to tatters.

Finally he rolled to a stop half on the gravel bank. Aside from the broken rib and too many cuts and scrapes to count, he seemed all right. His legs took his weight and he glided into the tall grass by the side of the road while the automobile slewed to a stop with a shriek of brakes two hundred yards up ahead.

Favoring his injured side, the Agent made his way as quickly as he could towards the airfield. Harsh shouts sounded on his right and the chase was on.

The Agent could make out the lights of the airfield dead ahead and he detected the drone of an aircraft engine. The distant crack of a stray pistol shot behind sheared off the tops of the high grass on his left.

He increased his speed.

The tall grass gave way to an open field. "X" launched himself across the expanse, his eyes riveted to the approaching airfield lights. His keen sense of smell revealed to him what his eyes could not see in the stygian darkness, but this did not prevent him from running into a warm, yielding form. "X" fell back on his rear and looked up at the hairy obstruction.

He'd run smack into a cow.

As the first light of dawn was breaking on the horizon, he dimly made out the dark moving forms of other cows bent low over the already short grass. He got up and began winding his way through the small herd.

Anther gunshot erupted, closer this time. And "X" heard the voice of Kovacs urging his men on. "This way, you fools!"

Over the sound of the slow moving cows, "X" heard pounding footsteps drawing closer. They were almost upon the Agent.

He needed to buy time.

Years ago, Secret Agent "X" had mastered the ability to hypnotize animals with his gaze and bend their primitive minds to his will. Stepping up to the nearest cow, "X" stared deeply into the bovine eyes of the animal. He tuned out the sounds of pursuit while he hypnotized the cow. It instantly followed his commands and trotted off towards Kovacs and the others.

"X" repeated the procedure and in moments he had several cows heading right for his pursuers. Moments later, he heard sharp exclamations of surprise and barked curses amidst the agitated lowing of the animals and he knew he'd managed to buy the precious seconds he needed.

He turned and sprinted towards the airfield.

Chapter Eight

The livestock allowed the Agent to reach the airfield unhindered. Still clutching his injured side, he clambered up the chain link fence and tumbled down to the wet grass on the other side.

The airfield was small with only two aircraft on the single runway. Dim lighting cast a wealth of shadows by which "X" was able to approach undetected.

There was a choice to be made, he knew, as he drew nearer to the idle aircraft. One of the airplanes was in Kovacs's service, of that "X" could be certain of. It was imperative to the plan forming in his razor sharp intellect that he determine which one. This was made somewhat easier by the clear company markings on one of the craft. "X" guessed that Secret Agent Y would want to play things close to the vest by commandeering a private aircraft and not a charter. And the unmarked aircraft had one engine buzzing, the cowling up as if being prepped for take off.

Thus the Agent scudded towards the unmarked craft as quickly and as quietly as he could. The running engine could be cut at any moment so "X" could not rely on the sound to cover his approach.

The plane rested near to the squat hangar/workshop and the interior lights etched the craft in harsh relief. Agent "X" slowed his approach, seeking the cover of a cluster of rusted oil drums some thirty feet from the airplane. He spotted a man standing near one of the plane's propellers watching the approach from the road. At least one other man was inside the shed if the clanging noises coming from within were any indication.

"X" went into action.

Quitting his hiding place, he sidled along the shadow's edge until he could put his back to one wall of the hangar. Several tense seconds ticked by while the Agent made certain the man near the airplane had his full attention on the road. Satisfied, "X" poked his head around the corner and saw no one inside the hangar.

"X" glided in.

The hangar was a mass of jumbled tools on rickety worktables and strewn all over the floor. He had to step gingerly around the mess lest he give himself away. Yet, at the same time, every moment was precious. Kovacs and his men would arrive soon shouting alarm. And when that happened the plan the Agent had concocted would be worthless.

The Agent's all-seeing gaze darted around the messy hangar and he spotted the man making the racket. He was a hawkish man, raw-boned and spindly inside the gray coverall that draped on him like a shroud. The man clutched a wrench in one bony fist and was wrestling with a bolt on an engine carburetor. The man had his back to "X" and was absorbed in his work. Outside the engine noise cut off.

The Agent crept up and was inches from the man when his luck went sour.

Disgusted with the unyielding bolt, the man threw the wrench away. He stood and turned, seeking a new tool and came face to face with Secret Agent X.

The man's eyes widened and he made as if to cry out, but the Agent moved with blinding speed. His arms lashed out, the hands stiff as two-by-fours, delivering stunning chops on either side of the man's neck. The stinging blows were not meant to bring about unconsciousness. "X" caught the man under the arms as he slumped and laid the man down on the dirty floor.

"Jerry!" a voice called from outside. "Will you cut out that racket? I can't hear if the boss is coming. Jerry!"

The Agent leaned over the prostrate form and hissed, "You are partially paralyzed. If you want me to undo what I've done, you'll agree to placate your cohort. Blink twice if you agree."

The man's terrified eyes fluttered up and down twice in rapid succession.

"X" placed his thumbs on either side of the man's scrawny neck. "Give a warning of any kind and I'll paralyze you for life."

The Agent pressed his thumbs into the nerve clusters in the man's neck. The scrawny limbs jerked and twitched.

"I-It's all right, Dave!" the man bellowed quickly, panic giving volume to his voice. "Keep watching for the Boss!"

"X" leaned over the man. "Tell him you'll be out in a minute."

"I-I'm coming out!" the man bleated. "Give me a sec!"

"Good!" Dave sounded relieved. "Maybe we can finally blow this joint!"

The Agent had all he needed from Jerry. With one precise blow he rendered the man unconscious. Next he stripped off the man's coverall and donned the greasy uniform. Before zipping it up, he withdrew his make-up kit. Working furiously "X" transformed himself into the prostrate Jerry. The Agent only had seconds to complete the impersonation and his skills were tested to the limit. He ran dye through his hair to turn it the same shade of blonde as his subject's. The work completed, he lunged for the engine carburetor and his deft fingers played swiftly over the device. Then, with it still in hand, he left the hangar.

"Good as new!" he called out in Jerry's voice as he approached the plane.

"About time!" Dave said, ducking under a wing. "Now where's the Boss?"

"X" hastily fastened the carburetor into place and slammed the engine cowling. Dusting his hands together, he began patting at the coverall for a pack of cigarettes.

He grinned at Dave. "I caught a snootful of machine oil back there. Gonna grab a smoke and some of this night air."

"Yeah, yeah." Dave waved Jerry away with one hand. "Just make it snappy."

"Will do."

"X" moved off. As soon as he was swallowed by darkness, he rose up on the balls of his feet and catfooted it towards the other plane.

He managed ten paces when suddenly he was caught in a flashlight beam. Guns cracked, spewing lead. "X" heard a bullet whiz by his ear, then a second slug dug a furrow along the outside of his left shoulder.

"I got 'em, Boss!" a voice shouted.

"Make sure, you idiot!"

The second voice belonged to Kovacs.

The Agent scurried out of the glare from the flashlight beam and ran flat out for the other plane.

Pistols barked behind him but the shots went wide. "X" crouched around the wing of the charter aircraft just as the door on that side opened in response to the gunfire.

The pilot was a large man, his shoulders filling the doorway. "X" dashed headlong up the stairs and into the craft, preventing the pilot from stepping down.

"Get this thing in the air!" "X" bellowed.

Before entering the aircraft, the Agent turned to look after his pursuers, ducking his head to see beneath the wing.

The action saved his life.

A bullet sizzled past where his head had been a moment before. But it did not pass cleanly. The bullet clipped Agent "X" in the temple stabbing tiny agonizing daggers through him.

He pitched into the arms of the pilot.

"Get… us…. up," "X" managed. "Fate… of… the… world… Arizona!"

Then all "X" knew was darkness.

Chapter Nine

"**G**ood morning, pal," the pilot said to "X" as he guided the plane into the morning sun.

Secret Agent "X" groaned and opened his eyes. The sun was blinding and he squinted against the glare. He reached up a hand and felt a bandage around his head. The motion pulled at a similar constraint around his torso and his nicked shoulder.

"Thanks for the repairs."

"Don't mention it," the big pilot extended a hand. "Name's Hale. Al Hale."

"Pleasure," "X" replied taking the hand but offering no name in reply. The pilot had wavy blond hair and movie idol good looks that ended in a square jaw like a paving stone.

Hale nodded curtly. "It's like that, huh?"

"No offense meant. But you know how it is."

"That I do."

"What's our heading?"

"We'll be hitting Arizona in an hour. Just like you wanted."

"You did the right thing."

"Now don't go getting all mushy. I'm due in 'Zona in a couple of weeks. Coming in a little early won't make much of a difference. One of the perks of running your own airline is getting to pick your destinations. Frankly I welcome a little something out of the ordinary. Been a bit too much of that lately. Ordinariness, I mean."

"You're doing your country a great service," "X" said, his eyes growing heavy.

"Glad to be of service to someone these days." Hale looked over at his passenger. "Care to tell me what it's all about?"

But his passenger was dead to the world, breathing evenly.

"Man alive!" Hale said under his breath. "And I thought only the job was a bore."

An hour later Hale gently shook Agent "X" by the shoulder. "X" awoke with a start, jerking upright in his seat.

"Easy, fella," Hale soothed. "You're still plenty banged up."

"X" shrugged off the restraining hand and rose up out of his seat. "Thanks again for the patch job and for getting me here in one piece. I've got to get going. Time is critical."

Hale shook his head and stepped aside to let "X" by. The Agent raced along the length of the craft until he reached the exit. He got it open and paused on the threshold to throw a heartfelt salute of gratitude to Hale.

"Take it easy, brother," Hale said, holding up one meaty paw in farewell. "It's a rough world out there."

"You don't know the half of it," "X" replied. "Pray you never find out."

And with that Secret Agent "X" was gone.

Outside, X's eyes quickly adjusted to the blazing sunlight and the wave of stifling heat that washed over him was welcome to his stiff muscles. The airport was a large facility with crowds already forming up for the first flight out.

The Agent slid off the bandage from around his head, felt no dried blood crusted in his hair and silently thanked Hale again for cleaning the wound before dressing it. With his soiled coveralls, "X" looked like one of the ground crew and moved unnoticed towards the terminal.

Once inside, he spied a man in a phone booth in a quiet area of the terminal. He was about the Agent's weight and build. There was a suitcase propping open the booth door so the man could hear when his flight was called.

"X" approached slyly and deftly slid the bag out of the booth, replacing it with an ash stand. The man, engrossed in his conversation, noticed nothing.

In the Men's Room, "X" exchanged his soiled, torn clothing for a black suit and navy blue tie, then placed a $20 bill in the bag to cover the man's loss before closing it.

Make-up kit in hand, the Agent set about adopting a new identity. As every second was vital and his hair was already blonde from his brief stint as Jerry, "X" took on the visage of the pilot who had saved him. He finished the transformation, dropped the kit into a pocket then eased out into the crowd.

After leaving the bag at Lost and Found, "X" dashed outside. A small parking lot ran off to one side and he headed directly for it.

Striding quickly between the rows of parked cars, he sought and found one automobile with a window half-lowered against the heat. Reaching in, he unlocked the door and slid behind the wheel.

In his pocket were a variety of skeleton keys to open even the most stubborn lock. But there was also a form of universal key which could start almost any make of automobile manufactured in the US. He stabbed the key into the ignition and worked the pedals and was roaring out of the lot seconds later. Agent "X" had a lot to accomplish and was drastically short on time.

What had begun as a simple operation to expose Joe Kovacs as a double agent had escalated to earth-shattering proportions. K-9's idea of forging evidence to discredit "X" in order for Kovacs to recruit him and reveal himself had worked to perfection. But no one could have guessed at Kovacs's connection to Leopold Otlet's secret army. The Agent could have used K-9's resources against this new threat, but they'd played out the first part of the mission too well and now "X" was utterly cut off from federal help. And the intricate networked he'd put together to wage war on crime has been smashed.

He was going to have to run down Otlet on his own. This was not the first time he had stood alone against a master criminal, but he could not recall a time when the stakes had been this high.

Road signs indicated he was approaching Phoenix and that suited him just fine though he had to reluctantly cut his speed for fear of being pulled over. The city was shrouded in early morning quiet, the traffic sparse. A glance at his watch revealed it was just after 9 AM local time. Good, he mused, the State Planner's Office would be open.

"X" parked across the street and trotted across to the stately edifice. Inside fans moved the stale air as he took the stairs two at a time down to the Records Office. There he found an owlish matron who blinked at him from behind her horn-rimmed spectacles. Her nametag read Mabel.

"X" adopted a suave, debonair attitude to match his movie idol appearance and stood before the woman. "Good morning, my dear," he crooned. "I wonder if you might assist me."

Mabel shyly looked him up and down. "Why, certainly," she cooed.

"I'm having a devil of a time with the water out at my ranch house. It's down to a trickle. And I suspect it's been diverted. I certainly was not notified beforehand."

"That's terrible."

"Yes. Well, I would like to take it up with the agent who sold me the spread and want some hard facts to throw at the scoundrel. Might I see the Waterworks Records please?"

Mabel, apparently dazzled by the dashing air "X" feigned, nodded her head slowly as her mouth dropped open and motioned the Agent to follow her.

Twenty minutes later, "X" had the information he needed and was back on the road. His guess had been correct. Otlet's private army would need a large, isolated tract for a Headquarters. To operate one quietly meant setting up out in the desert. The desert meant water. Oh, Otlet could bring in generators to power the core he'd created but for an operation of such immense scope, wells couldn't possibly supply enough water for all the inhabitants. The Waterworks files had revealed a recent major diversion of underground water for 'Military Use'. X, as a top-clearance agent of the government, knew of no such large-scale installation currently in operation outside Phoenix.

"X" had found Otlet's lair.

He pulled the car off to the side of the road a mile from the supposed military base. It was a sprawling collection of sheds and hangars surrounded by a high fence. A side road branched off the main highway and was the only approach. The cloudless sky and high, arcing sun illuminated the surrounding terrain which was flat as far as the eye could see.

The question before "X" now was how to infiltrate the facility?

As if on cue, a ramshackle, weather-beaten mail truck trundled up the highway and was slowing to take the turn off.

"X" leapt out of his vehicle and flagged the truck down. It slid to a halt on the dirt bank. The driver raised his mailman's cap and smiled.

"Hey, friend," "X" began pleasantly. "My car overheated and I'm wondering if you could ferry me in to that base so I can put one of their telephones to use."

"Sure thing." The man's smile widened. "Hop in."

Agent "X" walked around to the passenger side of the vehicle. He slid the door open and got one foot on the step when rough hands grasped his shoulders and he was hauled inside. The divider had been slammed back. Men leaned into the cab from the rear of the truck. Gun muzzles bristled around X.

"That's him all right!" came the voice of Mabel from the rear of the truck. "That's the dirty, lying skunk what tried to sweet talk me!"

One of the hard-faced men leered evilly at the Agent and put his gun to X's temple. "One false move and we'll plug ya!"

Chapter Ten

The ride into the complex passed in silence. Agent "X" had to endure the snake-like grins of the armed men around him as they confiscated his gas gun and the myriad of other devices he normally concealed on his person. Mabel sat in the back, proud as a peacock of her efforts that morning. "X" used the ride to memorize the layout of the place. He spotted the cavernous hangar flanked by generators running along one entire wall. There were sleeping quarters off to one side and what looked like a Mess Hall behind those. Armed guards stood ready outside every building. But the defining features of the entire base were the dozens of immense radio towers stabbing upwards into the clear blue sky.

"Talking to Martians?" "X" chided in the hope of loosening a tongue or two.

A gun barrel tapped "X" on the temple. "You'll do your talking to the Chief. Until then, put a lid on it. Or else."

"X" ignored the threat and returned to his inspection of the facility.

The truck pulled up outside the cavernous hangar and the gun-wielding men shoved "X" roughly out of his seat. The gunsels clambered down and surrounded him. Then they marched into the hangar.

In direct contrast to the blazing sun outside, the hangar was dimly lit and possessed a funereal air. The light filtering down from the lamps dangling from the high ceiling revealed vast rows of catalog drawers on the left taller than a person and a procession of desks on the right. "X" was marched up the aisle between these. Men and women moved like a human hive between the desks and the catalog drawers, which "X" could see contained 3X5 index cards. There had to be untold millions of the cards packed into the drawers.

At the far end of the hangar was a cluster of offices. "X" was brought to a halt outside the closed door of one of these and one of the men rapped on it with a gun butt.

"Enter!" came the gravelly voice from the other side of the door.

Mabel opened the door and Secret Agent "X" was shoved roughly inside. The gunmen needed no further instruction from their leader. They closed the door and left "X" alone with Leopold Otlet.

The two men studied each other. "X" noted Otlet's intense, bulging eyes and the white, slightly scraggy beard were at odds with the conservatively cut, black suit the man wore. Otlet's office was a cluttered, musty, cobwebbed affair with dusty stacks of books, files and manuscripts piled high to the ceiling. Otlet made "X" think of a great spider lying in wait, hidden by shadows.

And yet, the man flashed a hideous smile as he came around his desk to address "X" with his sepulcher voice.

"I welcome you to the City of the Intellect," Otlet croaked.

"X" wanted to put Otlet off balance and keep him there so he adopted an indignant air. "Is this how you welcome people to your city of the future? At gunpoint!"

Otlet looked genuinely offended and stepped back, the smile drooping. "A temporary measure, I assure you. The day will come when such crude precautions will never be necessary again."

"So you say."

"It will come to pass. I will bring it about!" Otlet stormed.

"Will this world be free of kidnapping, espionage, and murder?"

"Yes! Yes!"

"X" laughed and shook his head. "Keep dreaming, friend. From what I've seen, you're just another tin pot dictator. Like that clown in Berlin."

Otlet's eyes flared. His hands bunched tightly into fists. "His end is at hand. My country will be free!"

"In the meantime, you'll set yourself up as a world dictator."

Otlet opened his mouth as if to reply, then sighed. "I see what you are trying to do and I will not be baited. I could have had you killed outright, but my vision does not allow for wasted resources. So I shall appeal to you to join the cause. Anything less than this would be criminal."

"And what precisely would I be joining?"

Otlet spread his arms expansively. "The world of tomorrow!"

The man came towards "X" and put a hand on his shoulder to lead the Agent out of the office. Three guards outside the door fell into step behind Otlet as he and "X" headed up the aisle.

"This documentary edifice contains more than 20 million index cards and documents," Otlet began. "My archive brims with books, photos, posters, newspaper clippings and countless other artifacts. Only they will be counted in time. Counted, annotated and filed for easy reference. Such was the vision shown to me.

"No document can be properly understood by itself. It's meaning only becomes clear through its relationship to other documents. And vice versa. From this simple truth I came to realize that all of human civilization could be considered in this way. In my City of the Intellect, everything in the universe, everything of man will be registered as it is produced. The result shall create a moving image of the world. By combining radio, television, x-rays, cinema and microscopic photography the networked documents of human struggle will be cataloged. And it will be free to all. Everyone, from his armchair, will be able to contemplate creation!"

"The electronic telescope," "X" offered.

"Yes! You begin to understand! In my future world, anyone can merely submit a question by telephone through my telescope and the answer will be found here, then by televisor, radio, phonograph or telephone the answer will be transmitted. Information at your fingertips."

"And for this you require the Information Architects."

"Precisely. Anything and everything related to the human experience must be recorded and filed. No detail is too small. Not action trivial. Like the single snowflake that touches off an avalanche, nothing is insignificant."

The Agent could not help but be impressed by Otlet's vision though the man was clearly mad. "In this way you will drive the Nazis out of Belgium?"

"Not only that!" Otlet replied hotly. "Off the planet as well!"

"How?"

Otlet smiled ominously. "Come! I will show you."

Leopold Otlet gestured "X" up a side corridor. They came to an elevator, which they took down three levels to a gloomy subterranean chamber. A series of iron doors led off from the elevator. Otlet produced a key and unlocked one of the doors. He flung it open.

"X" saw Betty Dale huddled on a crude bunk.

"Betty!" he roared and stepped into the room.

Recognition dawned in her blue eyes and she leapt off the bunk to throw her arms around X. "I knew you'd come! I just knew it!"

He released her and his eyes blazed at Otlet. "If you've harmed her..."

Otlet held up his hands placatingly. "You misunderstand. Her presence here is my proof to you that nothing is beyond the scope of my electronic telescopes."

"Explain yourself!" "X" demanded.

"Were you not surprised by the quick arrival of the authorities outside the restaurant in Los Angeles despite your precautions?"

"X" admitted that he was.

Otlet nodded. "Now allow me to explain how it was done. It began with the reported presence of Miss Dale in Los Angeles. Then the waitress Miss Dale replaced made a telephone call to her babysitter. The operator noted the information as Rafael's is a restaurant you and Miss Dale have dined in previously. This information, insignificant on its own was coupled with a second call placed by the babysitter to her young man to come pick her up. In the unbridled haste of young love, he was stopped by a traffic policeman for speeding and gave a crazy story about a waitress at Rafael's being paid to step aside by some dizzy dame. The officer, also an Information Architect, reported that to the core and these seemingly useless nuggets of information, like so many links in a chain, were hammered together here until, in minutes, I knew with certainty that Betty Dale was at Rafael's for a clandestine meeting, presumably with you. Do you begin to grasp now the interconnection of all things?"

The enormity of Otlet's architects and the power they placed in his hands was staggering to "X" whose mind reeled at the implications. With a network of this kind, Otlet could rule the world.

"Impressive," "X" allowed. "And dangerous."

"Ah! You begin to see."

They left the cell. "X" had his arm protectively around Betty as they made there way back to the elevator.

"In time," Otlet went on. "I will have Information Architects spread out to the four corners of the globe. The correct detail at the precise time can bring fortune or ruin as I see fit, put someone in a position of power or crumble an empire. Already my Architects in Brussels are reporting on the Nazi occupation. Others in Germany who oppose Hitler's rule are feeding the core information. Troop movements, orders, hushed telephone calls, carefully worded communiqués, the seemingly random coming and goings of officers plotting to topple the regime – a billion trivial occurrences going on every second of every day. They are all, one by one, going into the core. By their own actions the Nazis provide the key to their destruction."

The stepped into the elevator and it rose upward.

"Very noble," "X" said. "What happens after you've eradicated the Nazis? Who next will be subject to your scrutiny?"

"Why, everyone, of course. Every scrap of knowledge will be fed into the core. In time it will replace the file cabinets you saw earlier. With it, I will have a world at peace. Wrong doers will no longer have cracks in which to hide."

They stepped out of the elevator onto the main floor.

"And you will decide who is right and who is wrong?"

"Someone has to."

"You can't play God!" Betty exclaimed. "No human being could!"

"There is a first time for everything."

Betty looked up at X. "We have to stop him!"

Otlet laughed, a gravelly rumble in his throat. "You can't stop me. No one can. As for you, Miss Dale, you are merely a bargaining chip. You were abducted to lure the former Secret Agent "X" here although that proved unnecessary. Either he becomes my greatest Information Architect or you shall be killed. Rather painfully, I'm afraid. Men!"

Otlet's guards closed in.

But Agent "X" reacted faster. He pressed down in a specific way on the right heel of his shoe, triggering the tiny air gun concealed inside. A small dart fired out of the gun into the shin of the man in front of him. The dart was treated with a non-lethal concoction that induced unconsciousness and the man dropped as if pole axed.

Before the man hit the ground, "X" was in motion. He shoved Betty towards a nearby staircase, which she hastily ascended, while "X" crouched to throw a shoulder into the nearest gunman. The Secret Agent hit the man solidly and the gunsel careened into the wall and fell, stunned.

The last of the guards dared not fire for fear of hitting Otlet, who backed away slowly as if mesmerized by the battle, so instead the gunsel wrapped his thickly muscled arms around the Agent's torso. The cabled muscles flexed and the arms constricted like twin pythons. One of X's arms was free and he jabbed his elbow repeatedly into the soft middle of the guard. Then, reaching up and back, he took hold of the man's collar, bent forward and executed a textbook judo throw. The man sailed over the Agent's shoulder, slamming into the man "X" had bounced off the wall. Both men sprawled in a heap.

This gave "X" a moment to stare after the fleeing form of Otlet who had regained his senses. No doubt the man was off to summon aid.

One of the men on the floor had retrieved the pistol and fired. The bullet struck the railing in front of X. This snapped the Agent out of his momentary reverie and he launched himself at the man. A stinging kick sent the gun skittering away. A stout jab broke the man's nose.

But the second man buried the sole of his shoe in the Agent's stomach and "X" was driven back, his broken rib like a molten steel rod inside him. The pain would have paralyzed anyone else, but the Agent's finely tuned physique was battle hardened. As was his mind. Long ago he'd learned to ignore pain, turn it off as one would switch off a light. However he deliberately favored his side, pressed a hand there and grimaced in agony for the sake of his assailants. The men took the bait and, with vicious leers twisting their misshapen features, closed in for the kill.

When they were in striking distance, "X" made his move.

Like a whirling dervish he seemed to be everywhere at once. He planted a shoe in the gut of one man while a devastating backhanded blow clubbed the other in the jaw. The blow knocked the man back a step and the Agent followed it with two piledriver jabs and another kick that laid the man out.

Agent "X" 'felt' the man behind him about to strike. He whirled around, grabbed the man by his shirtfront and hurled him head first into the wall. There was a wet smacking sound and the man crumpled and lay still.

"X" took off after Leopold Otlet.

Chapter Eleven

Once again time was against the Agent. If he could not end things quickly, Otlet could rally an army of faithful followers to his defense.

"X" ran along the banks of card files, dodging the clerks moving between the files and desks intent on their tasks. His passage did not go unnoticed. Several of the workers made as if to stop him, but he eluded their feeble attempts to halt his progress. He spotted Otlet up ahead as the man disappeared down a wide staircase.

Agent "X" increased his speed.

He hit the stairs running and hurtled down the short flight. The stairs ended at a pair of iron doors. Otlet had left them open in his unbridled haste and "X" streaked through the opening.

The doors gave on an immense, low-ceilinged room dominated by a massive structure that ran the entire length. The huge device resembled three cylindrical columns lashed together and laid lengthwise. Energy crackled over the smooth surface, casting the desks and worktables scattered about in an eerie glow. The room was intensely cold.

A rifle butt crashed between X's shoulder blades and he stumbled forward, falling heavily. Cat-like, he sprang to his feet and turned to face his attacker.

Six men pointed rifles at him.

Secret Agent "X" smirked at the firing squad facing him, then dashed to one side.

Fingers tightened on the triggers.

"Don't shoot!" Otlet bellowed, the smile sliding from his lips. "You'll hit the core! Hold your fire!"

This was exactly what "X" had been counting on. However there was no time to savor this small victory. As he scuttled around one corner of the core he came face to face with four more armed guards responding to the commotion.

In seconds "X" was bracketed.

Otlet came forward, a beaming smile pulling at his harsh features. "You cannot outsmart the all-knowing," he explained, condescendingly. He gestured at the gigantic device. "Every adventure of yours is on record, every police report that mentions your name has been collected here in the core. Each has been analyzed, classified, absorbed. Your tendencies are as well known to me as they are to yourself. Leading you into this trap was child's play."

"This isn't over," "X" said.

Otlet regarded him frankly. "No. I'm afraid it is. It was my hope to enlist you to my cause. I brought you here to see the opponent you face. With the core, I am unstoppable. And yet you persist in your attempt. Well, I have much larger matters to concern myself with."

Leopold Otlet gestured to the men who, prodding "X" with their rifle, guided him away from the core.

"Before you die, I want you to know that I am indebted to you. The false information your handler introduced for us to find was most convincing. I will have to make adjustments to my Architects. Also the averted destruction of Unit 6282 exposed a flaw in the core's response. The Unit, believed destroyed by the core, should not have functioned after you so cleverly re-assembled it"

A touch of sadness colored Otlet's expression.

"Goodbye Secret Agent X."

Otlet turned his back on the Agent and that was the cue to his men to open fire. They raised their weapons and took aim.

"X" wished Betty Godspeed and stared down his murderers.

Gunfire erupted in the complex.

Otlet pivoted. There was a look of surprise on his face.

For the shots had sounded right outside the door. Screams and yells could be heard at the top of the stairs. The doors flew open and Joe Kovacs and his crew stormed into the room. They all clutched pistols and rifles in their fists. Kovacs held a Thompson machine gun. The gun muzzles aimed at "X" suddenly swung around to face this new threat. Both groups, guns leveled, ceased moving in a frozen tableau. It was a standoff.

"Well," Kovacs roared, unfazed by the weapons. "What have we here?" He turned to X. "Secret Agent X, I presume? You got cute with the plane engine back in Los Angeles but it only slowed me down. Looks like I got here just in time. I would have hated to miss your end."

Otlet was outraged. His face beet red, eyes bulging, he stepped forward. "Kovacs, how dare you barge in here — "

"Save it, old man!" Kovacs interrupted. "I'm running things now."

"I'll see you in Hell first!" Otlet snatched up a pistol from one of the desks and held it tightly in his trembling fist.

The air crackled with tension as the armed groups stood facing each other.

"Don't make this any harder that it has to be, Otlet," Kovacs cautioned.

Leopold Otlet fired.

The bullet only grazed Kovacs's shoulder but that fact was lost in the barrage of gunfire that single shot unleashed. Suddenly the air was full of streaking lead missiles. The low ceiling turned the sound into the roar of canon. Men screamed and fell, blood flew. Bullets pinged and whined in all directions.

Agent "X" used the chaos to seek a means of disabling the core and put a stop to Otlet's mad scheme. But as he began to examine the device stray bullets did his work for him.

Squatting in one corner of the room was the cooling unit which maintained the wintry atmosphere. The machine was peppered with errant gunfire and it began to rattle. Black smoke belched out of it. The unit sputtered and died in a shower of sparks.

"You damned fools!" Otlet bellowed from behind a desk. "See what you've done! Now the core will overheat. It will explode! All is lost!"

Almost instantly the temperature in the room began to rise as the core produced incredible amounts of heat that had been held in check by the refrigeration unit how gone silent.

A couple of Otlet's men, aware of the peril, threw down their rifles and dashed for the doors but Kovacs's henchmen cut them down mercilessly. The doorway out of the room became effectively jammed with corpses.

There was no way out.

Kovacs took advantage of Otlet's momentary distraction and fired a short burst at the old man. Bullets tore into Otlet's stomach. The man groaned and pitched forward. Two more of his men fell before three of Kovacs's gunsels stuck their heads out at the wrong time and then were torn apart by bullets. Kovacs tried for the door but a hail of fire sent him sprawling behind a desk.

X, abandoning his attempt to disable the core, turned his attention to finding a means of escape so he could retrieve Betty before the explosion Otlet foretold claimed the lives of everyone. However, to find Betty it would be necessary to cross the killing zone in front of the door. An impossible feat, but he would have to make the attempt.

The Agent was about to do so when he spied a vent out of the corner of his eye. Crouching low as bullets spanged off the core wall, he scuttled towards it.

"Oh, no you don't!" roared Kovacs. He had also spotted the vent. He rose up, his Thompson machine gun chattered, loosing a deadly storm of fire. Otlet's men ducked behind whatever cover they could find. Some weren't so lucky and fell forward into fresh spreading pools of their own blood. This deadly hail of bullets came close enough to the Agent to make him seek cover behind a buttress holding the core in place. The brief delay allowed Kovacs to reach the vent a split-second before X.

Kovacs stood with his back to the vent, his machine gun pointed squarely at the Agent who was out in the open now a half-dozen paces from the next buttress.

"You lose," Kovacs crowed.

But before he could pull the trigger, the grate behind him exploded outwards, striking Kovacs in the back. He dropped his gun as he reeled. A slim form tumbled out of the vent.

It was Betty Dale.

But this was no time for a reunion. "X" lunged forward and snatched up the Thompson barrel first. He raised it like a club and swung it savagely at the head of Kovacs. The wooden stock split on impact and Kovacs sprawled, unmoving.

"Get back inside, Betty!" "X" ordered, tossing aside the shattered gun. "This whole place if going to blow!"

"We can't go that way," Betty countered. "I hid in the vent to avoid some men.

But it was angled like a laundry shoot. I lost my grip and slid down here. I looked up before I fell and saw sunlight!"

"An air vent from the roof," "X" finished. The temperature had risen to stifling levels. They sweated as if they were in a sauna. Sporadic fire could still be heard near the door. "That was the only way out. We're sunk."

"N-No…" a voice groaned behind them.

It was Leopold Otlet.

Ducking low, "X" and Betty rushed over to the sprawled man.

"I… I was… a fool," Otlet gasped. "Drunk… with… power. N-Now at the end I truly… understand."

He fumbled in his pocket and, with shaking hands, withdrew a key.

"My… private elevator." He gestured weakly. "Behind… panel. Take you to… my office. Escape!"

"X" took the key from the dying man.

"I-I'm finished…. Go!"

Heat radiated out of the core now. The air shimmered. Agent "X" and Betty began pawing at the wall in search of the concealed catch for the false panel. Betty found it and it clicked open. "X" thrust the key into the lock. The elevator doors parted and they hurled themselves inside.

The car rose with agonizing slowness. They could only stand inside and wait for the explosion that would finish them.

The elevator shuddered to a stop, the doors opened and they were in Otlet's office. "X" seized Betty's hand and they ran for all they were worth.

Crowds of the faithful dashed this way and that. There was a mad scramble for the exits. "X" and Betty made their way through the group towards a window.

The Agent snatched up a chair and launched it at the glass. The window shattered. Whipping off his jacket and winding it around one forearm, "X" cleared away the jagged shards in the frame like so many teeth and they were able to scramble out.

The mail truck still stood where Otlet's people had left it. "X" dived behind the wheel as Betty climbed in. Using his universal key, the Agent brought the engine to life and it roared lustily. He threw the truck into gear and stomped down on the gas.

The truck leapt forward, tossing Betty through the open divider. "X" guided the vehicle expertly through the panicked throng. Some of the faithful sought to clamber aboard but the truck was going too fast.

They reached the gate at last. "X" floored the accelerator and the metal grill of the truck crashed through the chain link fence.

Then the complex erupted in a massive fireball.

The blast wave barreled towards the truck, gaining inexorably. It smashed into the vehicle and sent it tumbling like a leaf in a hurricane. It rolled heavily three times, then came to rest on its side.

"X" shook his head to clear it. He was wedged in between the driver's seat and the steering column, which was askew. He painfully extracted himself. His first thought was for Betty's safety.

He braced himself in the open divider frame and peered into the rear of the truck. Mailbags were strewn everywhere, the sacks jumbled one atop the other. There was no sign of the girl.

In horror, he considered the possibility that Betty had been tossed from the truck as they rolled. He turned to stick his head out the shattered passenger window thoughts of Betty's torn, broken body lying in a heap on the sand tormenting him.

As he turned, he thought he saw one of the mailbag move. He stared at them and they heaved again.

"Betty!"

Agent "X" tossed the bags this way and that. Then finally the face of Betty Dale appeared. Her blond hair was in disarray, hanging down over one blue eye, but other than that she seemed uninjured. To "X" she had never looked lovelier.

The Agent helped her up. "The mail sacks acted like pillows and cushioned the impact as we tumbled."

Betty made an attempt to smooth out her disheveled clothing. "I'm going to kiss the next mailman I see," she announced.

"X" held Betty close to him. He guided her to the rear door, shoved it open and jumped to the sand. He turned and helped her down.

"It's finally over," Betty signed against him.

"Yes, the core and Otlet's minions were consumed in the explosion. Nothing could have survived. We'll have to round up his Information Architects though. That'll be quite a job. After I'm re-instated, that is."

A look of sorrow pulled at her flawless features.

"What is it?" "X" asked.

"Oh, I'm thinking of what Otlet said about the Nazis. Do you think he was telling the truth when he said he could end their regime?"

"Hard to say. The man was insane."

"But what if the Nazis become a greater threat to Europe? What if they one day threaten us? And the entire world? Could Otlet have stopped that from happening? Was the solution destroyed with him?"

"We'll never know," was all "X" could say.

And then they began the long trek to the highway.

THE END

THE "X" FACTOR

Having the opportunity to contribute a story to the re-issued first volume of these all-new **Secret Agent** "X" anthologies was a thrill beyond words for this writer. So when Ron put the word out that a third volume was in the works, he didn't have to ask me if I wanted to contribute, rather, he only had to tell me when he wanted the finished story. A chance to write "**X**" again? That was a no-brainer.

Or so I thought at the time.

You see, I had one problem with regards to my pulp fiction production: I didn't have a clue what evil **The Agent** should be battling. The problem was that Ron and I were ramping up the action as we brought *Ghost Squad: Rise of the Black Legion* to a rollicking finale and every pulp idea I had was geared to that novel and the captivating cast of characters we had created. When I turned my thoughts to the man of a thousand faces I got... nothing. Blank. Zip. Nada.

No worries I told myself, the *Ghost Squad* was almost completed and time was on my side. I wasn't concerned. **The Agent** possesses an uncanny "**X Factor**" which any writer can exploit if he or she keeps their writer radar tuned. "**X**" is such a multi-faceted character that almost anything could be turned into a terror only he can vanquish.

For a few weeks I kept telling myself this as nothing came to me story-wise. Then, out of the blue, a member of a pulp board I haunt put up a link to a forgotten genius named Paul Otlet who had conceived of a 1930s internet decades ahead of its time. This idea fascinated me and, after a little research, I was completely enamoured with the idea. And right from the get-go, I knew this Depression-era "internet" was meant for "**X**" to tackle. There was that "**X Factor**" coming into play yet again. A few pulp embellishments later and Paul Otlet's benign vision became Leopold Otlet's mad plot to take over the world. For the record, the electronic telescope laid out in the pages of the tale you've just read is precisely what the real Otlet conceived — I felt I owed the man behind this incredible invention that much. Had the Nazis not prevented Otlet from finishing his work, the world might be a different place today. My alteration was merely related to the use to which the device is used. For you trivia buffs, Paul Otlet's headquarters was located across the street from Leopold Park in Brussels. Take Leopold and Otlet, slam them together and, bang, instant villainous name.

While putting the tale together it occurred to me that Airship27/Cornerstone, as far as I know, is the only publisher regularly releasing new **Secret Agent** "X" tales and that the writers involved in the series were directly responsible for the character's legacy. As was the case with **The Shadow, Doc Savage** and the pantheon of Golden Age heroes, over time, the tales of these daring adventurers became almost a universe unto themselves. These heroes developed networks of informants and vast resources – all layered in gradually over decades by a host of writers penning the yarns, adding bits here and there.

Thus, as the modern keepers of the **"X"** flame, I felt it fell to us current writers to continue to develop the character. I'm not talking about revamping or "re-imagining" **"X"** for the 21st Century but rather of broadening his specific universe one small piece at a time.

Enter **Secret Agent "Y"**.

Branding **"X"** a traitor also fits in along these lines and both these elements, I hope, help to expand the universe of the character while staying true to the original classic tales at the same time. The ultimate verdict on whether I've achieved this is up to you, faithful reader.

As for the tale itself, have we seen the last of **Secret Agent "Y"**? That, too, is up to you. If you've enjoyed this tale (and I surely hope you did) then let Ron – the ol' Airchief – know. We aim to please with these modern pulp tales!

With **Ghost Squad: Rise of the Black Legion**, **Secret Agent X: Volumes One** and **Three** plus the forthcoming **Jim Anthony** and **Mars McCoy** anthologies, I truly feel like a pulp writer now, churning out purple prose to stretch the wonderfully lurid covers Airship's artists keep on creating. Writing pulp is a pleasure I never thought I'd experience and I plan on doing it as long as folks want to read it.

So, until next time, thanks for reading.

ANDREW SALMON is an Ellis Award nominee, lives and writes in Vancouver, BC. His work has appeared in numerous magazines, including *Storyteller, Parsec, TBT* and *Thirteen Stories*. He also writes reviews for *The Comicshopper* and is creating a superhero serial novel currently running in *A Thousand Faces Magazine*.

He has published five books to date: **The Forty Club** (which Midwest Book Reviews calls "a good solid little tale you will definitely carry with you for the rest of your life"), **The Dark Land**, the first of a series ("a straight out science-fiction thriller that fires on all cylinders" – Pulp Fiction Reviews), **The Light Of Men**, his first work for Airship 27/Cornerstone, which has been called "a book of such immense significance that it is not only meant to be read, but also to be experienced... a work of grim power" – C. Saunders. **Secret Agent X: Volume One** and **Ghost Squad: Rise of the Black Legion** (with Ron Fortier) constitute his pulp fiction debut at Airship27/Cornerstone.

Andrew's work will also appear in the all-new **Jim Anthony Super Detective** collection as well as the forthcoming **Mars McCoy** anthology. He is also preparing **Wandering Webber**, his first children's book, for publication.

To learn more about his work check out the Airship27/Cornerstone store (http://stores.lulu.com/airship27) and the following links: www.lulu.com/AndrewSalmon and www.lulu.com/thousand-faces.

AFTERWORD

Welcome to Airship 27 Prod. Phase Two. After a year of hard work re-editing and reprinting our first two *Secret Agent X* books, we are launching our third volume made up of four new stories never printed before. With the success of those first two books, it was clear to us that you, our loyal readers, wanted more thrilling escapades of pulpdom's greatest super spy. Little did we know way back then that we'd soon be parting company with our old publisher. That was a bad enough set back. Imagine our real frustration when that self same publisher opted not to continuing carrying these titles in his catalog. And by titles I mean all the Airship 27 books done up until then.

All too quickly most of the distributors carrying our books such as Barnes & Noble on-line and Amazon began to deplete their meager inventories of Airship 27 books. Soon they were simply gone, unavailable to our growing audience of new readers. So for the past year, Rob and I have been working fiendishly to get those first Airship 27 pulps back into print. As of today there remains only two left to reprint; *Captain Hazzard #1 – Python Men of the Lost City* and *Captain Hazzard # 2, Citadel of Fear.* No longer available from regular distributors, both these books are selling for insanely inflated prices by small, independent book sellers. The last time I checked with Amazon's listings, copies of *Python Men of the Lost City* were going from $65 on up. Whereas *Citadel of Fear,* what few copies you can find, are demanding $265 a copy!!!

I told you it was insane. It's also highway robbery. Upon learning this, I immediately started getting the word out any way I could advising our faithful customers not to despair, both books are being reprinting and will soon be available again. You have our word on that. Once all those earlier books are back in print, they will stay so. Again, that's our commitment to you for your continued support and encouragement.

Airship 27 Productions is growing every day and this book is a prime example. Of the four writers presented within these pages, only one is an Airship 27 veteran; the talented Canadian, Andrew Salmon. The other three equally gifted penmen are all new to these pages and for several of them, this is their first ever time in print. We guarantee you it will not be their last. What you have here are young men of various backgrounds with one common desire, to write classic pulp heroes and all of them have delivered far beyond my wildest imagination. The stories are fresh, original and innovative and yet all of them are true to the character as he was handled back in the 1930s, the heyday of the pulps.

Realizing we wanted to expand our line of titles, we decided a short while ago to let it be known we were looking for new contributors and hoped we might find a few daring souls to sign on. Much to my utter joy and surprise, within days of the word getting out, my e-mail inbox began getting filled with inquiries from would-be pulpsmiths wanting to know what they had to do to write for Airship 27 Prod. Within two short weeks we had recruited ten new amazingly gifted storytellers and as I write this all of are hard at work on either their first assignment or their second for us. Some of them, much like the old pulp scribes of yesterday, can really pump out hair-raising yarns in no time flat. Believe me when I say we've got some truly terrific, bloody purple prose coming your way in the months ahead.

2009 looks to be a banner year as you will be seeing more *Secret Agent X* (volume four is already in the works) plus *Sherlock Homes – Consulting Detective, Jim Anthony – Super Detective, The Masked Rider – Wild West Tales, Dan Fowler G-Man, Mars McCoy-Space Ranger* and possibly more *Lance Star-sky Ranger, Ghost Squad & Captain Hazzard* adventures if we can squeeze them in. Now that's what I call a full schedule. Still it is one we feel confident in completing because of your response to this book and all our past efforts. It's been one hell of a ride up to now and only seems to be getting wilder with each passing day.

Airship 27 Productions is dedicated to bringing you the finest new pulp stories ever. All our books are available via Amazon.com in print and Kindle versions. You can also pick up a $3.00 pdf of all our books at out website catalog: airship27hangar. com. Please do stop by and check out all our products if you haven't done so before. So we say adieu to Phase One and welcome to Phase Two.

Better buckle up!

Ron Fortier
11/12/2008
(Airship27@comcast.net)
(www.Airship27.com)

THE RETURN OF PULP FICTION'S GREATEST SPY!

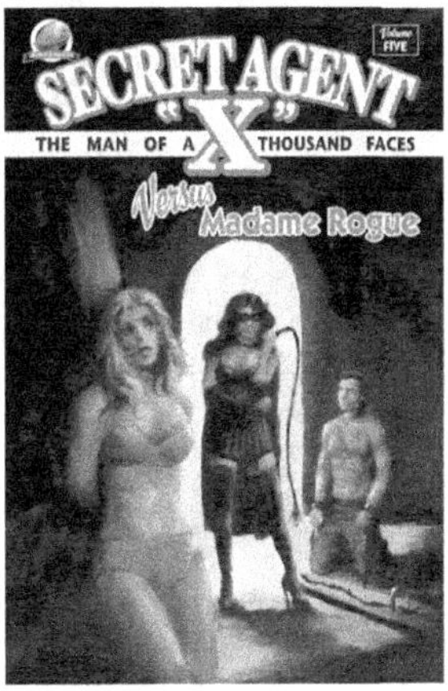

Pulse-Pounding Pulp Excitement
from Airship 27:

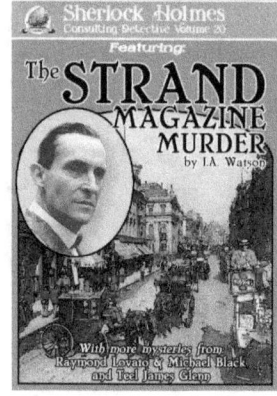

This is just a small sampling of the thrilling tales available from Airship 27 and its award-winning bullpen of the best New Pulp writers and artists. Set in the era in which they were created and in the same non-stop-action style, here are the characters that thrilled a generation in all-new stories alongside new creations cast in the same mold!

"Airship 27...should be remembered for finally closing the gap between pulps and slicks and giving pulp heroes and archetypes the polish they always deserved."
–William Maynard ("The Terror of Fu Manchu.")

Pulp Fiction for a New Generation!
At Amazon.com & www.airship27hangar.com

All Airship 27 Books are available for just $3/each at the Airship 27 online hangar! This includes some titles unavailable in print form. For the best in New Pulp reading excitement- *airship27hangar.com!*